Past Praise and Awards for Colleen Oakes

Winner—2014 Next Generation Independent Book Awards—
Young Adult

Award-Winning Finalist—2014 International Book Awards—
Fiction: Young Adult

"Most Cinematic Indie Books of 2014"—*Kirkus Reviews*

2014 "Best Indie Books of the Year"—*Kirkus Reviews*

"Oakes continues to weave literary magic as she pulls you
down the rabbit hole into a Wonderland like you've never
read before. Experience the world anew as you learn how a
young princess becomes the villainous Queen of Hearts."

—Chanda Hahn, *New York Times* and *USA Today*
bestselling author of the *Unfortunate Fairy Tale* series

Praise for the *Wendy Darling* series

"A dark twist on a familiar tale that readers will have difficulty putting down."

—*School Library Journal*

"Oakes superbly crafts both a story with wings and a Neverland with teeth, a story that will tempt any reader into never growing up."
—Brianna Shrum, author of *Never and Never* and
How to Make Out

"This twisted spinoff of a famous children's tale is filled with richly developed characters and fast-paced, eloquent writing. With *Seas*, Oakes delivers a stunning sequel to her *Wendy Darling* series. Stuck on board a pirate ship with the infamous Captain Hook, Wendy must quickly learn to face her true nature, and choose what kind of heroine she will be: sappy or strong, as she is swept inexorably toward a showdown with a chilling and maniacal Peter Pan. Oakes does a marvelous job slowly chipping away at her characters' exteriors to reveal what lies beneath, be it true heroism or malignant evil."
—Alane Adams, award-winning author of
The Legends of Orkney series

"If the first *Wendy Darling* pulled me away from familiar adventures in Neverland, Book 2 has me sprinting away from them... and I didn't know how badly I wanted that deviancy until it was too late. Oakes' delicious plot twists and rich revelations leave you just the right amount of full, but they mostly leave you crying out for the final installment in this micro-epic where Wendy's authenticity is the unquestionable star. Oakes' signature style of dark fantasy retellings is intoxicating, and the much awaited Captain Hook does not disappoint."
—Mason J. Torall, author of *The Dark Element*

"Described in lush, lingering detail, Neverland is all that Peter Pan promises: vibrant, gorgeous, filled with magic and excitement. But it also harbors unexpected dangers . . . perhaps none greater than Peter himself. While she is initially intoxicated by his charisma, Wendy's practical good sense, stubborn loyalty, and newly liberated fire give her the courage to defy Peter . . . only to land, in a stunning cliffhanger, in even worse peril. Dark, even horrific in its graphic bloodshed and psychological menace; but the nuanced portrayals—of a hero frequently excused by his whimsical glamour and a heroine too often dismissed as girlishly insipid—are riveting."

—*Kirkus Reviews*

"We are all familiar with the story of Peter Pan, whether from J.M. Barries' original 1911 novel or the many film versions it inspired. Oakes' tale, told form Wendy's point of view, breathes new life into Peter's story and makes it her own. This Neverland is far more mesmerizing and dangerous than Barries', and I was pulled in by the lyrical writing. Every time I opened the cover, I felt completely transported into Wendy's world. The perilous call of the mermaids, Tinker Bell's violent obsession with Peter, sinister Captain Hook—all compelling reasons to read *Wendy Darling*."

—*Middle Shelf Magazine*

WENDY DARLING

WENDY DARLING

Volume Two:
SEAS

COLLEEN OAKES

31652003167765

SPARKPRESS, A BOOKSPARKS IMPRINT
A DIVISION OF SPARKPOINT STUDIO, LLC

Published by SparkPress, a BookSparks imprint,
A division of SparkPoint Studio, LLC
Tempe, Arizona, USA, 85281
www.gosparkpress.com

Published 2015
Printed in the United States of America
ISBN: 78-1-940716-88-6 (pbk)
ISBN: 978-1-943006-00-7 (e-bk)

Library of Congress Control Number: 2015940086

Cover design © Julie Metz, Ltd./metzdesign.com
Author photo © Erin Burt

For Maine, who is the sun and the moon and everything in between.

"Proud and insolent youth," said Hook, "prepare to meet thy doom."

"Dark and sinister man," Peter answered, "have at thee."

—*Peter Pan* by J. M. Barrie

# Pan Island

Peter knelt beside John, the disgraced general now kneeling in the middle of a circle of Lost Boys, some looking confused, some angry. His tattered shirt was peppered with drops of blood that seeped down from his shoulders. Peter's red hair fell over his emerald-green eyes, once again their normal shade after having burned navy for the past three days following Wendy and Michael's escape. His voice, the one that had previously been screaming poisonous words of anger, now softened to a soothing tone.

"John. I want to believe that you had no idea that Wendy and Michael would be leaving. I want to, and yet, I don't." His hand clutched John's shoulder roughly, his dirty fingernails digging into John's pasty skin. John sniffled.

"I didn't know she was going, Peter, I swear! I knew she wanted to go, but I thought I could convince her to stay! I didn't know she was going to take a boat." He looked at the ground. "And I didn't know she would take Michael."

A tear dripped off the end of his nose as he sputtered, "Wendy's not that brave! I never thought she would go!"

Peter sighed, as if the burden of John's guilt weighed heavily upon him. He paced around John in a circle, speaking loudly. "You were right about that, John, Wendy is not brave. Wendy was scared. Scared of the feelings she had for me, that they were too much for her weak, womanly heart."

Peter stopped pacing and rose up above John, so that his feet were flush with John's head. The Lost Boys watched with awe. Peter raised his arms into the air.

"My sweet love only needed some time to think and Hook kidnapped her!" The Lost Boys shook their hands in the air with rage as they screamed and cried. Peter continued whipping them into a frenzy. "She could have been our mother! She would have been my queen! She was meant to take care of us!"

Two of the younger boys were crying. Peter's eyes narrowed as he looked down at John, the pitiful creature now sobbing at his feet. A grin stretched over Peter's face.

"Don't worry boys, we'll get her back when the time is right. The captain has no idea of what his foolish decision has brought upon him. And as for Wendy . . ." He looked out onto the horizon, watching a churning sea crash in on itself, the waves chasing each other into foamy oblivion. "Wendy will be mine. I just have to be patient." With a sigh, he sunk back down in front of John, lifting John's chin up to face him. A fat tear rolled down John's cheek. Peter flicked it away with annoyance. The warm Neverland breeze rustled the leaves around them, sending a small flock of pale-blue birds fluttering their way out to the bright turquoise sea. Peter's demeanor suddenly shifted. His intensity gave way to a playful tone, his clenched fists becoming open palms. He brought his face close to John's.

"John, I'm going to need you to do something for me. Something that will prove your loyalty beyond a doubt. You need to make me believe. You need to make your brothers believe."

"Anything!" whispered John desperately. "Anything!"

Peter smiled, his white teeth glinting in the twilight. "Good. And once you do this, I promise, I'll make you a general again. It will be like nothing has changed."

John swallowed. "Yes! Yes. Peter, I'll do anything you ask!" He reached out for Peter's hand and winced; the middle Darling boy's back still ached from the whipping he had received at the hands of the other two generals. He bit his lip to keep from whimpering. Peter stood up and pulled John gently to his feet.

"I'm glad to hear that, John. Very glad. You won't regret it."

John wondered where his sister was, and what she was doing at this very second.

Peter smiled wickedly. "Let's get started."

CHAPTER ONE

The iron shackles on Wendy's wrists shifted and clanged with each pitch of the waves as the *Sudden Night* fought its way through the churning sea around it. Most ships, thought Wendy, understood that they were at the mercy of the waters and made their peaceful way through them, riding each wave as a docile passenger. Not the *Sudden Night*. Captain Hook's ship, a black behemoth, burst through the waves with a relentless fury, not so much navigating its way through as challenging each one, daring the heaving sea around it to duel with each and every crest. It made for a violent ride, and when heavy chains bound your wrists to the wall, a particularly brutal wave could make life very painful. Wendy could feel the pitch of the sea growing hungry and attempted to protect herself by latching her fingers around one of several iron rungs that hung above her head.

"Michael, hold on, it's a big one!" she screamed, and had no further uttered the words when the ship pitched violently to the right. Her body lifted up and off the ground as it took to the air, her ankles twisting about below her, her ratted brown curls lashing across her face. A pocket of air floated underneath her, lifting her upwards and then—*slam*. The chains stretched out to their limit, which was followed by a painful wrenching as her body was flung forward but her arms remained encased. The *Sudden*

Night now pitched the opposite way, and her body was pulled back against the dripping black wall, wet with condensation and sticky with salt. Her face slicked across it before she fell to her knees. Some of it got into her mouth, and she retched. The skeleton chained in the corner watched them silently with a macabre grin, its bones endlessly rattling with the vibrations of the sea. The waves slowed momentarily as Wendy forced bile back into her throat.

"Michael! Are you alright?" Wendy attempted to rub her wrists under the chains. They were bloody and raw, their exposed redness painful to the touch but also terribly itchy, which meant itching was painful but beyond gratifying. Gritting her teeth, Wendy carefully began snaking her fingers up between the iron chains and her wrist, sighing with pleasure when her filthy fingernails met her raw skin. The salt under her nails caused a stinging pain to radiate out from the wound. She scratched with determination, making each rip count.

"Wendy . . . you said don't itch."

Michael, her tiny, normally bouncy five-year-old brother, was lying beside her, his wrists also bound by chains, tiny chains with small holes for the thin wrists, built to keep children firmly below deck, in this damp hell. Who kept chains like that in their brig? *Hook did. What a sick bastard.*

Wendy bent over her little brother as best she could, fitting him into the crook of her elbow, curling his body towards her.

"It's okay," she whispered. "It's okay." She was lying, and he knew it, which was why he ignored her and continued staring at the wall. His beaten voice rose up from the bowels of the ship.

"I wish we had never left Pan Island. At least we had a bed there."

Wendy closed her eyes. This was probably the hundredth conversation they had had about this, but she vowed to keep her patience. To a five-year-old, things like a bed and meals that weren't shoved towards them in dirty bowls were of paramount importance. She had tried her best to explain to Michael *why* she had taken him from Pan Island, *why* she had risked both of their lives to escape, knowing that Peter would not hesitate to use Michael's safety to manipulate Wendy into loving him. She tried to explain to this five-year-old how Peter had fallen dangerously in love with her: a consuming, obsessive, and greedy type of love. Peter wanted to own Wendy, and believed that he could force her into loving him. She had not told Michael though, how Peter had flown her up high above Neverland and dropped her, only to catch her just before her body slammed into the waves, or how he had told her they could never go home again. She had not told him about the bruises and wounds that he inflicted on Tink, the fairy blinded by her love into a prison of Peter's making. No, she would not scare him any more than he already was. Instead she had tried to impart to his five-year-old brain that Peter was very, very dangerous. Michael seemed to accept that fact, but was so miserable in his current state, that he couldn't do anything but turn into himself, constantly shivering against Wendy's side, his face pale and drawn. It broke Wendy's heart to see her cheerful and boundless brother now so afraid.

They had been down here for three days, counting the sunsets through a tiny port window that splashed endlessly with seawater, a window that was sometimes completely submerged in the sea. On the third day, Wendy had seen a small black fish with bright canary-yellow markings on its tail fin curiously nibbling at the window. She had pointed it out to Michael, and for a while, they made up a story about this fish, where it had been and where it was going, its fishy family and fishy loves. It had been a mistake. Talking about family had drawn them both back into sadness, and they cried together over their best memories of their parents, George and Mary Darling, people they knew they might never see again. When Peter had taken them through the nursery window, he had told them that time was different in

Neverland and that their parents would never even know they were gone.

That had not been the truth. Nothing Peter Pan said was the truth.

Every word that slipped out over his seductive tongue had been a lie, his devastating good looks and considerable charm bewitching the obvious truths about him. Their parents, Wendy had quietly come to understand, probably thought that all three of their children were dead. At the thought of their enormous grief, Wendy struggled not to come undone. *Why had they left? Why had she trusted Peter? Had they blamed Booth, the boy in London who loved her, for their disappearance?*

When they weren't causing pain, her memories were the only glorious escape from the salt and the darkness. With Michael curled on her lap, she would think of the way Booth had kissed her, or the way he read a book, his brow furrowed as he drank in every word of the novel, lost in the words on a page. Once as a child she had bounced an apple off the side of his head before he had noticed her standing before him. That would not happen now. She remembered how he had touched her face and looked at her, in that way that let her know that he believed in everything she was now and everything she would be, and he wanted it all. She remembered this and then she looked at the shackles on her wrist and remembered that she would probably never see him again. Wendy could feel herself pulling toward a silent state of despair that would have been all too tempting if it weren't for Michael.

Because of him, she had to keep her spirits up, and even if her voice faltered when she sang lullabies into the pitch-black gloom, she would keep singing. Because of Michael, she could especially not linger on John, the brother that she had left behind to Peter's insanity. John, blinded by his own need for Peter's approval, John who worshipped the flying boy with an adoration that bordered on the religious, John who had stated that Neverland was his home. The brother who could barely remember his life before Neverland. *The brother who had threatened her life.*

Unable to sleep most nights, Wendy sat awake with one arm wrapped around Michael, and somewhere in between her desperate prayers, she would swear that one day she would get both of her brothers home, back through their nursery window, back to their parents. Somehow, someday, a day when chains didn't bind her wrists and there wasn't a flying boy out there who desperately wanted to possess her, she would take them home.

But for now, they were here, in the brig, keeping company with a rotting skeleton.

It had been three days, three days of hell itself when the door at the top of the black wooden stairs burst open. Wendy pulled Michael into her arms protectively. It was probably the same disgusting pirate, she thought, a squirrely man named Redd with a tangled gray-and-ginger beard and jowls that seemed to pull his face to the floor. One of his eyes had been carved out, and in its place was a ragged, infected scar that oozed green mucus the consistency of tears. Redd repulsed her, but despite his disgusting appearance and the uncomfortable way he leered at the edges of her skirt, she was always glad to see him, for he brought the food. Seared fish and loaves of hard, knotted bread, a meal of Jesus's own making, were all they received, and for these, Wendy was immensely grateful. She now squinted at the top of the wooden stairs, hoping to see Redd's lanky gait. What she saw instead was a hulking silhouette, much larger than Redd, filling up the doorway. Her chest clenched with fear as the thudding sound of heavy boots made their way down towards her. His face edged into the light and Wendy concealed a gasp, pulling Michael ever tighter to her. She turned up her chin, hoping to hide the fear in her voice. Her hands shook at the sight of him.

"Please don't hurt him."

Smith looked down at her, his thick forearms covered with coarse black hair. Tattoos of angels and demons loped up and down his hulking arms, so taut they reminded Wendy of rocks. Upon them, demons leered out from behind trees, their forked tails waving their way down his veins as angels watched from above. Two large tattooed wings sprouted from either side of his neck, curling up to either side of his cheeks. Wendy swallowed, and felt a cold stab of fear as his dark eyes looked down at her. She had seen this man slit the throat of a child. *Kitoko.* His blood had splattered her face.

"Recognize me, you little brat?"

Wendy stared up at him, her hazel eyes wide in the dark. "You killed Kitoko. I saw you."

"Oh, was that his name? I didn't even know." Smith pulled out a long, thin knife and ran it underneath his chin. "I remember. I could feel his jugular give. Best feeling on earth, any pirate'll tell ya."

Wendy turned away, sickened, casting her eyes to the lengthening shadows on the walls. "That's what I thought. Now, you're coming with me, since we've got business upstairs. The boy stays."

"NO! NO!" Wendy struggled against him. "Michael has to come with me! Please. We stay together!"

Smith squeezed her arm. "Not today you don't. Captain wants to see you only. The kid stays here."

"No! No! Don't take my Wendy!" Michael was screaming now, holding desperately to Wendy's leg, crying hysterically, fear spilling fat tears from his cheeks. "Wendy! Stop him!"

"Michael!" Her face crumpled.

Smith was reaching over her now, unlocking the chains around her wrists and freeing her from the wall. Wendy struggled against him.

"Please don't do this! Whatever you are doing, please! He's just a child! He won't be trouble, I promise. You can't leave him down here alone!"

Smith grinned.

"He ain't alone. He's got Paulo to keep him company."

He shrugged towards the skeleton.

"He's shy—only wakes up when there's one person down here, according to pirate lore." He looked down at Michael. "But don't worry, he'll only eat your fingers. One by delicious one." He snapped his teeth together. Michael let out a bloodcurdling scream as Wendy was ripped out of his grasp.

She flailed against Smith's arms, trying to twist her way out of his iron grip. He let out a sigh. "Now you're getting hysterical, just like a woman. Calm down or I'll have to take your ear."

She felt his cold blade on her jawbone. He spun Wendy to face him, her body pressed hard against his chest. She squirmed uncomfortably.

"Where are you taking me? Please don't separate us. Please, he'll die alone! Please . . ." Michael was sobbing now, pulling hard against his chains, struggling to pull his wrists out of their grasp."Don't worry. I'll be gentle with him. He's too little to put up much of a fight. Kind of like you." She felt his hand creeping up the side of her dress. Feeling cornered, Wendy sank her teeth hard into his wrist.

"OW! You little bitch! You bit me!"

Smith looked down at her with disbelief before roaring with laughter.

"You bit me! I haven't been bit by a woman like that since the last time I was in Port Duette! And she was naked, so it hurt a bit less."

Then he slapped her hard. Her face snapped to the side so fast she worried her neck would break. Wendy felt her ears ringing as she hit the ground, the side of her face completely numb. She took a breath and shut her eyes to quell the tears that blurred her vision. Then she pushed herself up from the wet floorboards and turned back to Smith, her head swimming. Silently, she moved in front of Michael, her hands outstretched, her hands shaking before dropping her voice.

"Please sir, don't hurt him. I'm asking politely."

Smith sneered before twisting his voice into the British tones of a seasoned aristocrat. "Dearest Miss Darling, please accept my regards when informing you that you're on a pirate's ship." He dropped back into his normal speech. "Your etiquette don't mean nothing here."

Then, moving with terrifying speed, he picked Wendy up and threw her towards the stairs. "Now get up there. The captain wants to see you. He doesn't like to be kept waiting—trust me." He walked up the stairs behind her, ignoring Michael's hysterical cries as he pulled desperately on his chains.

"Don't leave me! Don't leave me!" he screamed.

Wendy shouted over Smith's shoulder. "Michael, I'll be right back! Tell yourself the story of the magic prince and the evil witch, and count how many times you can tell it! When you get to a hundred, I'll be back!"

Michael's tear-stained face looked up at her, his bright-blue eyes red rimmed with dark circles, his once-chubby cheeks sunken and hollow.

"Promise?"

Wendy looked up at Smith, who just shrugged.

"I can't promise, I can't, but I'll try my best! I love you Michael!" Michael collapsed into hysterical wails, burying his head in his hands. Wendy felt her heart shatter outwards like glass. Smith looked back at Michael with a nasty grin.

"Enjoy Paulo's company! He has a fondness for little boys!"

He slammed the door behind him, shoving Wendy forward onto the landing of a dim hallway. Michael's screams faded in her ears as they walked deeper into the bowels of the *Sudden Night*. They turned right, and then right again, making their way back to the center of the ship. Wendy was looking at her feet as she walked, and was glad for it when the floor of the ship suddenly pitched beneath her, and was able to fling herself against a black wall that left her hands full of jagged splinters. Smith didn't even stumble.

"Come on, girl."

The hallway opened itself up into a wide, circular hole before them. Wendy looked above her and gasped. Rising out of the dangerous opening at her feet was a massive spiral staircase, the stairs made of a polished wood and the railing made of . . . marble? Wendy reached out to touch it before letting out a shriek and leaping back. Curving away from her and up through the levels of the ship was a railing made of bones. Long femurs connected to the wooden balusters with the nubs of shorter bones, each one glistening white from the hundreds of hands that ran over them every day. Curled skeletal hands marked the end of each step, as if the hands were holding up each stair individually.

"Move!" Smith barked, and Wendy cautiously put her foot on the impressive structure. It was surprisingly solid. She continued to climb, trying her best not to touch the banister of bones, though with each roll of the ship, she was forced to grasp onto the smooth white handholds to avoid falling into the void below.

"You are barbarians," she pronounced with disgust, trying to shake a strange white flake off her shoulder that drifted down from above.

Smith chuckled. "We call it the Jolly Staircase and it sits right at midship. Why let the bodies of our crew go to waste? Once you are a part of the *Sudden Night*, you stay with us forever. These are the bones of my brothers." He patted the staircase affectionately. "Someday I hope to be part of the captain's bed frame. Most action I'm ever likely to see." He laughed to himself.

They moved higher. Wendy couldn't get over how large the ship was. The height alone was staggering as she counted the levels of stairs, each marked by a full skeleton slumped at the end of the banister, their knuckled joints pointing their way upwards, the next level of the ship painted crudely on their foreheads: 3 . . . 4 . . . 5. . . . The only glimpse Wendy had of the

Sudden Night was of its outer parts, when they had hauled her up in their massive black net. The ship was taller than any ship she had ever seen, and she had been struck by how far off the water they had climbed. Still, Michael had been blue and lifeless at the time, and all her focus had been on him, on breathing life back into his body. *And now she had left him in a dungeon that felt like death.*

"Alright, deary," crowed Smith, "this level be the captain's deck, deck seven."

"How many levels are there?" asked Wendy.

"Decks. And there be eight decks. The brig is in the bilge, lowest part of the ship."

Wendy struggled to catch her breath from the steep climb. She had been too long in that damp underground hell. Her muscles were weak, her head woozy, her heart terrified at what might follow. She didn't feel ready to meet the infamous Captain Hook, and yet, Michael's life depended on this meeting. Just the thought of him was enough to flood her hazel eyes with tears, and she fought back the memory of his terrified face, replacing it instead with Booth's face, and his firm and unwavering belief in her. *"Be brave, Wendy,"* he had said, and so she would be. For her and Michael's sake, she would be.

Smith continued, unaware that Wendy had stopped. "Turn right at the top of the stair and don't you complain none to the captain. He didn't have to pull you out of that sea, 'twas fine with the rest of us if Peter choked the life out of ya."

Wendy ignored him as she made her way up the final level. At the landing, a full skeleton, wearing an elaborate red jacket and a bejeweled hat adorned with a white feathered plume, welcomed her. "That's the last person that complained to the captain. I shoved a sword down his throat." Wendy shuddered, looking at the skeleton with curiosity and dread, red sapphires staring back at her from hollowed eye sockets. Without warning, Smith shoved her roughly between her shoulder blades and she fell forward into the hallway. The *Sudden Night* followed that with a violent rock that sent her tumbling against the wall. Smith barely moved, his feet grounded like roots into the lush tapestry that covered the floor.

"Welcome to the Captain's Deck."

Wendy looked around, literally thrust into a completely different surrounding. There was light here! Glorious, beautiful light. She raised her fingertips to touch it, the golden rays streaming in from circular port windows lining the hallway, their brushed copper finishes newly polished. The carpet splayed out underneath her fingertips was lush, so foreign in a place like this: curling fleur-de-lis of silvery greens surrounded embroidered men atop horseback, each adorned in blues and riding fiercely into battle. Orange blossoms dotted around them, culminating in a wild swirl of flora. The carpet reminded her of home and she felt the familiar pang of grief in her heart. Wendy let her fingers brush against a lone string that had sprung lose from the pattern. She began to pull herself to her feet. The boat gave another sudden pitch, and this time Wendy managed not go hurtling about to one side, her hands quickly finding a small brass knob that lay along an otherwise flat wall. There was only a moment of relief before the door pitched open and revealed an elaborate golden privy.

"That's where the captain takes his shits, he does. Sea legs you don't got, my girl."

Wendy narrowed her eyes as Smith gave a deep chuckle at her misfortune. She righted herself, trying to hide the humiliated blush rising up her cheeks. Her exhausted heart hammered inside of her chest as she stared at the enormous mahogany door at the end of the hallway. Smith saw her eyeing it.

"Ah, that be one of the captain's favorite treasures."

The door was a work of art, something that in London would have been worth thousands of pounds. A pair of wicked mermaids bordered the curved wood, their hands outstretched, as if beckoning Wendy closer, dangerous but alluring smiles dashed across their mouths. Their teeth were inlaid with white pearl. In the center of the door was a huge carving of a male fairy, flecks of silver falling from his hands, the metallic sheen dusting the bottom of the door, making light cascade down its curled wood. The fairy looked nothing like Tink, so weak and small. This fairy was all muscle, his body so perfect and so nude that it made Wendy blush at its indecency. There was a crown of stars around his forehead, his eyes closed, and his mouth open as if in song. The tips of his feet brushed the bottom of the door, his arms stretched wide, reminding Wendy of the crucifix that had hung above her bed in the nursery. Gigantic wings stretched behind him, texturing the wood, stretching out behind the boundaries of the door. He was glorious, and Wendy could almost feel the power radiating out from this inanimate figure, forever carved in wood. The ship creaked underneath them. Smith cleared his throat.

"Get a move on, landlubber. Captain doesn't like to be kept waiting."

Wendy's shoulders brushed the sides of the walls as she made her way to the door. She raised her hand to knock, but then looked back for Smith's approval. He was gone already, the lush hallway empty behind her. She clenched her fist and closed her eyes, trying desperately to remember everything she had heard about Hook, wondering how best to save her and her brother's lives. Michael's desperate face leapt to her mind and she blinked back hot tears. *I must not fail us.* Wendy took a long breath in, the prayers of her childhood falling from her lips without her consent.

"Our Father who art . . ."

A deep voice boomed out from behind the door and into the hallway.

"Neverland has no gods that can hear your prayers, foolish girl. Come inside."

Wendy swallowed her fear and pushed the massive door open, the fairy king swinging forward to welcome her into Captain Hook's quarters.

CHAPTER TWO

Upon stepping into the room, Wendy was instantly aware of just how disgusting she was. A wretched smell emanated directly from her skin. The curdling stench of salt and fish, of not bathing for five days, of the stress of being held in the damp dark against her will enveloped her. Captain Hook's room was making her feel revolting by comparison. Wendy had seen some elaborate rooms in her life in London; the wealthiest of her mother's friends invited people over purely to marvel at their lavish dwellings, their Gillows of Lancaster desks, their Louis XVI lounging chairs. Wendy had seen those rooms, bored out of her mind, sitting pretty on a couch, lost in a book as her mother discussed the social lives of the people around them.

Now, here on this ship in what was one of the most-lavish rooms she had ever seen, Wendy wished she could hear her mother's voice, going on about who looked inappropriate at the ball, who had run away with her teacher, who was failing at Father's bank. Her mother's voice did not come, and so instead Wendy waited in the silence, taking in the elaborate decor around her. Light wood, patterned in ever-widening spirals spread out from under her bare, blackened feet. A maroon rug filled the room, the corners marked with black tassels that lay limply against the floor. The back of the oval-shaped room served mainly as a showcase for a massive black marble fireplace. Two wooden boys, their backs bent as if they couldn't bear the weight, held up a long mantle that was covered with glass bottles of wine, each one set into an iron holder to keep them from rolling away. In the center of the mantle, an enormous stuffed crocodile held a ticking clock between its teeth, the sound bouncing off the richly wallpapered walls. Its beady eyes and peeling skin silently watched Wendy as she fidgeted nervously, waiting for the captain to speak. Rising from the top of the crocodile's head, a sheet of onyx-black marble glistened in the candlelight, like a wall of ink. The walls were covered by wooden bookshelves, ancient books piled in some places, neatly organized in others. Wendy was seized by how much she missed books, and by extension, Booth. It was all she could do to keep from pressing her nose against the pages, breathing in the oily scent of the paper, the clean notes of page and ink. Instead she stood still, staring now at the black flag that dangled from the glittering crystal chandelier, its tattered edges framing the stark outline of a single white skull. A disembodied baritone voice echoed through the room, its tone confident.

"That was my father's flag. Do you like it?"

Wendy had to cough to find her voice. There was an uncomfortable stirring in her lungs.

"Yes sir, I mean, Captain Hook. Sir." She winced.

A high-backed leather chair faced away from her, black and navy leather stitched together in flawless design, the two armrests carved in the shapes of roaring lions. On one side dangled a hand holding a glass of rum, the glass swirling every few seconds so that the liquor dashed up against the sides of the glass, leaving a thin amber film. He took a silent sip.

"Impressive room though, isn't it? I commissioned the best artisans in Neverland to furnish this room, and then paid them for their wares by not killing them." The glass disappeared and then returned, followed by a sigh. "Truthfully, it has turned out a bit garish for my taste, but it is a good room to drink in, to regret and dream, is it not?"

Wendy opened her mouth unsure of what to say.

"Speak, girl. And don't mutter this time. I can't stand children who mutter."

He gave a simple, short bark of a laugh, and had another drink.

"That's a lie. I really can't stand children at all. *Particularly naughty boys.*"

Wendy reached for her voice, clutching her hands in front of her. "Captain Hook, my name is Wendy Darling . . ."

"I know you who you are," he snapped. "Believe it or not, I know most everything that goes on in Neverland. It's a perk that comes from owning its largest town."

"Yes, sir. As you know then, my brother Michael and I are being held down in the ship's prison, the lowest room on the ship. . . ."

"You aren't in the ship's prison, you are in the brig. And, you haven't even seen the depths of the *Sudden Night.* There are worse places, believe it or not. You should see it simply as a holding room, a place where you pleasantly wait to speak with the captain."

"But the chains . . ."

"The chains are necessary, though usually the *Sudden Night* doesn't hold prisoners. You simply wait in the brig until I deign it time to speak with you. Then you either live, or you walk the plank. You'll find justice on the *Sudden Night* simple and unflinching."

Wendy lowered her eyes. "I understand, sir. It's just that my brother, Michael, he is only five years old, sir."

The hand swirling the glass stopped moving and Wendy felt dread rush into her chest.

"And what should that mean to me? That he is five years old. A nine-year-old Lost Boy killed one of my men with an arrow through the eye. *Children are not just children in Neverland, Wendy Darling.* You should know that more than anyone."

Wendy nodded, her mind searching desperately to the appropriate answer to each question.

"Answer me this, Wendy, is Peter Pan a child?"

She saw the cold look in his eyes before he had dropped her, sent her cartwheeling down to her death, only to teach her a lesson. She cleared her throat.

"No. No, he is not."

"Correct. First intelligent thing you've said today. Now, I'm going to ask you one more question and you will answer it. Consider your answer carefully, for your life and your brother's life depend on your answer."

Wendy's voice burst uncontrollably out of her throat. "Please, please! I will do anything. I will scrub the decks, I will sew your clothes, and I will cook! I will do anything, please, just don't hurt my brother, please spare him. Please, sir!"

The glass hovered a moment before slamming down on the lion's head, shattering into a thousand pieces. A drop of blood dripped from Hook's fingers onto the lavish carpet. His voice was coiled and controlled.

"Quiet! I will hear none of your emotional pleas. I said I would ask you a question, and you will answer it."

Wendy's heart pounded and there was a roaring in her ears.

"My question is simply this: give me one reason why I shouldn't kill you. Choose your answer wisely, because I've heard them all before."

Wendy closed her eyes, remembering everything that she had heard and seen since arriving in Neverland. He raised a single bloody finger and moved it back and forth like a clock pendulum, his tongue clicking.

"Ticktock, girl. I have waves to master and mouths to feed."

Wendy felt the boat move underneath her, the waves caressing and battering the *Sudden Night*. Her head jerked up just as Hook was beginning to speak again.

"If you can't—"

"You shouldn't kill me because Peter Pan is in love with me."

There was a silence in the room. The clock ticked its disapproval.

Wendy held her breath and watched as the bloody hand clenched once and then released again. Hook stood. His back rose up from behind the chair, taller than she had imagined, but then again, she had lived around just children for far too long. He had rich chestnut hair, short and shorn with a razor, flecked with gray at the temples and crown. A white collared shirt, crisp and clean hit the neat beard that covered the bottom half of his face and chin, these hairs also graying at the edges. He turned and the light slowly crawled across his face. Wendy gasped, only because he was so different than she had imagined him. Peter had described him as a monster, and yet, he was just a man—though a grown one. His face was hard, with sharp cheekbones that jutted out from firmly set cheeks, as if he was biting the inside of his mouth. Two large eyebrows slanted downwards over steely gray-green eyes, fringed with short lashes, his gaze intense and terrifying. Wendy realized with a start that he reminded her a bit of her father. The crisp white shirt was tucked into high-waisted gray pants, and the black boots that Wendy remembered seeing a few days ago on the deck hit him at the knee. A long navy military jacket dusted the ground at his feet. Though it was well taken care of, Wendy could tell that it was quite old. Four large medals in the shapes of stars and suns covered the left breast of the coat.

As she stared at him, Wendy guessed that he was in his late thirties. Her eyes followed the coat down to his left hand, and swallowed the lump in her throat when she saw it; sitting in place of his hand was a single hook, larger than necessary, and quite sharp, its silver reflecting the shifting light of the ship. Hook noticed her looking at it.

"Interested in the hook, my dear? I can show it to you closely if you would like." He turned it menacingly. Wendy immediately shifted her eyes to the ground.

"No. I'm sorry, sir."

"Sorry is a word you will no longer use on the *Sudden Night*. I run a very tight ship here, and we don't have time for apologies."

"I'm sorry, I mean I . . ."

Wendy stopped talking midsentence and Hook laughed. His rum-laden breath washed over her face.

"So Peter Pan is in love you with you, you say?"

"I do, sir."

"And how long, how long has Peter been in love with you?"

Wendy bit her lip, trying to remember how long they had been on Pan Island. "A few weeks, sir."

"Ah, but a few weeks on Neverland feels like years, does it not?"

"It does, sir. I'm actually not sure entirely sure how long I have been here."

"If you have been here a few weeks, than a few months have passed in the place you used to call home."

"Oh, no!" Wendy immediately thought of her parents and Booth. She quickly wiped a tear from her eye, determined not to cry in front of the captain.

"Women. Here take this." The captain handed her a black linen handkerchief. Wendy wiped her eyes.

"I'm sorry. Shoot! I mean, not I'm sorry. It's just been . . . my parents you see . . ."

"Yes. Everyone back home surely thinks you are dead. Which you almost were when we pulled you out of the sea, sputtering and sobbing. If we hadn't pulled you out—"

"We would be dead," said Wendy drily. "Peter would have killed me, and Michael would be at the bottom of the ocean." The thought turned her stomach.

"Ah yes, Peter Pan, Neverland's golden boy." Hook chuckled. "You've found out some things about Peter, have you?"

Wendy's eyes narrowed. "He's . . . evil. He's cruel and manipulative and insane. He . . ." She had a hard time even finding the words, so traumatized by the memory. "He dropped me. He dropped me, and I almost died. He said that he did it to teach me a lesson. He dropped me and threatened me, and told me that he would kill my brothers if I didn't love him. And so I left, I left. . . ."

Overwhelmed she fell to her knees. This was the first time she had spoken about what happened, and it poured out of her, though Hook's sneer showed that he was deeply disinterested in her emotions.

"I left my other brother there, John. I left him! He worships Peter, will do whatever he says, as if Peter has brainwashed him! He made him a general and it's blinded John to the truth." She paused. "Just like I was blinded, just like the Lost Boys are blinded. How could I not see? We should have never left our nursery window. Never."

She felt the captain's hook under her arm, yanking her up to her feet.

"Stand up, girl. Pull yourself together."

Wendy did, feeling ashamed at her outburst of emotion. Hook blinked.

"Peter has blinded us all, at one time or another. I know a little something about that."

Wendy shook her head.

"Peter is not a very good person."

At that, Hook burst out laughing, a deep chortle full of bitterness.

"That's quite an understatement. I feel sad for you, girl, so easily taken in by his beauty. I bet getting you to fall for him was as easy as luring a fish with a bucket of chum."

She felt ashamed, but also acknowledged the truth of his statement with a blunt nod of her head.

"I forgot everything when he brought us here. My parents, who I was . . . the boy I loved."

Hook's faced changed momentarily as he let his hook linger on her shoulder. Then he yanked it back from her as if she was on fire.

"Chin up, girl, you're not dead, and that's more than most people who have interacted with Peter Pan can say."

He sighed and rubbed his Hook against his forehead, eyeing

her as the fireplace behind him roared and sparked. Then with a groan he made his way over to a tall cabinet that was set inside the bookcase. When he opened it, Wendy saw easily a dozen glass bottles of wine, rum, and other libations as the captain took his pick. He drew out a small black wine bottle. Using his teeth, he pulled open the cork and sent a huge swig down his throat.

"Ah! Much better. Let there be no more talk of love. Now, about you and your small brother."

Wendy felt her skin tighten. She waited as the captain made his way back to his impassive chair. He sat down hard, the bottle clutched in his hand.

"I won't kill you and your brother today. Today. And it's not because I have a soft spot for children, so don't mistake my mercy for sentimentality. You may be of use to me, and I intend to learn everything you know about Peter Pan. But not today. Today is . . ."

He swirled the bottle.

"G'on, I'm needed upstairs. Judging by the way this boat is rocking we'll be hitting some rough waters later. Now, you will not be getting a free ride here. Both you and your brother need to find a way to be of use to the crew on this ship. Don't be underfoot, don't be stupid, and don't eat too much. If one of you falls off the deck into the water, we won't turn around for you, you understand?"

Wendy nodded, her heart flooding with relief. "Yes, sir. I promise that we will make ourselves useful and stay out of the way."

"Good. I'll have Smith set you up in a proper room, unless you would like to say in the brig with Paulo and the rats."

"No!" Wendy snapped, then changing her tone to a more polite cadence. "No, we would not like to stay down there."

"Now, before you go, I have to ask you one more question."

Wendy stayed silent.

"Is there anything I need to know about Peter Pan that might affect my men in the near future?"

This was a test, she could sense it, and therefore she didn't hold back, not even for a second, her voice almost interrupting him.

"Yes! Peter now has guns. Lots of them. He told the boys that he's preparing for a great battle."

Hook's voice dropped. He sounded worried.

"Ah yes, the guns. He's getting bored. I feared this was coming when he burned down our armory."

"He burned down the armory because I rejected his advances."

"Did he, now?"

Hook laughed. "I did learn something today, it turns out. Ah, it brings me joy that Peter Pan once again wants something he can't have."

"What do you mean?"

Hook's hand swirling the wine bottle stopped moving.

"Do not presume we are friends, Miss Darling, and that we are going to have chats. I could still decide to kill you. What you know about Peter Pan could fit into a thimble."

Wendy was intrigued, but stayed silent. Hook turned away from her.

"Leave me be," he snapped. "I have already wasted too much time talking to you, and I am beginning to wonder if you wouldn't be more help to me as a sacrifice to the mermaids' coral garden. They love virgin blood."

Wendy stumbled at his words as she made her way to the door, trying not to fly off her feet as the *Night* pitched suddenly to the left.

"You best get your sea legs about you soon. No one on this ship will coddle a girl with a broken ankle. Better to feed the fishes."

"I will," vowed Wendy, clumsily making her way past the huge door, the carved male fairy watching her with brilliant wooden eyes.

"Miss Darling," the captain was pulling his hook down his jawline, the bottle of wine in his other hand. He stared at her for a moment. "If your other brother attacks this ship with Peter Pan, or any other Lost Boys, make no mistake, I will put a harpoon through his heart and I will enjoy doing so. Do you understand?"

Wendy stood frozen, one hand on the door handle, the other clutching the edge of her filthy dress.

"Yes," she whispered.

"Good. Oh, and try not to get violated. That would be . . . an incredible hassle."

Hook turned away from her and walked to the fireplace.

"You're dismissed, Miss Darling."

She took once glance back at this mythical man, a man whose named was whispered among Lost Boys, a man whom she believed Peter actually feared. He continued to lean his head against the clock, his eyes closed, his hand and hook clutching at the mantle. The wine bottle was open at his feet, spilling out onto the carpet. She shut the door behind her. Smith the Murderer was waiting for her, his gigantic tattooed arms crossed.

"And, how did you find the captain?"

"He was fine."

"You do what he says, savvy? I'll not have a wench like you scuttle this ship, you hear?"

She nodded, her mind lingering on the captain's face when she had left. Troubled, she thought, as Smith led her down the lavish hallway and back down into the bowels of the ship via the bone staircase. That was how she had found the captain. Hook was many things, but troubled was the word that fit him best. Troubled and terrifying.

CHAPTER THREE

Smith led her back to the brig, where Michael was waiting for her, lying silently on the floor, his wrists raw and bleeding from where his chains had rubbed his skin. Wendy scooped him up in her arms and hugged him hard as Smith unlocked his chains.

"Say goodbye to Paulo, lad!"

"Be quiet," snapped Wendy. "Can't you see you've already done your damage?"

Smith raised his lip in a mean sneer but mercifully stayed silent after that. Wendy hoisted a still Michael over her shoulder, and he clutched hard to her neck.

"Don't worry," she whispered. "We're leaving."

Michael didn't say anything, but tiny sniffles began breaking her heart as they followed Smith through the endless dark interiors of the *Sudden Night*. As the made their way upwards—using the bone staircase that Wendy prayed Michael wouldn't notice—Wendy felt the vibrations of the waves pounding on sides of the ship and smelled the salty water all around them. It was in the very grains of the black wood, that distinct wanton smell of the salt. *It made her sick.* Smith turned a sharp corner, and Wendy bumped hard into his back.

"You running a rig, girl? Give a man some space."

Wendy backed up, Michael still wrapped around her back. Smith looked around, his eyes narrowed.

"Check the hallway," he instructed. "You never know where pirates are lurking."

Wendy leaned back and peeked around the corner. The hallway was empty, the tasteful wall decor of cutlasses rocking softly back and forth, the knives winking in the sunlight as they pitched left and right.

"Uh, there is no one," she replied, confused.

Smith grunted. "A lot of work for a silly girl and her cowardly brother."

Michael dropped down from her back, and plunged past her, his open hands coming down on Smith's massive leg, hitting him again and again.

"I'm not a coward! You're mean! I hate you! I hate you!" He pounded away, a hail of tiny fists, as Wendy tried to pull him off, fearful of what Smith would do in return.

"Michael, stop it this instant!"

He ignored her. Smith looked down at him with cold eyes as Wendy tugged at her brother, finally detaching him with a hard yank that sent them both tumbling back onto the hard floor. Smith grinned nastily.

"I like you a bit better now, you wee little scallywag! But touch me again, and I swear to God, I'll cut your filthy ears off!"

Michael shrank back behind Wendy. Smith huffed in their general direction and then turned around to face the dead end of the hallway. "I know it's somewhere here, if I could just get a moment of GODFORSAKEN peace to find it. . . ."

Smith felt up the sides of the wall, covered with strange knick-knacks—bells, locks, watches, gears, and wooden instruments.

"If I can remember . . . Ah, there it is."

He flipped a tiny iron casing upwards and underneath it sat a tiny black gear, barely the size of a pound, which Smith turned twice to the left. Wendy heard a click, and a thin piece of wood fell out of the door. Smith took it in his hand, and after making an obscene gesture with it, pushed it forward. To Wendy's surprise, the wall of locks and knickknacks swung open. Even Michael stopped sniffling for a moment as he watched in fascination as the hidden door appeared. Smith groaned, wiping his nose off on his massive forearm.

"The captain likes tinkering, that he does, especially with weapons."

He pointed his finger upwards.

"He likes making things that can kill flying boys. Like your brother!"

Wendy chose to ignore him, though his words made her heart tremble with thoughts of John, impaled and bloody.

"Is that where we are staying then?" she asked.

Smith grunted. "Sure is. Captain's orders. Flip up the lock, turn the wheel counterclockwise twice and the lever comes down. Push the lever straight in and the door will open. Now listen to me, close it tight behind you. This is a secret room, and we don't need every scurvy dog on this ship knowing where a pretty young thing sleeps, do we?"

Wendy understood instantly what he was saying.

"I'll bring you both breakfast in the morning, lunch is a roll and a fish, and dinner will be with the men up on deck. Keep an eye on yourself on this ship after nightfall. You won't be safe, unless you're with the captain or me. Though, it would be a stupid pirate who would cross the captain's orders, and he'd be signing his contract with bloody Davy Jones, but still." He grinned, showing his blackened back teeth, his breath washing over her, a mix of rot and wine.

"Men at sea have needs."

Wendy shook her head. "Thank you, Smith."

Taking Michael's hand in her own, she stuck her head through the door, where a few wooden stairs led down to a small room. Michael followed her before looking up at Smith with an intense scowl.

"I'm going to call you Smee," he said to Smith decidedly.

"Like hell you will," he muttered, before giving the little boy a shove forward, shutting the door behind them. "See you at dinner, little buggers."

He shut the door behind them, and Wendy heard the turning of the small wheel, sealing them safely inside. Michael was already making his way down the short steps.

"Oh, Wendy!"

Though any room in the world would have held more charm than the dank hell that they had been in the last five days, this room, for being tiny, was actually quite comfortable. Two short beds were tucked in the corner, one on top of each other, the bottom one so low that you practically had to bend at the waist to fit inside. Each bed had a straw mattress and a scratchy blanket thrown on top of it. Across from the beds sat a ragged armchair, though it must have once been beautiful, as Wendy could see the remnants of a red damask pattern. She spotted some bloodstains on the carpet, but they seemed quite old, and she decided not to linger on them. The room was flanked by wood panels that were pockmarked with tiny holes in the wood grain. Wendy ran her finger across them. It was the perfect size for the end of a hook. She shuddered, wondering what exactly went on in this room, this room that Hook kept secret, even from his own men. A single port window looked out onto the pitching sea beside them, filling the room with a reassuring daylight. Wendy breathed in the Neverland sun as Michael climbed all over the room exclaiming over the smallest things.

"Look, Wendy, here's a letter!" He pulled it out from under the bed. "There's some mouse poop, too."

"Well, don't touch it!" she deadpanned, thinking of what her mother would say if she knew her children would be happily sleeping on straw beds with mouse poop underneath them. She hoisted herself onto the upper bed and unfolded her legs, giving a happy sigh when her body uncurled. She hadn't known how much she had missed being able to lie down on a bed. Even her hammock on Pan Island hadn't been this comfortable. This tiny room, where you couldn't walk two feet without bumping your knee, suddenly seemed like Buckingham Palace. Michael curled up beside her.

"I think we are safe now," she whispered to Michael, before kissing his head.

"Was Hook nice?"

"No, he was not." Wendy answered honestly before pausing. "But he wasn't terrible either."

Michael's eyes sparkled. "Not bad like Peter Pan is bad."

"No. Not like Peter." Wendy closed her eyes, remembering the desperate look in Peter's eyes as he wrapped his hands around her neck, strangling the breath out of her just before the *Sudden Night* rammed into them. It was like he had wanted to consume her, consume her breath, her life. She had never been so scared, for in that moment, she had thought she would lose Michael. Her arms closed tightly around him.

"I'm sorry, Michael. Sorry for letting Peter take us away from our home. We should have stayed . . . we should have . . ."

Michael wrapped his little fingers around Wendy's slim ones.

"We wanted to fly, though. I did like flying. I hope we can fly with the pirates."

Wendy knew that wouldn't happen, but instead she stayed quiet as he prattled on. Flying. She couldn't even think of the sky, its vast open blue, terrifying as she had plunged through it, untethered to anything except the possibility of death. Her mind lingered on Hook, on his cryptic words. "What you know about Peter Pan could fit into a thimble." What did he know about Peter that fueled his hatred so? The man had enough ammunition to hate him as it was, with the constant battle of Lost Boys and pirates, and yet there was something else, something deeper. His words had been so soaked with hate, which could only come from a personal loss. *Was it that Peter had taken his hand?* Wendy clenched her hand, unconsciously, feeling the way the tendons pulled her fingers forward. Yes, losing a hand would surely do it.

"Michael . . ."

He was already asleep, finally safe, and finally warm. She wouldn't wake him. Instead, she pried the letter from his bunched up fist, folding it open quietly, working hard to keep her own eyes open.

Captain's Log
May 17, 1892

My dearest Easter,
It pleases me to say that the Jolly Rodger flourishes even in these caustic waters! We sailed out of the port of Shimoda, straight east until we pulled upwards into Alaskan territory. The wind and the waves seem to be on the side of our able navigators, pushing the Jolly Rodger onwards at a swift clip. Leaving behind a mild storm, we venture on, to places few eyes have seen in this dark North, a place of fearful night whispers and beauty that is so violent that it pierces your beating heart! As the green pines of

Barrow slowly vanish from sight, I set my vision on the adventure before me, a destiny. I am at once a pirate, a voyager, and a theater patron, watching this stage of harsh, sharp landscape unfold beyond our bow. Peaks of unflinching ice penetrate the glaciers that make their way timidly down to our sea, and seals dance at our helm, their slippery fins slapping the icy waters, as if they were playing a game with us.

The men spotted a pod of black-tipped whales rising out of the water to the east—what monsters lie underneath us I cant even imagine, here at the tip of the world. Though it be bitter cold (imagine had we come in winter! The madness!), I have taken to wandering outside for the sunset, wrapped in a silly amount of blankets. The sunsets are different here, they are paler, the deep black of the water melding with the cleanest air you have ever breathed, and a blue horizon rising out over the ocean like a great eye, calculating and precise.

*It makes me feel small, my darling. I
miss you."*

*Yours forever,
Arthur Tiberius Hook*

Wendy smiled as she reached the end of the letter. There was something uniquely comforting about reading in bed—it was akin to pulling a warm blanket over her mind. Even though she was a prisoner on a pirate ship, her brother was being held captive by a maniacal god-child, and she may never see her family or the boy she loved again, she could, for just a page or two, escape into the mind and words of someone else. She carefully folded the letter and placed it back in the torn pages of the deep-maroon journal, its cover frayed and loved. Arthur Tiberius Hook. That must have been Hook's father, and Easter—his mother? Did Hook know this letter had been left in here? It had been tucked deeply under the bed, so perhaps not. Wendy put the letter down before placing her hands on her neck. She could still feel the slight raised bruises of where Peter had choked her and with a shudder she withdrew her hand. Michael breathed warm and soft across her face, his filthy hair pressed up against her cheek. They were both disgusting. She snuggled against him and fell into the folds of soft darkness like an old friend.

CHAPTER FOUR

They slept for twelve hours, rocked hard by the *Sudden Night*, before gnawing hunger woke them both. After attempting to brush Michael's hair and her own, Wendy changed them into the garments that Smith had left for them outside the door: breeches and a loose tunic for Michael, a simple and conservative cream dress for her, and a shawl patterned with thick roses and shades of pale green that draped heavily over her shoulders. Wendy loved it immediately, as it reminded her of a time when she didn't reek of fish and other unspeakable filth. After they were dressed, Wendy listened at the door, shushing Michael, who was pawing at her legs and braying about how hungry he was. She heard nothing, and so slowly and cautiously, she unlocked the door and pushed the wooden lever outwards. The hidden door swung open quickly, and they tumbled into the hallway. Moving quickly, Wendy shut the door behind them, taking care to flip down the black iron casing to cover the tiny wheel. She looked down the hallway, trying to remember where the stairs were.

"Here, follow me," Wendy whispered.

They made their way down a long, straight hallway, listening to the constant clink of the knives that rattled on the walls as the ship battered the waves. They stumbled over their feet as the hallway swayed one direction and then another, Wendy fearing that the emptiness in her stomach would turn to nausea if she paid too much attention to it.

"Wendy," moaned Michael, "I'm so hungry!"

"I know. I'm trying to find . . . " she turned a corner and spied the bone staircase, "that!"

She had to coax him up the stairs, trying her best to explain why the rails were made of long femurs. As they climbed, the air became cleaner, and she smelled, for the first time since Hook had pulled them out of the sea, that cloying sweetness of Neverland air, the hibiscus and the sugar plants saturating the air. The feeling of life entering her nostrils was such as relief. Finally, they reached a heavy wooden door that lay horizontal at the top of the stairs. Light peeked in from above, giving the door a square halo of bright, natural light. Wendy took a deep breath and pushed the door open, emerging into the sunlight like a creature of the night. She was at once overwhelmed by the noise of the monstrous ship: waves battered against its side, sending the occasional spray of salty water up over the deck. There was the sloughing noise of the bristles that a pirate was moving back and forth with vigor over the black wooden planks of the deck, and the faint *knock, knock* of the rudder that moved effortlessly behind them. Above her, massive black sails snapped in the wind, unfurling their shrouds like a caress, retracting them again only to meet the wind once more. The ship creaked underneath her feet. Michael squeezed her hand with excitement, a happy grin on his face.

"Wendy! This is a REAL pirate ship!" It wasn't a pirate ship, she mused, it was THE pirate ship, larger and swifter than any she'd ever seen or heard of. The *Sudden Night's* curving deck was unlike any of the ships Wendy had seen at port in London, or in the many books that John read featuring pirates and deserted islands. Like a hand creeping up her spine, Wendy felt the intense eyes of the pirates on her, but she consciously decided not to focus on them. Instead, she let her eyes widen at the sight of what this ship really was, the truth of the *Sudden Night*: it was a weapon. The right side of the ship was lined with harpoons of all different shapes, loaded into round cannons that swiveled on the wind. Their sharp barbed lips gleamed in the afternoon sun, their cruel tips pointed at the sky. She counted twelve separate cannons, each loaded with dozens of harpoons of varying size and shape. Underneath the harpoons lay a coiled black net that stretched the length of the deck. Wendy recognized it—she had been hauled out of the sea by this net. She shuddered at the memory of Michael's lifeless body, and then without warning, pulled him tight against her body, hugging him close. He gave an annoyed sigh.

"Wendy, stop!"

At the ends of the net, there were two open baskets full of hand-sized cylinders, smooth stones, polished white. She reached for one. Her arm was grabbed roughly and she looked up to see Smith, his hulking form blocking the sun, the angel tattooed on his arm staring down at her with its naughty cherubic grin.

"I wouldn't be touching those. Those pearls have just a touch of gunpowder inside of them."

Wendy recoiled.

"See, if we can't shoot a harpoon through the Lost Boys chest, we can blow their eyes out of their skull, singe their skin! Just about everything on this ship is about as dangerous it can be, for a good reason. The Lost Boys attack from the sky—and we have to be ready for them."

Smith raised his eyes.

"See that man there, in the crow's nest?"

Wendy followed his gaze to the center mast, where a cherry-wood basket lorded over the deck.

"That's Hawk. We call him that because he always has his eyes on the skies. That is his whole job. And when he sleeps, Owl takes over at night."

Smith stood up straight, his hands on his broad waist.

"Can't ever not watch the skies. They've tried to take us before, but the captain is smart, and he knows what he's looking for."

He grunted.

"Peter Pan and his brood of psychotics."

Wendy brushed her tumbling hair out of her face.

"They aren't a brood of psychotics. They are boys. Children."

"Well, if I could kill me one of those boys a day, I would be a happy first mate."

"You're utterly revolting."

"Indeed, I am."

Smith beat his chest with one hand before letting out a loud burp.

"C'mon, I'll give you the tour and introduce you to a few of the men." He gestured to Wendy's wildly blowing hair. "Pull that back. You're on a ship now, girl, not at some namby-pamby boarding school where your curls need be bouncing all over the place!"

Once a small group of the crew had assembled, Smith instructed them to stand in a line. All eyes were on Wendy, a disturbing bunch—sunken eyes with dark bags underneath them, red rimmed and jaded. Pirates, she would learn, were always tired.

Some of the pirates were quite ordinary, cheery-looking chaps with loose-fitting tunics and leather belts, who stared at her with a hopeful curiosity. The older men mostly looked miserable, as if nails had pierced through their shoes, obviously uncomfortable at her presence onboard. Their uniquely terrifying names rolled off Smith's blunt tongue and into Wendy's waiting ears like a persistent drip of water. Bloody Blair, Wu, Svengili. Voodoo, an impossibly tall black man, whose cocoa skin shone in the sunlight, except for his arm, which had been badly scorched and was now covered in hideous scars. He nodded kindly to Wendy as Smith ran through the names. Olathe, Bouff—a squatty man, with piggish eyes and a belt with a dozen different knives hanging from it. Redd, the one-eyed bastard that she had met in the brig leered at her, his eyes resting hungrily on her collarbone. Black Caesar was a very white man dressed in all black, pale and gaunt, as if he had one foot on the other side of the grave.

Hawk came grumbling down from the crow's nest for the introduction, and was joined by Owl, his twin. These two reminded Wendy of the pictures of robust circus performers with their long, curling mustaches. Owl wore gigantic, bottle-cap spectacles, while Hawk had none. Attempting to be magnanimous, Wendy stepped forward to shake their hands.

"I hear you watch the sky."

Hawk reached forward shyly before his face turned cruel.

"'Tis wrong having a lady on board," he said quietly. "You'll curse us all."

He squeezed her hand tightly, cruelly. Wendy kept the smile frozen on her face, her hand in midshake. Hawk turned away from her and began making his way back up the rope ladder to the crow's nest, grumbling loudly about Wendy as he went.

"She'll be the death of us! Best to throw her overboard, I say. Let the crocs have a taste."

"Oh, shut the hell up, you cur-infested lout," snapped Smith. "We've all had it with your prophecies! About a quarter of them come true, and those are only the ones that are already gonna be true, like we're having fish for dinner tonight!"

The rest of the pirates roared. Wendy turned back to Owl, the quieter brother. Wide eyes blinked out from behind thick spectacles. Wendy smiled at him to no response. Smith let out a barking laugh.

"He can barely see, girl. He's blind as a bat."

Wendy's face must have betrayed her, because a bunch of the men burst out laughing. Owl stepped shyly forward. "My lady, though I can't see your face, I am guessing that you are wondering how a blind man sits in the crow's nest, and how this blind man is going to keep you safe from one devilish Peter Pan."

Wendy bit the inside of her cheek, but weighing her options, decided to go with honesty.

"Yes sir, I was indeed wondering."

"I like an honest girl."

He stepped closer to her, and Wendy could see that past the thick spectacles, his eyes were a milky white, as if a cloud of fog had descended into his irises. "I protect you with these." His grizzled hands reached up and tapped his ears.

"Peter Pan is quick, and he is smart. During the day, we can see him from afar and aim our harpoons, but at night, or in a fog, he might be able to sneak up on the ship from the water, or from the air directly above us. He wouldn't dare come on us during the day, but night is a dangerous time for enemies of Peter Pan."

Wendy's heart went cold at the thought and her tongue failed to make intelligent words come out of her mouth.

"Yes, yes. I suppose it would be."

Owl leaned forward, and Wendy smelled his rotten breath, reeking of spoiled milk and cheap wine. "Peter Pan can do those things, but Peter Pan cannot defy nature. He cannot silence the air around him that parts as his body sluices through it."

Owl made a slicing motion with his hand, then brought it up and down in waves.

"As he flies, the air swirls around him."

He pursed his lips together.

"Whoosh, whush, wheeww . . ."

Then he banked both of his hands. "Peter Pan likes to fly very fast. Not slow. He sounds different than a bird. A bird flaps. It goes *phhffftt*, pause. *Phhfft*, pause. Peter goes, *whush*, continually. *Whush, whoosh, wheeeeww,* as he's descending. No flaps. The air parts for him like he's a king, and down he comes." His eyebrows narrowed. "And then we aim the cannons at him. One day, he'll forget. One day, maybe now that you're here, he'll drop down into our range. And when he does."

Owl raised his finger to the sky.

"Bam."

Wendy nodded.

"My brother, Hawk, he watches during the day. Sharp eyes, but also sharp ears. But me . . . I listen at night, and in the fog. I hear, everything. The slithering beasts of sea, hungry for food, hungry for mates. Birds, desperately flapping for land, their wings giving out too soon. Mermaids, singing their ethereal and deadly songs in the depths. And I hear Peter Pan. In fact, I heard him last night."

A chill shot through Wendy. *No, no.*

"He was out to the east, circling. Watching our ship from a great distance. He had two others with him, not as skilled. Clumsy fliers, loud. He was very agitated, his movements sharp, hard, and reckless. He wants you. I can hear it in the wind."

Wendy curled her hands into fists, willing herself not to be afraid.

"He may want me, but he does not have my permission to take me. I do not belong to Peter Pan. Or any man, for that matter."

Owl gave a toothless grin as the a few men around her gave a hearty, "Hear, hear!"

The older man reached out a shaky hand for her, and Wendy, overcome with a thankfulness for his incredible gift, kissed his palm. Owl's face registered surprise, and a blush ran up his weathered cheeks, mottled with burst blood vessels. He shyly yanked his hand back. "It's a pleasure, my lady."

Smith looked with disdainful incredulity at the men mooning at Wendy.

"WHAT IN THE BLOODY HELL is happening here? Have you never seen a girl before? Ain't you got a ship to run? Hop to it men! At the ready before I cut your ears and wipe my arse with them!"

The pirates all scuttled away. Smith turned to Wendy. "That's enough jerking around for today. Let me show you to your work."

"I'm not going to work! I'm going to stay on the deck and be a pirate!" declared Michael.

His arm darting out quickly like a snake, Smith reached out and picked up Michael by the collar of his shirt, raising him up until their eyes were level. Then he stomped over to the side of the ship and held Michael out over the water.

"Stop! Stop it!" Wendy cried, to no avail.

Michael whimpered as he clutched desperately to Smith's arm.

"Are you planning on staying on this ship?" he asked Michael. Michael whimpered.

"Yes, sir. Yes, Smee."

"Then you work. There is no free ride. No nannies here, no playtime. This isn't Pan Island. Will you work?"

Michael nodded, fat tears running down his cheeks. Without a second glance, Smith tossed Michael down, where he landed hard on his bottom on the deck. He whimpered for a moment before his attention was quickly diverted.

"Smee, what's that?"

Michael pointed to a large metal structure beside him on the boat, iron carved like a curled hand, reaching upwards from the deck. The sharp talons of fingers splayed out at the end. Sticky webbing stretched in between the fingers, thick rope that had been dipped in something—syrup? Tar?

Without warning, Smith reached out and boxed Michael's ears. Michael let out a horrible cry.

"That'll teach you to call me Smee again, you filthy rat bastard."

"Stop! You hurt him!"

Smith narrowed his eyes at Wendy.

"You going to cut his cheese up for him too?"

Wendy ignored his barb, while thinking that she had, indeed, cut up Michael's bread before.

"Now, let's begin—what do you scrappy sea bass know about ships?"

Michael pushed forward.

"I know that there is such a thing as a poop deck!"

Smith narrowed his eyes.

"Ignorant, as I imagined. Spoiled, little, rich Londoners who ain't never been anywhere near an actual ship."

"So there's no poop deck?" Immense disappointment fell across Michael's cheeks, red from the biting wind. Smith sighed, his hands tracing one of three giant knives that hung from his leather belt.

"Yes, there is. Follow me and don't dawdle, you pox-faced krakens. . . . Captain never told me I'd have to be a nanny. . . ."

As they walked quickly down the deck, Smith pointed out the various parts of ship, Wendy trying desperately to remember the names of each feature as they went.

"This here side is the port side. If you are facing to the front of the ship, port will always be on your left. That way if you turn around, it's still port. Got it?"

Wendy and Michael nodded.

"This side is the starboard then."

"Why it's called the starboard?"

"Why don't you stop asking your lollygagging, stupid questions and get a move on?" the pirate grumbled as he shoved Michael forward.

A short man, dressed in ragged finery, his head covered with unruly gray curls, stepped forward.

"If you would allow me to explain, Smith: it's called the starboard because back in the olden day, before rudders, they had to steer the ship using the stars for navigation." He pointed off the starboard side. "And they steered it from the starboard side. It's the side that the stars favor."

Smith grabbed the man by his coat, pulling him close to his face.

"You mean to show me up on my boat, Barnaby? That voice of yours makes my skin stand on edge, makes me feel like you look."

The man quivered in Smith's hands.

"No, no Smith, I was just trying to help!"

Smith threw him roughly to the ground. The man landed on his knees in a pile of squirming fish, gasping their last breaths. A small tin box bounced out of his pocket and sent gears scattering across the deck.

"Pick those up. And if you know so much, you can give them the damn tour, you nattering wretch!"

Barnaby straightened his coat. "With pleasure."

CHAPTER FIVE

First Mate Smith stomped away, grumbling about the day he could throw them all overboard. The man brushed off his coat before pulling some glasses out of his pocket. He was small and ferretlike, with a twitchy nose and a pinched face, as if he was smelling something unpleasant. He seemed like one of the bankers at her father's old firm, that is, except that his hands were black. Not dirty, like all the other busy hands she saw around her, but black as coal, as if he had dipped them in ink. He stuck out one of his shiny black hands and Wendy, with some hesitation, reached forward and shook it.

"Don't worry, won't come off on ya, lass. I tinker, that's what I do, and that involves grease and grime. Though, it doesn't help that my hands were burned in a coal fire. Makes the black stick to them a bit more, I'm afraid."

He held his hand up, and she could see the skin pulled into fine rivulets of scars, running from palm to wrist. She swallowed her initial shock and smiled kindly at him.

"Wendy Darling, I presume?"

It was so nice to hear someone speak in that polite dialect of home that she almost wept.

"Yes, and this is Michael."

"Hello, little sir. Welcome to the *Sudden Night*. I'm Barnaby, the ship's navigator. Though here in Neverland, I fear I'm of little use."

Wendy smiled and Barnaby beamed at her.

"I'll have to tell you about that thankless job some other time, for I fear if I do not quickly give you a proper tour, Smith will have my black hands dangling from the foremast."

Wendy looked down the ship to see Smith angrily staring down at Barnaby, raw hatred splashing over his rough features.

"Yes! Well, I heard Smith explaining starboard, didn't I?"

"Yes, he had just started."

"An easy way to remember it is, 'Starlight, star bright, starboard is on the right.'"

Michael began singing along softly to the familiar tune. He smiled and turned his face to the sky, the sun washing over his pale features as he sang the rhyme softly to himself. It was the first time since they left Pan Island that she thought her little brother might actually be alright.

"The starboard side is also where you will most likely find the first mate, the captain, and the higher-ranking pirates. The side opposite the starboard is called port. It means passage or entrance. For example, we most often dock at Port Duette on the port side."

"Ah, I see."

As they walked forward, Wendy noticed the eyes of the crew glaring hard at her as they pretended to go about their work. Smith raised a long whip that he had been coiling around his arm.

"Anyone fancy a lashing? Keep your eyes on your work, mateys!"

"Stay away from Smith." Barnaby lowered his voice. "He is neither a kind nor forgiving man."

Wendy remembered the way he had slit Kitoko's throat, the way the blood had poured out of his neck like a broken pipe. She shuddered.

"I know well that he is not."

"Well! Shall we continue? The basic parts of the ship are

common, be it a pirate ship like ours, or a vessel of the Royal Navy." He scratched his nose, wiggling it back and forth afterwards, his black hands pressing a filthy rag up to his mouth. "Though in my opinion, the *Sudden Night* could take any ship, Navy or otherwise."

Wendy swallowed, hoping to remember it all.

"Don't worry, my lady, a ship is nothing more than a system of rigging and sails. All any crew does is attempt to keep the parts of the ship running smoothly. If each man does his job, the rigging and the sails do theirs and we sail on, to rape and pillage, and what have you."

Wendy bit her lip. Barnaby leaned over.

"Don't worry, Miss Darling, we don't do much raping. Mostly pillaging and fighting amongst ourselves. Now, do you know any other parts of the ship?"

Wendy shook her head, ashamed at her lack of knowledge in this area. She thought of John, raising his wooden pirate ship up and down on invisible waves, playing in front of the nursery window while she read in her bed, his silhouette bathed in the light of the gray moon. *John would have been great at this. But she had left John behind, still in Peter's clutches.* She said a silent prayer that he was safe and that Peter had not taken out his anger on her brother, that John's intelligence would hopefully keep him safe. As she stood on the rocking deck, sticky guilt wormed its way through her heart at abandoning him. Barnaby continued, oblivious.

"If you look above you, you'll see the masts."

"And the crow's nest!" piped up Michael. "Even I know that!"

"Good job, little chap! That is the crow's nest. It's where we watch for weather, but mostly for flying devils."

Barnaby paused.

"Er, I mean . . . Lost Boys."

Wendy looked down.

"Of the masts, there are three masts. The foremast, the

mainmast, and the mizzenmast. The foremast is the first mast at the front of the ship; can you see it, Michael?"

Michael jumped up and down, obviously thrilled.

"I do! I see it! And the next mast is the mainmast. And what do you think that does?"

"Balances the ship?" asked Wendy.

"Not necessarily. It provides the support to the other masts, but it also anchors the sails and gives stability to the bowsprit, which is that long piece of wood protruding from the front there. . . ."

Barnaby trailed on while Wendy found herself lost in his words, overwhelmed by the monstrous ship around her. Her eyes followed his finger to the front of the ship as he droned on to Michael, held in rapt attention. The ship creaked, and she raised her eyes to take in the masts that Barnaby had pointed out. Huge black sails billowed outwards, their breasts swelling full with salty air. The mast rocked overhead, the sail following suit, a quiet dance between two willing partners. The pirate named Hawk currently sat perched on the crow's nest, his eyes trained on the sky. Her eyes followed the mast down to the port side, where black threaded ladders ran up and down the sides of the masts, anchored to the deck by thick copper hooks. Every few feet of ladder, a pistol or a scabbard was tied neatly to the bottom side of the rope, facing upwards, without hilt.

"That looks rather dangerous, all those weapons just sitting there," blurted Wendy.

Barnaby gave a short, polite laugh.

"'Tis, quite dangerous. Each man on this ship has at one time or another impaled himself on those." Barnaby raised his blackened hand and rolled up his coat sleeve to reveal a three-inch-long scar. "Mine was last year, just over there. Didn't hurt too much, plus it meant I was one of the crew officially. They help when you are fighting enemies who can fly. You never know when you'll need a weapon." He looked carefully around the ship before dropping his voice to a whisper.

"Some on this ship would call the captain paranoid, but I tend to disagree. The captain's careful, though at times I wonder what he thinks we're fighting exactly. Those boys are dangerous, but they aren't that smart. Killing 'em is pretty easy." He stepped back. "Sorry, Miss Darling. I didn't mean to imply . . ."

Wendy shrugged, sick of apologies about John, her own toxic grief enough to wrestle.

"Please, Barnaby, continue with the tour."

They strolled towards the front of the ship, passing the cannons that lined the edge of the deck, their crested points reminding Wendy of the iron fences back home in London. Barnaby saw her eying them.

"Makes it hard to land on the ship when you can't do so without impaling your own feet."

They made their way up to the front of the ship, called the bow, as Barnaby explained. Michael looked around.

"Where is the wheel?"

"Aye, that would be in the back of the ship, below the poop deck."

Michael laughed. "A poop deck! I knew there was one, Wendy."

"You did." Wendy climbed up the stairs to the bow of the ship, nothing between her and the jagged black spears that pointed outwards, their ends tied together with a long piece of curled wire.

"Only the captain really knows what this does, but I imagine it's quite spectacular."

Wendy looked down from the ship, her eyes focusing down, beyond the bowsprit, where the figurehead of a mermaid led the ship forward. Carved from what looked like the ivory cliffs of the Teeth, her outstretched hand reached for the horizon. Long curls of hair cascaded around her body, covering her breasts and body. A wide fish tail, perfectly molded from the pearly crusts of oyster shells curved down the outside of the ship. Her eyes were made of black pearls, a ruby for her mouth. Both of her hands were stretched forward, palms facing outward, as if she were pushing the waves away from the boat. She would have been lovely if it weren't for her terrible curved smile that stretched the sides of her mouth around razor sharp teeth.

Michael stepped back. "Scary," he declared, and Wendy agreed. "That's Queen Eryne of the Mermaids. She's a ruthless beauty if the stories are to be believed." He gave a shiver. "We'll be sailing past the Gray Shore on our way to Port Duette. My least-favorite part of the island."

"Why is that?" asked Wendy, looking out to the turquoise sea that was now lapping gently at the sides of the *Night* in a lover's embrace.

"You'd be okay with the mermaids, I imagine. Unless you're a virgin."

Wendy whirled on him, her patience worn thin from her time in the brig.

"You are improper to ask, sir!"

He stared at her for a second before turning away, stuttering. "I'm sorry, I didn't mean to be improper." He itched his nose twice. "I only asked because while they use the bones of men to make their coral garden . . . they use the blood of virgins to feed it."

Wendy looked at him in horror before blurting out. "A mermaid tried to take me once. Peter saved me." Her hair blew around her face as she turned back to the sea, unable to face her little brother, who stared up at her, his face full of confusion.

"Saved you for his own purposes I imagine, knowing Peter Pan," Barnaby said quietly. Wendy flinched, remembering Peter's desperate face, as he had choked her in the water. She looked numbly out over the bow to the crystalline sea that stretched endlessly before them, the white caps barely summoning a gentle murmur of a wave. Barnaby, however, did not pick up on her wish for silent reflection, and continued prattling on.

"Well, I'm sure the men are glad you are here now, at least they have something decent to look at as we sail towards Port Duette.

I'm sorry, that sounded uncouth. Again, Barnaby, with your words! Ha! What I meant was, even if you are a woman with no knowledge of sailing, you are lucky to be the captain's guest, for this is the most-magnificent ship, the most magnificent I've ever seen, the best of the Scorned Fleet."

She turned, a strong wind rushing up from the waves causing bumps to rise on her bare arms.

"The Scorned Fleet? What is that?"

Barnaby rubbed his hands together before leaning casually against one of the giant metal claws that protruded from the side of the boat, like it was nothing more than a park bench in Kensington Gardens.

"The Scorned are the five ships in the captain's fleet. There is the *Coral Plunder* under Captain Reed Bonney, the *Vicious Seas*, manned by Captain Jaali Oba, *Viper's Strike*, its captain being Captain Xian Li, and the *Undertow*, the wicked Captain Maison. And our *Sudden Night* of course, best girl in the sea!"

"And what does this Scorned Fleet do?"

"Well, the *Night* and the *Undertow* sail primarily around Neverland, making sure things are kept in order on the main-land. The *Coral Plunder* and *Viper's Strike* sail the border islands, and *The Vicious Seas. . .*," he paused, "well, *Vicious Seas* does whatever the hell it wants."

"The border islands?"

Wendy paused, hope alighting on her tongue, its taste like thick honey, before bursting forth with excitement.

"Can they sail out of Neverland? Can you sail away from here?"

Please say yes, she prayed silently, please let him say yes. Barnaby turned his curious eyes upon her eager face.

"Now that would be too easy, wouldn't it? There is no leaving here lass, I'm afraid. Neverland has a very strange pull to it. Every year, a different ship in the fleet tries sailing out as far as they can possibly go, to test the boundaries. Every year it's the same story— once they hit a certain point, right around the 413 nautical mile mark, the water starts pulling backward. You push against it, and when you do, the sky suddenly erupts in a maelstrom of thunder, lightning, and wind, blowing you backwards, turning your ship from its headwind. The sails heed the call, and before you know it, you are heading back the opposite direction, no matter the skill of your captain—or your navigator. The compasses spin, and the instruments go mad. Mile 413 is a damned ship graveyard, with odd magnetic pulls and real magic working together to make a sailor's life hell. We lost the *Howling Hoard* and the *Banshee's Milk* there and God knows how many smaller, islander boats."

He shook his head. "Good men, they were, on the *Howling Hoard.*"

Wendy's face fell. "So you can't leave. Ever."

"Well, there's plenty of smaller islands between here and there. Hundreds of 'em, all ready for plucking."

He gestured his arm out towards the East.

"The main island is the biggest though. Don't have much reason to be anywhere else. Hook has control of Port Duette, though things might be a'changin'. . . ." Barnaby looked around fervently, as if protecting his words, before he looked out at the water lapping at the front of the boat, Queen Eryne's open arms embracing the horizon with a horrific scream.

"Forget I said anything, will you? Regardless, It's a lovely little prison though, isn't it, and no better way to see Neverland than from this deck right here. At night, when the clouds hover just over the surface, and the twilight comes in hungry, you can't tell the difference between the sky and the sea. You'll never see anything like it again." He gave a curt cough, wiping his mouth with one of his blackened hands. "Well, Darlings, shall we continue the tour?"

Wendy barely heard him as her heart had made its way slowly down her body, through the *Sudden Night*, and was now resting on the bottom of the voracious blue sea at her feet, so deep was her disappointment. *Was Peter truly the only one who could leave Neverland? Would she truly never see her parents and Booth again?* She was tumbling down into herself now, her hands shaking as they clutched at the deck, uttering a quiet cry under her breath. *Booth. Booth. I am trapped forever.* Barnaby watched her reaction with interest, absolutely misjudging the reason for her sorrow.

"Oh, do not fear, my lady, I will be going with you on the tour. I shall protect you from any untimely advances."

Wendy nodded, swallowing the sob that was making its way up her throat. "Thank you, Barnaby, I would much appreciate it."

Barnaby took them towards the rear of the ship, "aft to the stern," and said he'd show them the "poop deck," to Michael's juvenile delight. "The quarterdeck is usually reserved for the ship's officers," Barnaby told them as they mounted the stairs to the raised deck. Wendy thought it was actually quite beautiful. There, Barnaby even allowed the Darlings to look upon the cherrywood wheel that loomed over the entire ship, a singular eye of God, manned by Smith.

"See the wood? See how smooth it looks? It's because it has bent under the captain's fingertips. That wheel, it knows what he wants before he does, mark my words. This ship knows its captain, and if you try to do something that he doesn't agree with, it'll fight you."

Wendy did enjoy looking at the wheel, the rich wood glistening in the sunlight. When Smith turned it, she could feel the tiniest adjustments under her feet as he moved the wheel back and forth. The boat rocked a bit, and Smith looked up, annoyed at their presence.

"Barnaby! Get those landlubbers off this deck, or so help me God, I will feed your entrails to starfish. Show them the rest of the ship and be done with it. The men have work to do, and so does she."

"Aye, aye."

"Barnaby! How many days away are we from Port Duette?"

Barnaby took a minute to look at his compass, looked out at the sea, looked at an ancient gold pocket watch, and then out to sea again.

"I would say we are within three days of Port Duette, Smith."

"Port Duette?" Wendy's ears perked up.

"Yes, my dear. Captain Maison wants to have a little chat with Captain Hook."

Smith reached out from the wheel and roughly grabbed onto Barnaby's hand, twisting it sideward. The older man yelped and fell to his knees.

"I've had about enough of your prattling voice today. Shut your gossipy schoolgirl mouth and go about your business."

Wendy's brain was leaping from idea to idea. *Port Duette? Would it be possible to escape this ship, with its filthy men and staircase of bones?* Barnaby limped away from Smith, and Wendy could see a bitter anger simmering behind his eyes. She tried to distract him as they went below deck.

"Only three days until Port Duette? Can that be true?" *Three days until they could escape this hell. Anyone could make it three days.*

"Aye. We're about two hundred miles out." Wendy looked up at the sky. The idea of escape was tantalizing, but Port Duette was practically a neighbor to Pan Island. And Peter Pan. She shivered at the thought. Barnaby reached out his arm for her.

"Do you need a coat, my dear?" Wendy shook her head. Michael, who had been miraculously silent for most of the tour, now piped up.

"For heaven's sake! More of the ship! C'mon, Wendy!"

Wendy took one last look at the sea before ducking below the deck, loath to enter again into its dark hallways and lurking corners. Barnaby was a chipper guide, asking questions about Wendy's history and entertaining Michael with gruesome pirate facts.

"Did you know, that Captain Horatio once sliced off a man's

lips and sewed them to his back, since he was always speaking of mutiny? Did you hear the one about the pirate who fell in love with the sea, and filled his lungs every night with seawater, in hopes that it would one day make him able to be with her forever? He drowned in his own body."

Michael's face was pinnacle of delight, but Wendy found these morbid tales turned her stomach. What once had fascinated her now disgusted her. Death was real, violence was jarring, and she had seen enough horrors to know that these tales were based on dark realities.

"That's enough, Barnaby" she whispered as they climbed the staircase of bones, Michael jumping happily on each step.

"This is where the captain stays—his room is at the end of the hallway here."

"Oh yes. I've seen it already."

Barnaby narrowed his eyes at her.

"No one gets to see the captain's quarters, but Keme, our esteemed cook, and Smith, on the rare occasions. No one gets to see where the captain sleeps, not even his many whores."

Wendy didn't know what to say, so instead she just turned her head to look out the porthole window on the starboard side of the ship.

"You must be important, then."

Wendy shook her head, her voice dull. "I'm just a girl."

"I heard you are much more than that. I heard that Peter Pan is in love with you."

Wendy let her eyes drop to the floor.

"Perhaps."

"And that love was so terrible that you ran to Hook?"

She shook her head. "Hook came to me."

"Well, isn't that a nice coincidence? That the captain just happened to be there when you needed him." Wendy's eyes widened. She hadn't given too much thought to how Hook knew she was escaping that day. Her concerns had been survival and Michael, the only things in her head that she had room for. She whirled on Barnaby.

"Hook has a spy!" Her eyes widened. "Abbott!"

Barnaby made a slow movement of zipping his lips. "Now that ain't for me to say, Miss Darling. Best ask the captain on one of your special visits. Can you really be surprised? We are pirates, after all."

There was a surprising venom in his voice, but when Wendy looked back at him, he was smiling and cheery, showing Michael one of the many dumbwaiters that brought food up from the belly of the ship to the deck.

"Now, this leads down to the kitchen, where you'll be working, least, that's what Smith said. Shall we go take a gander?"

Wendy couldn't think of anything she would like less than cooking meals for these filthy men who took pleasure in killing children, and yet, found herself nodding all the same as the *Night* roared toward Port Duette, parting waves in its stead, slicing the Neverland sky into two with its towering black mast.

"Put us to work," she repeated, remembering Hook's warning. "Nothing would please me more."

Barnaby gave her a strange look. "I doubt that's true."

CHAPTER SIX

The kitchen was located below decks, on the port side.

"This is where the captain says you'll be working." Wendy looked around with a grimace. The room was tight, small, and dark, with grainy wooden walls, riddled with knots that seemed to look at her with curiosity. Cast-iron pots and pans swung overhead, and a tattered box of mixed silverware rattled on a shelf. A large tapestry flapped back and forth on the wall, its elaborate embroidery piquing her curiosity. Wendy walked over to it, tilting her head to read the inscription as she brushed dust from the fabric with her hand. "The *Jolly Rodger* and the *Atlantic*." A brown ship with a fiery-red jewel as its figurehead battled the waves in the scene depicted, its sails at full mast in a curled wind. The same flag that she had seen in the captain's chambers, a white skull on a black background, flapped at the top of the mast. As she looked at it, she remembered Peter's story about burning the *Jolly Rodger*, told high above the trees in Centermost. She had been so dazzled by him then, his presence, his charisma. It had all been a glamourous show.

"The *Jolly Rodger*? Peter burned that ship, correct?"

Barnaby nodded his head.

"Aye, and about a dozen good men with it. 'Twas a dark day, that was; a massacre."

He shook his head, the memory darkening his face.

"I wouldn't bring that day up to the captain, though, that being the day he lost his hand, and his father's boat. That'll get you thrown overboard."

Wendy swallowed her next five questions and continued looking around the room.

Fifty or so barrels lined the walls, each roped to the walls with the same thick black netting that had pulled her from the sea. Barnaby was much less interested in the kitchen tour than he had been about the above-deck tour. He pointed aimlessly to the barrels. "Got your salted and dried meat and fish in there. The men like them spiced pretty well. Apples and some root vegetables are kept in that room there, past the barrels. We're probably pretty low, but we'll stock up at Port Duette. You can ask Keme about it."

"Keme?"

"The cook."

Barnaby leaned forward, his voice hushed. "Don't be afraid of him, my lady. He's big but harmless, and can cook a fish fifteen ways till Sunday, which is all that matters to the captain. Also, he doesn't speak, but he'll let you know what he needs."

"And I'll be his assistant?"

"Yes. You and the boy, both."

Wendy looked over doubtfully at Michael, who yanked a dead fish out of a barrel with a delighted squeal. *That meant her. No need to pretend otherwise.*

"I'm sure we will be fine. Why doesn't he speak?"

Barnaby smiled, his small nose twitching. "Well, there are a number of theories, but my favorite is that he is bound by some ancient Pilvi curse."

Wendy looked at him. "Pilvi? As in Pilvinuvo Indians?"

Barnaby gave her a grin. "Ah, yes, I'm sure you've heard of them, heard Peter mention them a few times, have we?"

He rubbed his hands together.

"I'm glad you are surprised. You'll find the *Sudden Night* is full of happy surprises."

He wiggled his eyebrows at Wendy in a way that made her uncomfortable. She turned away, pretending to inspect the barrels, which were meticulously labeled in a language that she could not read.

"Yes, it's true—we have the last Pilvinuvo Indian on our ship, though he is mute as a rock. I'm sure Peter Pan would love to get ahold of him, which is why he stays below decks most of the time. It isn't safe for him anywhere else in Neverland—well, he's sort of like you in that way!"

Wendy curdled inside.

"Keme is loyal to the captain though—cooks his meals, delivers his food right to his chambers, most of the time. Rumor is that the captain has something on him, something that made Keme commit his life to serving the *Sudden Night*."

Barnaby laughed before rubbing his black hands through his white hair. "Don't we all." He paused, and the air hung awkwardly between them. "Well, I'll leave you to it then. Keme will probably be down in a few minutes. Darlings, would you like one last stop on the tour? The weapon room?"

Michael sprinted to the door, screaming yes. Wendy turned away, wanting a minute to herself.

"I'll pass, Barnaby, thank you."

He looked immensely disappointed, but Wendy found that she couldn't care less. Barnaby gave a short bow and left with Michael in tow. The girl from London let out a long breath and sunk down at the rough wooden table. She stretched out her arms along the grainy wood and let the tears she had been holding in fall silently from her eyes, puddling on the knotted wood. *No way home. No way out. How would she ever get her brothers home, if you couldn't leave Neverland without Peter Pan?* She blew the air out of her lungs, wishing for the nine hundredth time that this was all a dream.

An apple rolled down the table, stopping in front of her arms. Wendy jumped up from the bench, slamming her head hard into one of the cast-iron pots that rocked above her. She opened her mouth, and let an undignified word fall from her lips. "Damn it!" She rubbed her head with her hand, instantly ashamed of her language before looking up. A giant stood silently in front of her, shrouded in shadow. Wendy let out a cry and backed up slowly. The giant stepped forward. He was well over seven feet tall, and massively round. He dwarfed the kitchen around him as his monstrously huge figure tried to make its way towards Wendy. Wendy continued to back up.

"Are you . . . ?" She sniffed sadly, struggling to regain control of her emotions. "You must be Keme."

He silently moved towards her, pushing her backwards until she was pushed back over a barrel of fish, their silvery scales sliding over each other with a nauseating flapping sound. Wendy raised her hand, hoping her politeness would ward off whatever was happening. Her heart pounded in her ribs.

"I'm Wendy, I hope that I can be a help to you."

The man continued to stare at her silently, his body pressing her up into the barrel, so far that her hands were slipping over the fish, their scent permeating her skin. She raised her chin, unwilling to be pushed any further.

"Back up! Now! Please!"

The man stared at her before nodding his head once. A large finger, easily the length of her face reached out, hovering in front of her nose before reaching up to swipe the tear from her cheek. Wendy stopped breathing for a moment, resuming only when he stepped back from her with a sad smile. His face was soft and pliable, the same doughy substance as his large body. Round, saucer-like eyes peered out at her, the dark brown core flecked with strands of gold. His skin was the color of tree bark, a soft brown, peppered with freckles. Long black hair was swept under a red-and-white rag, and he smelled of pepper and salty sea air.

Even though he obviously wasn't in his prime, Wendy could see that the genes of the Pilvi Indians were strong, carried through his handsome features and exotic coloring. He smiled shyly at her before backing up with a bow. Wendy dislodged her hand from the bucket of fish with a groan, shaking it in front of her. The gentle giant opened his mouth in a soundless laugh, throwing his head back and pounding his hand on the wooden counter block twice before turning away from her. Wendy cautiously circled back around the counter to where he was standing.

"I'm supposed to help you, down here. In the kitchen."

Keme nodded once and handed her a huge kitchen knife. Wendy had never in her life been allowed to hold a knife that large, certainly not when she had rarely joined Liza in their kitchen in London. Keme walked over to the barrel and plucked up a dead fish by its tail, its mouth hanging open, its red lips stained with mottled blood. Wendy held back a gag. Keme plopped the fish in front of her and then motioned for her to cut it with the knife. She shook her head. He grinned, shook his head back and forth, and then proceeded to show her how to slit the fish up the belly, its insides spilling out across the wooden counter top. Wendy gagged, once and then again.

"I cannot. I cannot. I can do potatoes, but . . ." She uttered the word that she had been yearning to say to this entire ordeal. "No. No."

Keme watched her silently before taking the fish from her with an understanding nod. With long strokes, he pulled the scales back from the fish easily, and laid down a much less disgusting sight of two cleaned fillets. He gestured to a bucket of water and made the motion of washing. Wendy let out a sigh of relief.

"Yes. Yes, I can do that, at least."

Keme slapped her cheerfully on the back and moved his head side to side, as if he was hearing silent music in his head. Wendy decided that she liked him very much, very much indeed. She took the sickly looking fillets from him and doused them quickly in the bucket of fresh water. Keme showed her how to rub an onion peel quickly over the skin, how to sprinkle a handful of seasonings over the bunch and top them off with a dollop of yellow salt, and how to line the fillets up in front of a dangling iron cauldron. When Wendy had washed her hundredth fillet, Keme motioned her over to watch him load the fillet into a spherical iron cauldron that dangled from several large silver chains. Using his hands, he gestured to the cauldron and then swung his body back and forth, his hands in a circle. Wendy understood immediately.

"It moves with the motion of the ship."

Keme nodded before motioning to Wendy that it was hot. She shook her head. "I don't believe we have these where I come from."

Keme shook his head and then crooked his little finger before pointing to his head.

"Hook's invention?" Wendy grinned. "I'm not surprised. Have you seen the weapons on deck?"

Keme opened his mouth to laugh again before shaking his head and getting back to work, prying open a barrel of apples and setting onto them with a serrated knife, his skilled strokes perfectly slicing the apples in just four deft moves. A burst of crisp apple skin filled Wendy's nostrils, and she breathed it in like air. Here, in this tiny ship kitchen, she had somehow found one thing that smelled like home. Her eyes teared up, but she kept on working, helping him now with peeling potatoes, thankful for this thoughtless task that let her linger on a particularly delicious memory: Booth, winking at her slyly before tossing her an apple from his bag, like it was some sort of extravagant gift. She caught it in her hands and looked up at him, but he was already walking back to his father's shop, whistling a lilting tune, his bag full of books before disappearing at the corner. She looked down at the apple. *He had taken a bite already, and the white of his teeth marks were shiny and wet.* Wendy had looked around fervently to see if anyone were watching. No one was, and so she lowered her mouth to the apple, pressing her lips against the spot that she knew his had been. Her heart pounded and her knees gave a quiver as her tongue traced the grooves in the apple, feeling like such a naughty girl.

Back on the *Sudden Night*, Wendy felt a blush spreading up her cheek. Keme watched her with a sly smile before he turned back to the job at hand. The next four hours passed quickly, with Wendy up to her elbows in fish and potatoes, and Michael toddling around whining before he finally fell asleep, curled up against a pile of potato sacks. After their exhaustive work, with nary a break in sight, Wendy helped Keme load all the food into a dumbwaiter that rocked back and forth in the kitchen, her sore hands setting steaming fish and potatoes onto wooden square plates and sending them up to an unknown hand on deck.

By the time dinner was prepared, Wendy was drenched with a sticky sweat, and her hands reeked of fish up to her elbows. A sense of accomplished pride shot through her exhausted limbs as she reached down to feel her dress, hard and cracked with brine. A smile cracked over her face as the satisfied feeling of being needed and useful started to wash over her. She lingered on it for a moment before the reality set in that she was utterly disgusting and now it was time to go up on deck and eat with the men. She wiped her hand across her forehead and began her climb up the bone staircase, femurs rattling as she went. Finally, she emerged onto the deck, her breath catching in her throat as she took in the stark contrast of the blackness of the *Sudden Night* against a milky-white evening sky, splattered playfully with pink clouds. The water was blue gray, lapping at the sides of the boat with playful licks. On the deck, long pieces of plywood were shoved together haphazardly to make a table, the planks resting on barrels.

Next to the table, a thin pirate with stringy black hair and a long nose was lighting a pipe, his stumped leg resting on the edge of the chair. He caught Wendy's eye and she looked away quickly.

He grinned as a delicate puff of white smoke curled out of his mouth and rolled up his face, his words dripping out lazily.

"Been awhile since I've been served by a lady. Feels right."

Then he reached out to grab her behind but stopped short when Smith's furious face caught his eye.

"I'll take that hand, Shady Wick."

Wendy deftly side-stepped his reach. Keme tapped her on the shoulder and gestured to the pile of plates waiting for them on the port side. Wendy tucked back her hair and began grabbing plates, setting them in front of the men as quickly as she possibly could. The meal was basic—two fish fillets, a pile of potatoes, a slice of apple—but it looked delicious, and Wendy felt her stomach rumble with disappointment when she put the last plate in front of a pirate who looked equally as ravenous. Keme motioned to her to stand by him, and she did, with her hands crossed behind her back, just as he did.

They waited. None of the men touched their food. Finally, Smith cried, "Avast!" and all the men stood, the rickety bench pushed backwards with an uncomfortable screech. His face emotionless and cold, Hook emerged onto the deck, his black boots clipping the deck with each determined step. Wendy watched as he walked towards the table. His eyes looked forward, not taking in the steaming plates of food, nor the men who watched him with hungry eyes. He walked straight to the starboard side and looked out at the waves on the horizon. Then, pursuing his lips, he whistled a low note and heard one in return from the crow's nest, where Hawk was keeping watch. The captain spun on his heel.

"You men may eat. Enjoy your meal."

Some of the men dug in, while some bowed their heads to pray. Hook stared at them long and hard, his dark eyes burrowing into their thinning hairlines. "Fools," he muttered before turning heel and heading back the way he had come.

"Keep on, starboard tack steady, and watch the stern. The closer we get to Port Duette, the more the wind changes."

"Aye, aye, Captain!" replied the crew, speaking as though they had one voice.

Hook nodded once, confirming that he had been heard.

"Smith, see to it that the bow is recoated with the gloss tonight."

Smith stood, his impressive mass towering over the men who greedily shoved fish in their faces. Still, he was not as tall as Keme, who watched everything with a happy smile. "Aye, Captain."

"Good night then, men. May the Neverland night be kind."

As he walked past Wendy, the captain leaned forward. "You stink of fish. Wash up and meet me on deck for a drink in two hours. You'll be fed only then."

At the mention of a drink, Wendy bit down on her lip, unsure of the nature of his request. Hook saw her hesitation and scoffed back a laugh.

"Don't worry, child, I have no interest in wooing you. Not when I've had a woman carved by the shores of Neverland. Your brother stays below."

Wendy mumbled, "Yes, sir" and felt the silver hook's cold prick on her chin.

"I appreciate it when people are on time."

"Yes, sir."

"Good." Without another word, he clicked his way back below deck, but not before he reached out a hand to Keme, patting him once on the back. Then he disappeared back below deck, as quickly as he had emerged.

It was only then that Wendy felt the collective sigh of relief escape from the crew, and their conversation and laughter rolled forward with ease. Barnaby offered her a bite of his fish, but she refused outright, not wanting to contradict the captain's orders. She felt many an eye on her neckline, but she kept her head high, staring straight ahead as Keme did, reassured by his huge presence beside her. She enjoyed listening to their banter, so offensive that she often struggled to keep her mouth from dropping open at their lewd jokes and litany of curses. *Oh, how her mother would blush!*

After a half hour of hearing about mermaids breasts, her attention turned to a conversation happening at the end of the table, quietly, between Redd, Smith, and Voodoo.

"Aye, what does the captain think will happen at this meeting of the Scorned?"

"It's none of your business," hissed Smith, eating half a fish in one bite.

"You keep your mouth yammering, and you'll be dancing the hempen jig tonight," added Redd.

Voodoo grinned, showing shimmering white teeth marred by a single rotted one, square in the front. "He doesn't mean it, Redd. He'd miss your pretty face!"

"No, I wouldn't," answered Smith, pulling a fish bone out of his teeth. "I wouldn't think about you for more than ten seconds I reckon."

Redd leaned in. "I've been hearing whispers at Port Duette. Whispers about the captain and Captain Maison. Something 'bout a debt."

"Aye, that's because Maison owes Hook his life. Hook spared him once, carried him to the healers in Port Duette while he was bleeding all over the place. Maison has forgotten his debt in his pride. He's a sick man, Maison is. You've heard about *the line*."

Smith and Voodoo gave simple, short nods. Redd cleared his throat.

"I reckon Maison has been talking to Captain Xian Li, trying to get the *Viper's Strike* to turn its loyalty. Won't happen." Smith calmly picked up his knife, spun it between his fingers and without warning, brought it down hard into the meaty side of Redd's palm. The man let out a painful scream as blood began dripping through the open wooden slats of the table. Wendy's legs gave a quiver beneath her, but she kept her face impassive to avoid betraying her horror at the sudden violence. The other pirates went silent before suddenly appearing very interested in their food, their lidded eyes glued to their plates. Michael was sniffling beside her at the end of the table, and Wendy reached out her hand, patting him softly on the shoulder, refusing the instinct to pull him protectively into her arms.

Smith leaned forward and pulled the knife out of Redd's hand with a hard yank, and the older pirate held up his shaking hand, blood streaming down his wrist, fleshy pulp folding out from the center. Smith didn't even look at him as he speared one potato after another, shoveling them into his mouth with vigor.

"The captain's business is the captain's business, is that understood?" He wiped his mouth on his sleeve.

"Yes sir!" echoed back from the table.

"Ballast pigs," Smith uttered. "See to your wound." Redd stood now, shakily making his way below deck with another pirate, who Wendy guessed was the ship's healer, holding his hand above his head. Wendy looked up at the sapphire sky to avoid looking at the sickening trail of blood that now glistened on the deck. Keme smiled at her and patted her head absentmindedly. Smith wiped his mouth, slicked the blood off his elbow, and threw down his napkin.

"Good fish, Keme. Bit overcooked."

Then he made his way to the Quarter Deck, humming a happy tune, and tossing his knife in the air, blood flecks dusting his hand with each catch. Wendy turned away, ashen-faced. The rest of the pirates paused a moment and then went back to eating, whispering quietly amongst themselves of inconsequential matters, the sea, the air, women.

Keme motioned to the door to head below deck. Wendy felt a wave of relief wash over her and she bowed her head, leading Michael back inside, down the spiral staircase of bones, down curved hallways, into the hallway that led nowhere, and finally, after turning the tiny black lever, made their way down into their room. As Michael played with his toes, she happily pulled off her stinking dress and washed her arms, face, and hair in the small basin of rose water that had been set out for her. The smell of reeking salt and scale slid off her skin like a sheath, and she shivered happily to be clean once more. Michael climbed up onto the top bunk and began regaling her with tales about what he had learned about the ship, and the things he had seen.

"Barnaby said that the keel is below the hold; it's like the spine of a skeleton." Michael gave a shiver. "He also said that this boat is haunted by the ghost of Hook's Dad, Tiberius. He wanders the halls at night, crying out for Hook and for the blood of all men at sea."

Wendy let out an exasperated sigh. "He should not be telling you those stories."

Michael flopped back on his bed. "I like scary stories."

Wendy shook her head, not needing to tell Michael that they were living in an actual nightmare, a place where pirates stabbed each other and killed children. She turned over on her bed.

"I'm to go on deck and have a drink with Hook tonight; will you be okay here by yourself?"

Michael frowned, clearly not happy at the idea, but to Wendy's surprise, he kicked his feet in the air and shrugged.

"We're on a boat. You're still here, even if you're gone."

Wendy smiled before pulling herself up to look at his soft face. Her heart gave a tiny tug.

"You're growing up before my eyes, little Michael."

Michael kept his eyes on his feet, which he wiggled slowly, watching his toes curl and flex.

"I miss John."

Cloudy tears blurred Wendy's vision. "I know. Me too."

"I miss Mama. And Nana."

"Me, too. Shall we sing something that reminds us of them?"

A sob choked Michael's throat. "Yes. Please."

"Alright." Wendy sat down on her bunk and cleared her throat, letting her voice, which sounded less girly than she remembered, fill her mouth.

The meadow is silent
Little one, little one
Bluebells sleep, and roses keep
As you say good night
The night is silent
Little one, little one
Foxes wake under the setting sun
As you run towards slumber
The day is done
Little one, little one
Moon above shimmers with love
And God be with you when you dream

Michael surrendered to sleep, and Wendy lay awake, her thoughts crowded and loud. *What would happen to them? Were they safe? What was John doing at this very moment? Booth? Her parents? Would they ever imagine that she was lying on a bunk in an infamous pirate ship, rocking back and forth in the waves, barely noticing them anymore?* She didn't fall asleep, instead let the hours rock by on the shifting waves below. When it was time, she pulled on the long-sleeved white nightdress that had been left for her, tucked her hair back into a tight ribbon, and pulled a tartan blanket around her shoulders before quietly slipping out the door, locking it behind her, making her way up to the night, and to Hook.

CHAPTER SEVEN

When she emerged, she was taken aback by the clusters of stars blazing so bright that it was if they had all been spilled out just above the ship, their reflection blanketing the water. They reminded Wendy of that night with Peter in the lantern, when she had almost lost herself, and so she looked away, focusing instead on the reliable ugliness of the harpoons and torturous devices lining the sides of the deck. She ran her fingers along a sharp bow fixed with tiny jagged teeth that flexed with the creaking waves. Hook's voice carried down from above her, next to the mainmast.

"It's called the cutter. If someone tries to board our ship, we send this down the pontoon bridge and suddenly, no one has ankles anymore, so it's an easy fight. It's bloody, but it does the job. Bit of light mopping up afterwards."

Wendy shivered at the description, the blanket dropping from her shoulders.

"Good evening, Captain."

"Good evening, Miss Darling. How did you find your first day on the *Sudden Night*?"

Filthy. Exhausting. Terrifying. "It was fine."

"I have no patience for liars, Miss Darling."

Wendy took a breath. "It was terrible."

This made Hook grin, his tightly wound face unfurling a bit. "For a wealthy socialite, I imagine it was."

"You don't know anything of my life," snapped Wendy.

"I know enough," Hook said quietly. "Walk with me. And take the blanket, it can get quite chilly at night."

Wendy picked it off the ground, and followed Hook's heavy boots as they began making their way towards the helm.

"I'm going to give you some information this evening. Normally, I am not a trusting person, and it takes years, years, to gain my trust. There are two people that I trust on this ship, and you are neither of them. However, current circumstances, and a change in the wind has blown me to an inevitable conclusion: I must choose to trust you, because time does not allow it any other way. You will have but one opportunity to lose it, do you understand? And when you do, you will lose much more than my respect. A brother perhaps."

"Yes, sir." Wendy pulled her shaking hand underneath the blanket.

"Yes, Captain." His reprimand was firm.

"Yes, Captain."

"So, what I tell you is to be kept in complete confidence. You may not tell your brother, you may not tell anyone else aboard this ship. You will swear to me, before your God that you will not speak of what is spoken here between you and me."

Wendy thought for a moment. "I will not swear to God, but you have my word. Unless what you tell me pertains to my welfare, or the welfare of my brothers. You cannot expect me to not act in our best interest."

The captain raised his hook and scratched his eyebrow. "I suppose that's fair, clever little girl. Have a seat." He gestured lazily to a worn bench on the side of the helm. "You're relieved," he said to the helmsman, who promptly walked away from the ship's wheel, handing it over to Hook.

"I'm going to tell you, over the next few nights, everything that

I know about Peter Pan. You will do the same. We will share our information in hopes that someday we can repay the suffering he has caused us. In return, I offer my protection for you and Michael. Is this a fair deal?"

Wendy felt the tiniest tendril of hope curl out of her heart. It curled in the shape of Booth. "Yes."

Hook sighed. "I will tell you what I believe to be important."

A wave leapt up from the sea, splashing her playfully. She pulled her blanket tightly around her, watching Hook's silhouette as it bent around the ship's wheel, moonlight filtering through its holes.

"My father, Arthur Tiberius Hook, was the captain of the *Jolly Rodger* for thirty-six years. He sailed the waters around the Americas, India, and Asia. He was good man, and a fine pirate who treated his men with respect. My mother died of consumption when I was quite young, and he took me on the boat with him, trained up from when I was five. He had loved my mother greatly."

Wendy remembered the book of letters she had had found in her room. *Dearest Easter* . . . She had been dead already when he had written the letters. It made her heart ache with longing.

"I learned to read, to write, to sail all within the confines of the *Jolly Rodger*. The ship was my home, and my father . . ."

He paused for a moment, staring straight ahead.

"And my father was my hero."

He spun the wheel and Wendy could hear the slight rocking of gears underneath adjusting, turning, their creak whispering to the water, which answered in return, the boat heaving port side.

"In May of 1892, my father set sail for the Alaskan Territory. He had been hired by a mysterious Scotsman to explore the farthest reaches of the seas. My father had at first refused, but the benefactor offered a staggering amount of money, more than my father and his crew would make in five years of work. It was too good to refuse, and after outfitting the *Jolly Rodger*, my father sailed us north, farther north than anyone had ever sailed before."

He gave a sigh. "Words cannot describe what wonders we witnessed there: ice towers that pierced the sky, dwarfing the sun, their insides sharp and blue, a world of jagged angles. It was as if life itself was frozen at that point, as if time had ceased existing that far north. The *Jolly Rodger* was a ghost passing through something ancient, never to be seen by human eyes. It was freezing. Parts of the ship began crusting with ice, and my father was beginning to see the folly of this fool's errand. He had been given coordinates from the Scotsman, coordinates that he had tortured out of a local woman rumored to be a witch. We sailed on, the *Jolly Rodger* pushing forward, against the ice, against behemoths that slept under the waves and cried at night. Several men went to sleep on the deck, never to wake again. My father had no sooner made the decision to turn back when we saw the light."

Hook raised his right hand, stars peeking out from between his fingertips.

"A purple light, glistening off the pillars of ice that surrounded it, whirled, the ice around it turning to shadows. Ice mountains hovered above the deep, somehow a part of the water and not of it at all. My father was screaming for the *Jolly Rodger* to turn, but it was a moot point—the light had begun pulling the ship towards itself, and our nautical instruments went mad. The ship came about and was being pulled in backwards." He shook his head. "Our ship was swallowed by the light as though an egg through the serpent's mouth. My father . . ."

His voice faltered once, before he coughed and continued. "My father at the very last moment, abandoned the wheel and threw his body over mine. That was the last thing that most of the men remembered. But I didn't. I saw . . ."

"You saw the portals? The windows?"

Hook turned his head towards Wendy. "Yes. I saw the windows, the whirling stars, the circling light overhead, like fragmented glass. I watched as our world of ice and black water dispersed in a haze of stars and light."

He spun the wheel back to the starboard side, resting his hook easily on a worn knot in the wood.

"When we woke, we were here, in Neverland, in these turquoise waters, about three miles off the mainland. We had gone from a frozen hell of death, to a warm paradise that was ripe for the taking. The crew was delighted—my father was not. He realized that he had not been searching for treasure all this time, but he had been the experiment of a rich nobleman, and that we were trapped in Neverland forever, unable to sail away, trapped in this godforsaken land for all eternity!"

He slammed his hook down on the wheel, chipping a tiny piece off one of the handles. Then his eyes found Wendy, sitting at rapt attention.

"That's when Peter Pan arrived, a flying boy! Imagine our rapture! He landed on our ship perhaps a year after our arrival, bearing fruits and treasures from the mainland. The crew fell all over him, astonished at his power of flight, at his gifts, and his knowledge about Neverland. My father, unfortunately, was one of them. He was charmed by this boy, as was I, and we quickly became the best of friends."

Wendy gasped. *Hook and Peter? Friends?*

"Don't look so shocked, Miss Darling. Remember, I was fifteen years old and desperately lonely for anyone my age, and here came a boy who could fly, who could fight! We spent months as each other's only companions, and he taught me to master different weapons— the sword, the spear, the bow. In confidence, Peter told me how he had gotten his power, how he had saved the fairy Tink and she had gifted him with her powers—flight, speed, and strength—a bond that can never be separated, not as long as Tink lives. Peter and I grew closer, and it delighted my father that I had a friend my age, as I had only been around grown men all my life. Peter took me flying every afternoon, showing me the different parts of the island, though we never landed. The Neverland Sea from above is a rare delight, is it not? I still remember it to this day."

Wendy swallowed, remembering the first time that her eyes swept over the vast ocean of turquoise and the creatures that wiggled beneath its clear surface, like shimmering green glass.

"Yes. It is."

Hook's smile disappeared.

"I have never laughed so much in my life than those first few months that I knew Peter Pan, and likely never will again. It was a golden time, although I see now that Peter's seeds of evil were already being planted. Like a creeping root, Peter and my father became closer and closer. Peter took a great interest in learning nautical charts and mapping the stars, something that my father was passionate about. They would spend hours together, while I pulled my weight on the ship, bitter that I still had to work while Peter flitted about. Peter had never been close to his father—the wealthy Scotsman who had hired us . . ."

"But Peter was poor!" Wendy felt guilty for interrupting, but felt her objection burst out from her lips. "Peter told me that he was poor, that his family lived under a wealthy Scotsman, and that his brothers had pushed him into the river by his house."

Hook scowled. "Clever boy. Peter Pan is a liar, but he is also quite intelligent, and so he always mixes his lies with truths, so that details sound clear and confident. Peter was born the only son of Davis Wickerly. He was a spoiled brat, who enjoyed bullying the children of serfs. His father was a cruel man, and so Peter was a cruel child, even then. He clung to my father, and slowly, I began to see that it wasn't a friend that Peter wanted. No, Peter Pan had enough friends already, in fact, Pan Island was full of friends that Peter had brought here for himself. *What Peter wanted was a father, and he wanted mine.*" Hook's voice changed.

"I am still unsure of the details of that day, but I woke to the sound of yelling in my father's cabin and the breaking of glass. I heard my father tell Peter to get off the ship and never return, and Peter saying that he would live to regret this. I had barely climbed out of my bunk when my father came bursting into my room, his sword drawn, his eyes wild. He cradled me in his arms and told me to come back to his chambers and to stay there all day. He wouldn't talk about what happened with Peter, but told me to stay put. And so I did, out of respect for my father's fear. Two days passed, and finally I was allowed to come onto the deck. The *Jolly Rodger* was never quiet, and yet all was still when I emerged. I turned to look and was surprised to see the mainland, but even more surprised at what I saw next—another pirate ship. The *Sunned Shore* was manned by a small group of friendly chaps from the surrounding islands—good men with families and truly terrible pirates. Still, my father enjoyed their randy company."

Hook seemed disturbed at the memory, his throat croaking.

"And what had silenced the noisy crew of the *Jolly Rodger*? It was that the *Sunned Shore*—a fairly large vessel—had been turned upside down and was now resting on the tops of the trees just off the shore, their branches crumpled underneath its great weight. Water still streamed from the boat, and from the mouths of thirty or so dead men, some hung upside down, some dead on the ground thirty feet below it, their bodies trapped between branches and the broken boards of the ship. Painted on the side of the boat, in bright-yellow paint, were the words 'From the fatherless.'"

Hook yanked the wheel of the ship angrily, and a wave splashed over the side.

"My father's mouth was agape as he reached for my hand. '*Peter Pan could not have done this. He could not have. How could he . . . ?*' He was cut off, for Peter Pan landed hard on the ship's hull. Standing atop the upturned vessel, he glared as if he had his foot on the throat of a felled opponent. Wisps of black steam wafted off his skin. His navy eyes were narrowed and his face seemed more angular, like an angry wasp. He drew his gold sword and charged at my father. My father was many things—a navigator, a captain, a pirate, a lover of gold—but sword fighting was not one of his strengths. I screamed for him to let him fight me, but my father would not. The crew gathered around, their weapons drawn, but they weren't quick enough. Peter sliced at my father, once and then again, before leaping up in the air. *He was so fast.* His kick caught my father in the chin, throwing him off balance. My father stumbled backwards, and Peter took that opportunity to shove a sword through his heart. It was over in seconds. The old man never had a chance."

Wendy closed her eyes and wiped the tear from her cheek, imagining her own papa, unevenly matched against Peter's unnatural prowess. "I'm so sorry," she whispered.

Hook's jaw clenched and his hands tightened around the wheel.

"Don't be sorry. I have no use for pity. My father died in my arms. Words were said, blessings given, foreheads kissed. Peter Pan watched it all from high in his sky, watched as my father passed away from this world, a man who had shown him only kindness. And then he flew away, and I would not see him again for years. I vowed that I would build on my father's legacy, that I would one day run Neverland, and I would force Peter Pan into hiding, into shame. And when that was done, I would kill him. I found out later from Smith, my father's young first mate, that Peter had asked my father to kill me, so that he could be his only son. My father had laughed in his face, before seeing that he was serious. He then banished him from the ship and told him never to come back. My father had chosen me, and paid for it with his life."

Wendy continued to wipe tears from her eyes. She understood the allure of Peter Pan, how his presence was like the sun, and when it was pulled back, you found yourself in a cold darkness. She also understood what being the target of his rage—or his lust—could do.

Hook reached down, pulling up a bottle of wine from a small knapsack resting against the railing. With his teeth he yanked out the cork, spit it out, and took a deep, refreshing gulp. Then he pulled out two glasses and poured some of the dark red wine, a heavy tonic that sloshed with the movement of the ship. After handing a glass to Wendy, he paused and raised his glass.

"To Arthur Tiberius Hook."

Wendy thought a moment before raising her glass.

"To papas."

She drank long and deep before she felt the tip of the captain's hook press down her glass.

"Easy girl, I don't need you feeding the fish tonight."

Wendy nodded, feeling the warmth of the wine coating her throat and filling her belly.

"That must have been hard, losing your father like that."

"Yes, well, that is how it is that I came to meet Peter Pan. It is important to our future that you understand this story."

Wendy tilted her head. Her thoughts came one after another, but there was one in particular that stood out.

"How did the *Sunned Shore* come to be upside down? Certainly it couldn't have been the Lost Boys?"

She had asked the question hoping to look naïve. Of course it wasn't the Lost Boys—they could barely get dinner on the table for themselves. Hook shook his head.

"No, it wasn't the Lost Boys. Even with all of them, they could not have lifted the ship. And how would they get it out of the water?"

"Tink?" Even as Wendy uttered her name, she knew that it wasn't Tink. Tink was fast and powerful when she wasn't kept under Peter's thumb, but she didn't think the fairy could carry a ship.

"Then how was it—"

Hook leveled his eyes at her, and she held rapt by his intensity.

"Since you have come to Neverland, there has been a question on your heart, a question that presses on the soul of every person in Neverland. You might not recognize it yet, but it is ingrained in the shores of the island and the waves of the sea. Something is off here. You know it. You felt it with Peter."

Wendy shook her head out of frustration. Everything he was saying was true. There was something in the water, something in the air. A whispered secret. When she had been under Peter's spell, it hadn't been obvious, but now that she had been away from him, she found herself repeating a strange phrase: *What is . . . ? What is . . . ?*

She opened her mouth to say it now, but was cut short by a shrill whine from above, as Owl whistled down three strained notes, followed by a cry. "PAN!"

"Get down!" shouted Hook, pushing Wendy the ground, crouching over her, pulling his sword quickly from his scabbard.

"Bayonets to the helm! COME ABOUT!"

Wendy heard a grinding sound ring up from the deck below her cheek and the spears on the deck spun clockwise until they all were pointed inwards, their sharp barbs gleaning in the moonlight, focused on the space directly above Wendy and Hook. Every weapon on board was now turning.

"Fire a warning shot!" Voodoo sprinted over to a large black cannon and pulled a lever on the side before shifting it upwards dramatically. A blossom of blue fire erupted from the top of the mizzenmast, shooting straight into the sky. Its fire caught onto a long coil of rope that hung loosely from the peak of the mast. Voodoo began turning the lever hard and the flaming rope began to whirl in a wide circle, its flaming length enough to cover the width of the *Sudden Night*, like a protective flare. Wendy saw the shadow of a figure, arms folded, high above the flaming coil.

"Fire only if necessary! I will not waste weapons on his childish antics," Hook ordered. "But if he comes any closer, shoot to kill!"

Wendy's heart hammered. The *Sudden Night* was still, with only the sound of lapping waves, the thrumming of the sea. Then Wendy saw something falling from above them, a white diamond in the night, a dim flickering against the star-filled sky. It was tracing its way down from the stars, the flaming coil showering her face with light as she watched it fall.

"Get your weapons men!" Hook ordered. "Be ready!"

Wendy watched as the white object plunged towards the deck, passing through the whirling flame from above, now bringing with it a shower of tinder. Wendy lunged for the bucket that rested upon the helm before feeling the captain's hook on her arm.

"We have nothing to fear from fire," he hissed. The object fell down to the deck, where it landed hard in the middle of the ship, its hard impact echoing up the deck, its pieces exploding outwards. Wendy took a step forward.

"Wait," ordered Hook, as the pirates descended onto the object. "Wait. I want him to see it burn out." Wendy watched silently as the flaming object flickered a few times. Finally, it gave a flutter and went dark, the shiny gloss that covered the *Sudden Night* doing its intended job. Hook reached down and picked up the object before turning to Wendy.

"I believe this is for you, my dear." It was still smoking in his hands, and covered in small flecks of ash. A necklace. Creamy white pearls were strung together with silver wire. After looking at the necklace, they both raised their heads to the sky, Wendy flinching when she saw a shadow pass over the moon. Peter was a boy whose lips she had kissed, whose hands had felt her form, a boy whose every muscle she had worshipped. He now filled her with deep horror. There were a few minutes of silence and then Owl called down, "He's gone."

Wendy stepped forward. "Let me see the necklace."

Tied around the base of the pearls, its singed corners flapping in the wind, was a small note. Wendy unfolded it slowly.

"*To Wendy,*" it read, in Peter's messy scrawl, "*I dream of you.*"

At the bottom of the note was a bloody fingerprint, and with a whimper, Wendy noticed that the note had been tied to the necklace not with a brown ribbon as she originally thought, but with a lock of stringy brown hair, a brown that wasn't too far a shade off her own. She and John both had their mother's hair.

Chapter Eight

Two days passed at sea for Wendy, two days of cooking fish, shelling oysters, mixing spices, and picking rotten apples from a barrel, thus bringing light to something her father always said, "One bad apple ruins the whole bunch." There was an exhausting routine to cooking for the crew, and Wendy fell into it easily, enjoying the mindlessness of it all, and also Keme, who was a comfort even in his stillness. The quiet of their work, with the sluice of the knives, the slap of salting fish, gave Wendy time to think, to linger over what had happened to them since they had arrived in Neverland. Mostly, her thoughts lingered on three men: Booth, Peter, and John, but her worry about John far surpassed her worry about the other two: the guilt in her heart was like a dull thud that colored everything around her. He was a little shit, to be sure, but his damaged heart had been open wide enough for Peter to stroll right in. Desperate for information, she had, against her fears, made her way to Hook's chambers on her third night on the ship, her hands tracing over the grand carving of the fairy king before she knocked twice. The door yanked open; Smith glowered down at her.

"It's the girl," he said, clearly annoyed. "Should I kill her?"

"Not today, Smith. Perhaps later," replied the captain dully from inside the room. Smith turned back to her.

"What in bloody hells do you want?"

"I need to speak with the captain, please. It will not take long."

"Captain's busy, as you can see."

He stepped aside, and Wendy could see five pirates inside of Hook's chambers, all leaning over his drawing table, covered with maps and dusty, rolled pieces of papyrus. Hook didn't even look up from the table, though his heavy eyebrow arched in her direction.

"What is it, girl?"

Wendy raised her voice, refusing to be intimidated by these men even though they had most likely killed someone in the last month.

"May I speak with you privately, Captain?"

"Not now, perhaps tomorrow before we dock at Port Duette."

Wendy tried to defer.

"Yes, that would be fine, except that—"

"I am very busy!" Hook snapped. "As you can see! So if you please . . ."

Wendy was done being polite, so she practically shouted her request into the room, knowing that it would get his attention.

"I would like to have your spy on Pan Island send back a report about my brother. I cannot live anymore not knowing his fate." She paused and took a breath. "Please."

The two men stopped talking and looked over at her with amazement—and annoyance—at her boldness.

"You have interrupted a meeting of great importance for a boy of little," Hook snapped. "Your brother's loyalty lies with Peter right now. We know that he is alive, but that he has been missing as of late, probably being held and maybe tortured by Peter. I would say your useless prayers loudly, Miss Darling, for things are not looking good—for any of us."

He stood up abruptly, and thundered towards her, where, with a rough shove, he sent her reeling out into the hallway, his hook scratching the bridge of her hand. Once she was outside his chambers, he sighed with exasperation before whispering in her ear.

"I'll look into it more, but do not ever interrupt me again, or I'll let you watch your brother walk the plank, I swear it." His eyes focused on hers with unnerving intensity. He wasn't lying.

Wendy nodded. "Yes, Captain."

Then he loudly proclaimed, "Get the hell out of here! This is no place for a woman."

Smith looked over his shoulder, his hand tossing a dagger into the air. Five miniature pirate ships rested on the face of a dusty map in front of him.

"And bring us some bloody damn tea, while you're at it!"

The fairy door slammed shut in her face. Wendy begrudgingly headed down to the kitchen and fetched peppermint tea for the men, slamming the cups down against the long butcher block. She considered spitting into their cups before she remembered her manners and that her veil of politeness was the only thing standing between her and these barbarians. She placed the tray of tea in front of the captain's door, knocked, and then ran away, not anxious for another interaction with Smith.

The next day, as she served the men on the deck their dwindling meals of shellfish and apples boiled in cinnamon water, Hook silently passed a note into her hand. Wendy barely made it below deck before she unfolded the paper, her hands shaking with anticipation as she read three small sentences: *"John alive. Peter out flying with him often. General again."*

Wendy crumpled the paper against her chest, full of relief that seemed to flutter out from her very pores. *He was alive. If he could fly, he was not gravely injured. Peter would not give him flight if he was angry with him. John was alright.* She let out the breath that she had been holding for weeks, the fear in her heart uncurling like a fiddle fern in the sun. With this reassurance, she was able to focus more on the question that Hook had asked her, the question that did, indeed, press on her heart.

What is . . . ? What is . . . ?

She was still unable to get more than those words—that were

now a voice in her head—while she scrubbed pots or strolled along the deck, breathing in the sea air. Barnaby passed her on his way to the helm, and she figured it was worth a try.

"Barnaby."

"Yes, my dear."

"May I ask you something?"

"Anything, my lady."

Wendy struggled to not roll her eyes. Barnaby, in his compliments and his gaze, was always very direct.

"When you first came here, was there a question on your heart? In the seas and in the sky?"

Barnaby's bewildered look confirmed just how insane she sounded.

"Well, my dear, I'm not entirely sure what you are talking about. Best to lay off the wine probably." He chuckled, looking at Wendy for confirmation. She stayed still, a stray strand of hair whipping around her eyes in the strong wind.

Barnaby pushed up his glasses as they stood over the bowsprit. Michael was running circles around them, playing with a paper ship he had folded earlier that day. The robust salty air kept blowing it out of his hands, which sent him scurrying after it, much to the reluctant smiles of the crew working around him. A smile crept across her face. It brought her joy to see Michael playing again, to be able to be a child once more, and though his screaming nightmares woke her each night, he seemed better with each passing day. He missed his mother, and Wendy did as well. She had taken for granted the world in which adults fixed every problem, in which her parents kept her safe. The worries of children were swallowed into the very grownup-ness of their parents, and children were the luckier for it.

"Shall we continue our stroll?" Barnaby offered his arm, interrupting her thoughts. Wendy looked backwards, and seeing the scowl upon Smith's miserable face, declined.

"I'm sorry. I think I am needed below decks to prepare your dinner."

Barnaby shook his head. "It's a shame, a damn shame, that a woman of society like yourself is meant to salt fish and chop carrots!"

Wendy laughed. "I don't mind it so much. I like Keme's company, and for the record, we are all out of carrots. Tonight will be squid with stale bread." The look of devastation on Barnaby's face made Wendy laugh.

"Michael, are you alright?" He ignored her as he climbed onto the squat base of a cannon, holding his paper ship high in the sky, its sails fluttering along with its behemoth parent's snapping high above.

That evening, Hook requested her company on deck once again. Wendy headed up once the sunset appeared in her port window, wrapping herself in the same heavy blanket before stopping at the kitchen to make herself a steaming cup of thistle tea, a small reminder of home with each slow, heavenly sip. She followed the stairs up to the deck, barely even noticing the bones now. She relished the tangy scent of the night sea, so sharp and clean in her nostrils. The sky was the color of a blood orange, dripping into the sea, which had taken on a crimson shade in the strange light. Hook stood on the rail, his free hand wrapped around a downed line.

"The Pilvinuvo Indians call this light *bomvi-nato'si*—sunfire. It's magnificent."

Wendy looked out at the water. The color unnerved her—she much preferred the clear blue of the sea to this molten cauldron, but she nodded anyway, able to appreciate the beauty even when it reminded her of the blood that had dripped down Kitoko's throat. The captain didn't turn away from the sea of sunfire as he began his tale of the evening, his voice low, exhaustion creeping out from his very bones.

"The last time we spoke, I told you of my history with Peter Pan, how I came to loathe him, and why I have sworn my life to defeating him."

"Yes."

"Well, that brings us to the current day, and the climate, my dear, as they say, is a bit tumultuous." He closed his eyes for a moment. "We are running out of time, all of us. Peter is a ticking time bomb, *ticktock. Ticktock.*"

He waved his finger back and forth. "One tick too far, and all of this . . . ," he gestured out in the direction of the island, to the sea, and the bloody sky, "goes away."

His heels clicked as he leapt down from the side of the ship, reaching for a half-drained glass of wine. He took a long sip and peered over his glass at Wendy.

"Have you never wondered, Miss Darling, why a pirate, and a grown man, would entertain the youthful notions and challenges of a maniacal child?"

Wendy shook her head no, but she had, indeed, wondered this very thing. This was an obsession dark, and from what she could tell, without true reason. Hook had been introduced as Peter's sworn enemy, his great nemesis, and she had just accepted it straight from Peter's charming mouth, just like so many things. At that thought, embarrassment crept up her face, and she raised her hands to cover her cheeks.

"Well, he did kill your father, who sounded like a very good man indeed."

Hook's blinked twice, and his mouth parted in surprise. It curled back up into a sneer a moment later, but Wendy had seen it.

"Yes, Peter did kill my father, and that is enough to hunt a man for his lifetime. However, what Peter and I do, isn't a hunt, as much as I would like it to be." The captain pulled out his sword and ran his hook down it, slowly, the metal grating into a high-pitched whine. He raised an eyebrow at Wendy, eyes simmering with malice.

"Every morning, upon waking, the first thing I imagine is running my sword through his belly, and up into his ribs, watching him flail like a fish on a spear, unable to free himself, unable to fly away."

Hook paused before a terrible smile stretched across his face.

"I wouldn't speak to him, but I would watch him watching me watching him die. It would be, in a word, *glorious*. For my father and for so many others."

He dropped his scabbard, sheathed it beside him, and looked over at Wendy's shocked face.

"I'm sorry to be so frank, Miss Darling, but I need you to understand that I want nothing more than the death of Peter Pan. It's important that you comprehend that fact."

She nodded.

"I do." *Dear God.*

Hook turned and leaned against the railing, his hook clacking out an erratic pattern on the wood.

"You've been to my vault, I believe." Wendy was unsure of what to say. She had more specifically *broken into* Hook's fault.

"I, er, Peter had . . ."

"I know you've been there, my dear. I saw you, through the lenses of my spyglass. I saw Peter carry you away, your face covered with the blood of that general, your body limp in his arms."

Hook's eyes focused on the horizon.

"Seems like Peter goes through generals pretty fast, wouldn't you agree?"

"I would." Wendy let her thoughts linger on Oxley, Abbott, and John. *Always John.*

"I know then you've seen inside of the vault, the hallways of water, the room with the hanging cage, the music room, among many others."

Wendy shook her head. "Yes, I've seen it and hope to never again. It was a horrible place."

She shook her head at the terrible memory, of Darby's screams as he drowned behind a locked door, at Kitoko's face when Smith had opened his throat in a wide, red grin.

"A horrible place indeed—almost *too horrible*, would you say?"
Wendy paused, her mind replaying glimpses of the inside of
the water-logged vault.

"Whatever do you mean?"

Hook actually smiled at that.

"Would you say that the vault has a certain theatricality to it?"
Wendy leaned back against a bow chaser that flanked the helm.
She thought of the small skeletons that hung from the vault, the
red birds that beat in their empty rib cages, of the grinning skull
with its dripping green eyes, of the jagged wooden teeth and the
rushing river that pounded its surf between them.

"You could say it's dramatic, I suppose, but you're pirates. I've
been on this ship for a while now, and I have heard some stories
that I will sadly never forget, stories of murder and ghosts." She
paused. "Pirates are a very dramatic people."

Hook laughed, deeply. It was a foreign sound and Wendy
enjoyed it immensely.

"You're right, Miss Darling—we are pirates, and we do love an
occasional gruesome murder, but we don't need a skull-shaped
cave to murder people. Trust me, you really can do it with anything handy—" He looked directly at her.

"Say, a teacup. A spoon through the eye. The handle of a
cannon . . . a hook." Wendy's smile disappeared, and she slowly
put her teacup down on the deck.

"The truth is, Miss Darling, is that the vault is purely there for
Peter Pan's entertainment. It drives his imagination and his greed.
Its purpose is to give him a goal, to give the Lost Boys something
to raid, which happens every few years when they finally gear up
to it. The vault, and its treasures and its dangers, are all part of
the elaborate game that I am playing with Peter Pan."

Wendy, forgetting who she was with, leapt to her feet, her face
flaming with anger.

"People died there! *Children* died there!"

"Of course by children you mean Lost Boys. And of course

they did. The game is very real, even if it is just a game. People must die, or it ceases to entertain. The stakes must be real. Peter is able to be manipulated by a deft hand, but the boy is not stupid."

Wendy threw out her hands. "So the vault is just what, a playground for Peter?"

Hook's voice dropped.

"Have you ever seen a kitten play with a ball of string?"

Hook smiled, large white canines gleaming under the emerging moon.

"The vault is a ball of string for a very strong, very evil little kitten."

Wendy shook her head.

"But the liquor . . . it was there. We took it all."

Hook shook his head, a vein in his temple pulsing.

"Do you really think, Miss Darling, that I would store my treasure in a place that could be so easily found, that was so accessible from above? I'm the richest man in Neverland. I own every building in Port Duette, and a few on the outlying islands. I run a brothel, a tavern, a butcher, a bakery, a bank, and a dozen other, let's say shadier, side venues. Would it be wise then, that I would keep all my riches in a place where Peter Pan could stroll in with a few Lost Boys and take it?"

Wendy had seen the riches of this ship, stored in quiet corners, chests that overflowed with gold, and smaller signs of wealth here and there: the antiques in Hook's chambers, the newness of the weaponry, his boots that always reflected the sun. She knew now that the *Night* and its riches reflected only a snippet of what Hook owned, what the *Sudden Night* owned. Anger rose inside of her, boiling alongside with the red sea. She took a step towards him, tired of being a polite girl.

"Then why would you risk the life of your own men, and those boys, for a game? They were children, and you killed them! You had no right, you horrid, horrid man! Why not let Peter be, why even tempt him at all?"

She ran her hands angrily through her hair, tears choking her throat, unleashing the horror she had seen.

"Smith slit Kitoko's throat right before my eyes! Say what you will about Lost Boys, but you plot grown men against children, children who are following a leader that controls their every move, and you take their lives, as part of what, a game?"

She was done being nice, worrying about her every step.

"Peter is a monster, but so are you for engaging him! Their blood is on your hands."

Hook took one quick step towards Wendy, closing the gap between them.

"Peter killed seven of my men that day, Miss Darling. Seven. One using only his feet. Seven grown men, as you have reminded me, so don't act like I am killing some innocent lambs."

He dropped his voice, his dismay obvious.

"If anything, any man sent up against Peter is the lamb to the slaughter."

Wendy jerked her chin away towards him.

"Why, then? Why?"

Without warning, Hook grabbed the collar of her dress, crumpling it underneath his fingers as he pulled her towards him. His voice dropped as he whispered in her face.

"Well, that is the question, isn't it? Why do I play this game with this boy, this Peter Pan? Why bother with the blood, the calculating, the vault, the constant need to make sure that our rivalry stays strong?"

The ship rocked underneath them, the figurehead of Queen Eryne pointing to the sky for a moment before slapping the ship down upon rough, hard waves. Hook released her as they both flew sideways and Wendy grabbed onto one of the rope ladders leading up to the mast to steady her balance. Hook took a moment before smoothing out his jacket, once again in control.

"Do you not think I could kill Peter Pan if I wanted to? Why not just send my best men up the wild tangles of Pan Island to slit his throat while he sleeps? Why didn't Smith shoot his pistol directly at Peter while he was on the vault?"

When the captain turned back to her, his eyes were glowing. "Why haven't I loosed my cannons on Pan Island and burned that godforsaken island to the ground? I could do that in the morning and be having wine and cheese by noon." His voice grew louder, more agitated. "Why, if Peter were standing here now, would I not kill him? Why has an entire people fled from his emerald gaze? *Why, why, why?* Look at me child, and tell me why. Why, God damn it!?"

Wendy shook her head.

"Answer the question!"

It was there, it was in the back of her throat, and the tip of her tongue and yet, nothing. It was infuriating, chasing this question around like a fictional rabbit. Wendy's voice exploded from the place she knew the answer should be.

"Argh! I don't know, I'm sorry! Just tell me! I'm tired of these questions!"

Hook gave a disappointed shake of his head.

"As am I. I cannot tell you the answer, for if you do not know the question, I cannot explain the answer. It will come. It took me years to ask the question, and I saw the *Sunned Shore*, upended, the blood of pirates on the trees. I am sad to say that we do not have years. We may not even have months," he sighed.

"I am tired of this game with Peter Pan. I grow weary for hope. I have lost almost all, and I stand to lose even more."

He faced her, reached out his hook, and traced it silently across her hairline, the edge of it skipping over her skin, its blade sharp, but never cutting.

"I pulled you out of the sea that day because I believe you are our last hope. *You must be.*"

He closed his eyes and stepped back.

"Good night, Miss Darling. You may return to your quarters."

"Please, no! Let me stay. Tell me more and perhaps the question will come to me."

Hook rested his hand on the deck of the ship, his thumb tracing small circles.

"The question must be asked by you, and only you."

"This game," Wendy snapped, "is just as foolish as your other one."

Hook moved so fast that she didn't even have time to react, for one moment he was turned away from her, looking out at the sea, and the other he was leaning her over the edge of the ship, his hook pressing hard into her collarbone, her face looking out to sea.

"You don't make demands on my ship, Miss Darling, do you understand?"

Fear raced through her chest as she realized just how close she was to the water, how she could see a silent, watery death from here.

"Yes, Captain."

She swallowed, her heart thumping wildly against the inside of her chest. He stepped back, brushing his navy jacket with his hand, straightening his sun-shaped medals.

"My apologies. Please see if Keme needs any help in the kitchen before you go to bed and give him my regards."

Wendy swallowed, hoping to find her way back to normal conversation.

"You seem quite fond of him and yet, you never seem to visit the kitchen."

Hook's eyes met her own and he stared unsteadily into them.

"Because Keme reminds me of what I have lost." With a sigh, he turned away from her, his voice resuming its normal commanding cadence.

"We arrive early tomorrow in Port Duette. I will have clothes set out for you in the morning, for you will be joining me for our venture into town. Port Duette is a ruthless place, and I dare say that Michael leaving the boat would be terribly unwise. Children are ripe for the plucking in Port Duette, and I can't promise his safety, in fact I could almost promise the opposite. There are much worse fates in Neverland for Michael than being a guest on the *Sudden Night*. With only a handful of crew, he'll practically have the ship to himself—as long as he doesn't *break* anything."

"Yes, sir." Her heart sank. There would be no escaping Hook if Michael wasn't with her. It was simply a fact. She closed her eyes. But then again, where would she have gone? Where would they be safe from Peter? Sadly, there was no place safer than this ship of bones, no greater protector than Hook, despite his weary cruelty.

"Good night, then."

"And Miss Darling? I apologize for my anger. My concerns, as of late, are grave."

"I understand."

"You don't, but you will."

She left the captain standing alone underneath the stars, the weight of his worries stretched across his shoulders, so heavy it pulled his head towards the sea.

Chapter Nine

"Wendy, Wendy, Wendy!" Michael was jumping on her stomach.

"Ow, Michael, get off!" She pushed his legs, which seemed to be growing longer every day, off her body, and he slumped onto the floor of their quarters, landing with a loud bang.

"We're here! We're here! I think we're at Port Duette!" His sandy little head blocked the round port window in their room.

"I see the white sand! Remember Peter said once that it was made of earls!"

"Pearls. Not earls."

Michael considered this for a minute. "That makes more sense." His giggle turned into a pout, followed by a whine.

"Wendy, I really want to go!"

Wendy had told him last night that Hook wanted him to stay on the boat. What she believed would be a huge battle ended fairly quickly, with Michael curling up in her arms and admitting, "I don't want any more danger. I'll stay."

At first she had been surprised, but as he had stared at her with his bright blue eyes, her hands on his cheeks, she realized that Michael felt safe on the *Sudden Night*, and that his sense of security at the moment was a bit shaky. He had also seemed thrilled at the possibility that the boat would be his own for that golden day.

"Do you think . . . ?" He had seemed pensive at first, his bravery growing. "Do you think I could touch the wheel?"

Wendy smiled. "I'm not sure. You may have to stay below deck with Keme. There will be some crew left on the boat still."

Michael shook his head, so sure of his own adorableness. "They'll let me touch it. Hawk said I could."

"Oh he did, did he?"

"Mmm-hmm. He promised."

"Well, Hawk and Owl will both be staying, so perhaps that is true."

Michael went quiet and then whispered, "Wendy?"

She knew the question even before he asked it. "Yes, Michael?"

"You'll be safe, right? In Port Duette."

How did one answer this question? There was no promise of safety in Neverland, none that she could give without lying to him outright. The illusion of safety that had carried her through her entire life was chipping and falling away, pieces of a broken mirror that now revealed her innate brokenness.

"I hope so. I'll be with Captain Hook the whole time."

Michael was fiddling with a wooden yoyo that a pirate had given him, an item that never left his pocket. "Why do you need to go?"

Wendy had asked herself the same thing, but she knew that the more she knew about this world and the way it worked, the better. It was her unspoken fear that they would have to stay here forever, but if they did, she would not be the wide-eyed girl she was when Peter brought her here. She needed to see the truth of Neverland, its working cogs and machinery, so that if she needed to make a life here for her and her brothers, she could. And by God, she would.

She did not tell Michael any of this.

"There are things Hook thinks I need to understand. Things about Peter, and Neverland. Things are quite confusing here, aren't they?"

Michael nodded. "They REALLY are."

"Well, I don't want to be confused anymore, Michael. I want to understand. And to understand, I need to go into Port Duette."

Michael looked down at his hands. "Is this about Peter Pan?"

"Yes."

"He's not good, Wendy."

"I know he isn't. But I truly don't think he can get to us here. It's strange but I believe the *Sudden Night* is the safest place for us to be right now."

Michael smiled. "We have all these mean pirates to protect us."

Wendy knelt down before him, her heart sore at telling him these truths, truths that a five-year-old should never have to bear. "There are a lot of pirates, and they may protect us for now, but they aren't family. Don't forget that. *You and me, that's who we trust, you understand?*"

Michael didn't meet her eyes.

"What about John? Do we trust him?"

Wendy considered the implications before she tenderly voiced her answer.

"Not while he is still with Peter. He would not hurt us, I don't think, but when he is with Peter Pan he makes poor choices."

That was the understatement of the century, she mused. Still she continued.

"But he's still our brother and we love and pray for him every night, don't we?" Michael nodded, and then, just like that, his interest shifted, Wendy finding herself thankful for his juvenile attention span.

"Do you think that when I'm on the boat by myself that I can climb up to the crow's nest and drop something?"

Now, blinking in the early morning light filtering through the port window in their small bunk, Wendy felt a pang in her chest about leaving him.

"Don't forget, I'll be back tonight, Michael."

His head bounced around as he looked at Port Duette.

"Yup. There's buildings, Wendy! Buildings! They look . . . sad. Ooohhh, but the sand is so sparkly!"

As Michael prattled on about Port Duette, Wendy quickly washed her face in the basin and opened the small package of clothing that had been placed outside their door that morning, by a grumbling Smith.

After declaring, "Hook must be joking!" she began putting on the curious clothes; black pants, baggy at the top, but cinched at the knee into a sort of tight-fitting stocking that slipped over her calves. Brown leather boots went all the way up her up her leg, hitting her just above the knee, with complex leather laces that she looped around various metal hooks on the sides of the shoes. Next she pulled her arms through a long-sleeved mustard-yellow tunic, its button holes stitched with a beautiful black ribbon that trailed between her breast and down the middle of her back. A crisscrossing leather sash went around her waist and up over her shoulders, crossing in front of her collarbone. A low-slung black belt, with a spot for a sheathed dagger went around the widest part of her hips. After braiding and twisting her hair into a tight bun, she placed a brown leather pirate hat onto her head, adorned with a single blood-red ribbon that trailed down onto her right shoulder. She looked in the mirror above their tiny washbin. Michael squealed.

"Wendy! You look like a real pirate!"

Wendy made a face in the mirror. "I look ridiculous." *She did, however, like the hat very much.* She took a step, feeling each inch of the clothing hanging heavy on her body, pulling in places it shouldn't. She looked longingly at her light, simple dress, hanging on the back of her bed. She sighed. "It will have to do."

She took Michael's face in her hands. "I want you to be good while I'm gone. Be safe. Don't go anywhere alone—make sure you are with Keme if you are below deck, and with Hawk or Owl if you are above. Do you understand?"

Michael nodded. "I do, Wendy."

"I love you, more than all the stars in the sky." She kissed his forehead quickly before turning to leave, her heart twisting in her chest.

Chapter Ten

Wendy Darling made her way above deck, where all the pirates were scurrying like mad, prepping the ship to dock. Hook was at the wheel, Smith yelling out frantic directions as the *Sudden Night* made swift headway towards the port.

"Aye, we have a quartering sea, lads! Secure the lines, we're along shore and all in the wind!"

She felt their bemused stares as she walked past them in her disguise, their faces acknowledging just how silly she felt in this costume, like Michael wearing her father's smoking jacket. She joined Barnaby on the port side, and after checking that her many leather sashes were still in the right place, her mouth dropped open at the view of the shore.

"It's . . ."

She was speechless.

Barnaby turned to her with a laugh.

"Oh, Wendy! It's you!" He adjusted his glasses. "I didn't even recognize you. You look just like one of us, dressed in your long clothes. How very disappointing! I had grown quite fond of your dresses among these sad frocks." He gave a shy smile before turning back to the water, his voice lowering.

"It is quite something, isn't it? The Bay of Treasures. I never grow tired of looking at it."

He was silent for a moment before giving her hand a reassuring squeeze. Wendy didn't like the feel of his sweaty hand around hers and pulled away, but her eyes never left the island in front of her. She remembered seeing this bay when they had flown into Neverland, a shimmering diamond coast, but when it rose up above her, tangible and stark against the turquoise water, she found it hard to breathe in the face of its beauty. The white sand welcomed the ship like a mother curling her children into her soft arms. The curved bay—like a crescent moon—was anchored by a long stretch of beach that glimmered in the morning light. Blinded by the reflection, several of the pirates were shielding their eyes with their hands, but even with her eyes burning, Wendy found herself unable to look away. The pearled sand was hypnotic, its color shifting with the light as it refracted over the shelled surface. The sea lapped gently at its edges, the contrast to the white sand brilliant and extreme, colors that shouldn't exist pushing against her thick lashes. It was the purest of whites, like fresh milk; the light delighted to be playing across its surface, privileged and giddy. The untouched beauty of the sand set off the ugly sight of ship carcasses that littered the west end of the bay, huge hulking pieces of wood, their rotting insides filled now with birds and seals who raised their barking voices to greet the *Night*. Barnaby leaned closer to her, his putrid breath smelling of wine.

"The Bay of Treasures has the most-terrible reputation for wrecking ships with less-skilled sailors than our own—only the most-experienced captains can navigate this shore, one that climbs an ungodly amount in a matter of twenty yards. The pearled shore that you see comes from the mermaids' coral gardens, which run underneath all of Neverland seas. The shape of the coral pushes the pearls up and onto the shore, after the water rips them into flakes. Makes for a beautiful welcome, but if you take your ship over that coral too fast, you'll rip a tear right in your hull, like splitting a banana. Those ships ran high 'n dry."

Wendy heard a terrible creak run underneath the ship and gave a shudder.

"Shouldn't you be helping him, then?"

Barnaby shook his head.

"I'm no help here. Only the captain knows how to get this monstrous ship in and out of Port Duette."

Wendy raised her eyebrows. "Why wouldn't you tender the ship?"

Barnaby laughed. "Because Hook will not tender the *Night* in his own town. Tendering is a mark of weakness. That's why you see those ships tendered there." He pointed to the west end of the bay, where Wendy could see three large ships anchored just off shore, though none were as big as the *Night*.

She squinted. "Which ones are those?"

Barnaby leaned over the side before pulling a long spyglass out of his pocket. "Ah yes, that would be the *Vicious Seas* on the left, *Coral Plunder*, and *Viper's Strike*. No *Undertow* yet. That's . . . interesting."

Voodoo walked up next to Barnaby, who eyed him suspiciously.

"What do you think it means that Maison is not here yet, old salt?"

Voodoo shook his head. "Aye, can't be nothing good. Hook's bound to blow that man down."

"Quiet on deck!" roared Captain Hook, and the entire *Sudden Night* fell silent as the captain deftly turned the ship, his face furrowed in concentration, a drop of sweat falling down his neck as he leaned right and left, turning the wheel with tiny, calculated movements. The port side swung north before righting itself in rigid movement that barely kissed the wood underneath their feet. Wendy watched Hook as his eyes darted left and right, observing and listening to the waves, his feet wide, as if he was feeling the pull of the waves up through his legs, and pushing that into the wheel. He turned the ship again, a small movement to the left, and before he raised the wheel up with his hook, he waited a moment and then unleashed the wheel, letting it spin rapidly in the other direction. The *Sudden Night* swung wide, and Wendy found herself clutching the sideboards as it pitched across the waves, its port hurtling sideward towards the pearl sands.

She stumbled, Barnaby falling roughly against her, his arms wrapping around her waist to keep them both upright. She squirmed away, and he looked embarrassed, a red flush rising past his gray whiskers.

"I'm sorry, I'm sorry, my lady!"

He was having a hard time standing as well, though some of the other pirates seemed to barely notice that their ship was cresting a wave, headed on a surefire course to collide with the very shallow shore.

"Prepare to dock, the wind is onshore, smartly now, men!" screamed the captain, and the men scrambled to their stations, some running to the shorelines, others scurrying like spiders up the ladders. The ship barreled, unapologetic, towards the shore, waves parting before her berth as she drifted gently sideward to bump against the outstretched wooden dock.

"Secure the lines!" Hook yelled.

The men quickly answered with a robust, "Aye, aye!"

She glided forward, and the pearl shores welcomed the *Night* home with a scraping sigh. As the men threw various ropes overboard, some leaping out and onto the deck with surprisingly steady legs, the ship settled down into small, gentle sideward rocks, the water easing it to shallower shores, giving her the rest she sorely deserved.

"Land ho! Drop the anchor!" cried Hook, his voice raising over the clamor of excited voices above deck. The men were moving all around her now, like a swarm of busy bees tending to their queen, the familiar routines of docking working like clock-work. The rest of them heaved heavy loads upon their sweaty backs—bags of rotted fruit, of ammunition, and of treasure to trade—crates filled with cheese, salt, fish, soap, books, and, of course, liquor. Out of the corner of her eye, Wendy saw Black Caesar was carrying a huge white bag over his shoulders that was moving. Wendy had begun walking swiftly towards him when she saw Michael scurry past the mast, carrying a hunk of bread before he disappeared below deck with Keme. She turned away from the writhing bag, uncomfortable, but no longer worried that it contained her younger brother. As the men scuttled off, happy to be coming ashore and moving their sore legs, Wendy watched from the deck, her eyes burning with the reflection of the pearled sand. Barnaby took her arm.

"Will you join me, my dear? Port Duette has many fascinating sights, but I must confess that none are as lovely as you."

To her relief, Captain Hook stepped between them, and Barnaby was shoved roughly backwards by Smith, who looked terrifying in a full black coat, adorned with grinning white skulls, over a quite cheery blue-and-white striped shirt. The captain looked regal, wearing the navy coat that she had first seen him in, black pants, and high brown boots, his clothes ironed and crisp. Adding to his intense presence, the hat that she had once seen on the Jolly Staircase was perched upon his head, a flare that framed his brow. It was a deep red, like coagulated blood, and curved down in front of his eyes. The sides of the hat arched up like two parting waves, each lined with strands of a gold-filigree ivy, richly textured and obviously expensive. The tip of the cap arrowed outwards in a giant white plume, made of ostrich feathers that quivered in the wind like the delicate spine of a bird. Hook saw her eyeing his hat.

"Only when we meet with the Scorned."

Smith turned away so the captain would not see him snicker. He was too late and the captain whirled on him.

"Shut yer mouth, Smith, or I'll string your old mother up by her wretched toes."

"Yes, Captain."

Hook did not return the smile, but steeled his eyes on the port.

"The *Undertow* hasn't arrived yet. I'm not surprised."

"Want me to just kill him for you? Maison?" Smith twisted his mouth sideways and ran his hands lovingly over his dagger—the same one, Wendy noted, that slit Kitoko's neck.

"I wouldn't mind. That man needs a good flaying, and it's about time we taught him a lesson for his insolence."

"Not today, Smith. But I'll keep that in mind." Hook gave a heavy sigh. "He's here to try to negotiate himself into being the admiral of the Scorned."

Smith snorted. "Unlikely. The *Night* would make mincemeat of his ship if he tried, and I would take his hands before he could ever reach the wheel."

Hook paused, his eyes shifting east, towards the faint outline of Pan Island.

"I would say, unfortunately, it's more likely than you may deign."

Hook wrapped his hand around Wendy's upper arm. "Ms. Darling, you will be accompanying me in Port Duette. You may not stray from my sight, do you understand? This is not like London, with its decorative shrubs and stationed policemen where you may wander about freely. Your purpose here in Port Duette is to listen and learn, to observe. The Scorned and I have business here, and you will be my companion and witness."

Wendy nodded, shaking her arm free, annoyed at his presumption that she would just wander away, like some silly butterfly.

"I will go freely with you, but I am not your prisoner."

Hook's eyes darkened. "You're right, you are not, but you'll have to excuse me for taking precautions. Everyone in Neverland knows that we are docked here for the day." His eyes darkened. "Everyone."

Wendy felt the cold rush of panic twist in her stomach. *Peter.* How was it, that when she hated him, when it was he that she feared the most, that there was still some tiny infuriating part of her that would feel relief to see his lovely face? She hated herself for it, hated how Peter's animalistic charm could manipulate even her powerful reason. It disgusted her, made her want to scrub her body raw at the thought of him, just to rid herself of the hold he had on her. Her body betrayed her at the thought of his smile, and then counterbalanced, staying flush with the hatred of him. She took a step closer to Hook.

He lowered his tone, "That a girl. Let's see to it that you don't die."

Without another word, he began making his way across the deck and off the ship, walking in between the lines of men that waited on the wooden dock for their captain to touch dry land, their heads bowed in obedience. Smith followed behind him, followed by Wendy, who was trying to walk with as manly a gait as possible with hard, long steps and wildly swinging arms.

"Will you stop?" hissed Smith. "You look like a bloody monkey."

"Shut up," Wendy snapped back, surprised at her own impoliteness. She immediately apologized. "I'm sorry. I shouldn't have said that."

"That was the first piratelike thing you've said since you've been here—that is 'til you apologized," snapped Smith, with something that vaguely resembled pride.

Wendy smiled underneath her wide hat.

The zig-zagging dark wooden dock led across the sand, which up close took on a rainbow sheen, the pearl grains reflecting particles of light. They stepped off the dock and made their way up the shore (which made a delightful crunching noise underfoot, like cracking nuts between her teeth) up the beach, towards a wide arch made of haphazardly piled beach wood that welcomed them into a thick canopy of emerald trees. Hanging sideward off the arch, a messily scrawled sign creaked out its lone warning in the breeze:

Welcome to Port Duette.
You've been warned.

CHAPTER ELEVEN

Underneath the archway and its creaking sign was a narrow path into the wood; a dark oak barrel, roughly the size of two short men, sat squarely in their path. The pirates circled around the barrel, most making sure to leave plenty of space between them and its grimy surface. A rancid smell hit her full on in the face, and she gagged involuntarily. Smith grinned nastily before taking pity on her and handing her a handkerchief, which reeked of sweat, but it was still better than the sweet, putrid smell that rose up from the barrel.

Black Caesar leaned towards her. "Don't be embarrassed, lass. We're all used to it by now, but the first few times, these pirates were heave-hoing all over the place."

Wendy smiled behind the handkerchief.

Hook dangled a key out in front of him. "Black Caesar, please take our taxes, and let's be on our way."

The pirate grinned, showing his yellowish teeth and rotted gums.

"Happy to, Captain."

With the help of two other men, they turned the barrel over with a hard thud, revealing a gold padlock on the bottom that was attached to a circular slat in darker wood. Black Caesar took the key from Hook before unlocking the padlock and setting it quietly in the sand. Then, moving slowly and cautiously, his hands found a small finger groove in the wood and turned it, twice clockwise and then once backwards, his fingers spinning over the wood. The small circle slid over the opening and a tiny hole appeared in the wood. Bloody Blair and Voodoo began shaking the barrel back and forth between them, and soon coins began to shake loose, hundreds piling on the ground with loud, rattling clinks. Hook leaned back, satisfied.

"Ah, that's the sound of it. I love the sound of empty pockets."

Smith leaned over towards Wendy. "If you want to visit Port Duette, ye must pay the captain."

"What's to keep people from stealing it?"

"Have a look. Well, go on."

Wendy took a few cautious steps towards the barrel, stopping abruptly when she heard the faintest of terrible sounds: hissing, followed by the sounds of hundreds of legless bodies sliding over each other.

"Look inside," whispered Voodoo, his brown eyes large with excitement. "Watch our little friends move!"

Wendy knew that she rather wouldn't, but she carefully raised herself up on her tip toes and peered over the top as Voodoo dropped a lit match into the darkness. In the flash of light, she saw them, hundreds of thick black snakes, writhing as one nightmarish form, heads and tails and bodies, entwined, squirming and reaching towards the light, their yellow eyes lit in the sudden flare. Wendy leapt back, her heart exploding at the horror of it, and she watched, nauseated, as Black Caesar— moving very quickly—ripped off the lid of the barrel, threw in the writhing bag that he carried on his shoulder, and shut the lid quickly behind it. The hissing grew louder, and the barrel began rocking violently back and forth as Wendy heard terrified shrieks.

"Rats from the ship. What else we gonna do with them?" Black Caesar shrugged. "And if someone tries to steal it, or doesn't pay the captain their taxes . . . then we don't need no rats to keep them fed, do we?"

Wendy felt her stomach churn with revulsion and turned to Hook, hoping that he would wink, or give some sign that Black Caesar was fibbing. He didn't, and she felt a rivulet of sweat trickle down her forehead as they shuffled forward in the sand, making their way around the barrel. From there, the pearls underfoot turned into coarse brown sand that twisted into an emerald maze of low-lying trees, their branches heavy with moisture, and their leafy arms reaching for the crew. They walked for a few minutes, weaving their way silently through the trees, and Wendy began to sense a change in the air. The humid wetness of the island was sloping off her skin as they neared an opening in the trees and her nostrils were filled less with the smell of the sugar-scented beach and more with the odors of life—steaming fish and onions, burning wood, dust underfoot. Humans.

The path wove west, and the trees parted to reveal a tapered road made of the same pearls that littered the Bay of Treasures, only these were black, gleaming like ink in the unforgiving sun. Just as she was beginning to feel out of breath, the road branched out into the streets of Port Duette, mere feet separating town from jungle.

Wendy looked above her, at the buildings that loomed overhead, all of them leaning forward just a pitch, so unlike the sturdy square buildings that made up London. In that city, there had been an order to things, one building usually like another. Here, it looked as though a child had stacked the buildings together, shoving them into one another until they stayed, buoyed by the pressure between them. They leaned against each other, like weary travelers, holding each other up with the weight of their collective exhaustion. The body of one building leapt into another, windows split between them with rickety pieces of iron ore, wood planks nailed over doorways to make walkways to second-level entrances. Parts of marooned ships had been used in most of the buildings. The carcasses of the ships lost to the bay were now bedrooms that hung perilously over the street or curved roofs that once bore the weight of a keel. Masts—now wooden awnings—draped with mouse-eaten drop cloths blew in the wind, and somewhere in the town, a wind chime clinked several dull notes.

This surely was a town built for pirates, Wendy thought.

People of all colors were milling about in the road, selling trinkets or tree nuts, but when they saw Hook and his crew, they scattered, pushing to the sides of the street or scurrying up into buildings, tucking tail as they ran, like cockroaches in the light. Hook marched out front, the plume of his hat bouncing as he walked, Smith behind him, and Wendy behind them both, her head tucked down, the hat protecting her face from the curious eyes that peered from behind every broken window and battered awning.

Hook stopped, looked around, cleared his throat, and shouted "As you were!" and the street sputtered to life again, merchants creeping back out cautiously, their wagons waving with jeweled bangles, dripping honey candles and gleaming weapons. Crowds thronged around them now, everyone vying for the captain's purse. Wendy watched the vendors with fascination. Some carts held treasure: gold boullion, ruby goblets, and heavy gold rings carved with the heads of dragons, while still others steamed with food: seared fish wrapped in leaves with pieces of fruit, ripe melons topped with white cream, hard flakes of maize dipped in pepper sauce. The sight of each one made Wendy's mouth water terribly, but she forced herself to keep her eyes straight ahead and off the winding alleyways that stretched off of the main road like curling fingers, their dark corners leering at her with the horrible prospect of Peter. A cart rumbled past her, the skins of a dozen sea snakes dangling from iron hooks, red with black markings, golden rings on black, subtle green with brown peppered dots. Wendy thought she was going to be sick. She stumbled, but Smith caught her arm.

"Don't throw up on us, girl, we need you to walk straight."

"I'm sorry" Wendy whispered. "I don't know what's wrong with me."

Smith grinned and yanked her upwards, and they continued walking at a brisk pace. "I do, it's that you ain't got your sea legs yet and you're on land again. Feels strange at first—too steady. Now you're spinning."

Now that he mentioned it, Wendy did feel the solid ground under her feet, unshifting, unyielding, and she wished it would rock, or sway, just ever so slightly. She had gone from a giant tree that creaked ever so slightly in the wind to a boat that bent the sea to its will, and now, for the first time in a long time, she was standing on ground that didn't shift in some indiscernible way. Bile rose in her throat.

"Choke it down!" ordered Smith, and so she did, appalled and disgusted, but thankful to continue on without causing a scene. He passed her a canteen, and with a long sip of cold water, she began to feel better, ordering herself not to think about the ground beneath her feet or the strange, disorienting buildings above her.

With Hook leading the company up the street, Wendy focused on the sudden steep slope of the road, forming a narrow path that fit one person at a time. As she climbed, Wendy took in the view of Port Duette from the opposite end of the shore—from here she could see that the buildings were not only leaning against one another, but that they were stacked upwards in levels, moving back from the shore, each level less wealthy than the one before it, the buildings less stable, the space between them darker and more ominous, like a yawning sigh. The thick canopy of trees pushed between the buildings in what she guessed was a constant struggle of man and nature, with nature pushing the poor back further and further into its swallowing depths, back further into the shadow of the mountain until it swallowed them completely.

Wendy's calves felt a twinge of pain as the climb increased

between the narrowing buildings. When she looked backwards, she was now able to see the huge body of the *Sudden Night* looming over the town like an angry god. It rocked gently on the waves, the mast creaking so loud that she could even hear it here, a half mile from the ship. At the top of the road, the buildings on the left gave way to a low-lying stone boundary that let passersby view the sea with ease, and Wendy found great comfort that she could see the cresting waves lapping at the horizon. Edging away from the shores, the road continued to narrow and climb, the inhabitants of Port Duette gradually falling away from the company. Their group rounded a bend, and from there Wendy could see that the road ended at an elegant stone portico. Past the low-lying buildings was an open abyss—a steep drop-off that cascaded down into a dense cluster of palm trees far below. Above the building, a thin waterfall cascaded down from the mountain, its spray of water passing directly behind the stone home. Open archways surrounded the length of the building, and lush clumps of bright pink and orange flowers climbed the widely spaced pillars. Churning swirls of hunter-green ivy danced underneath the arching stone, and clumps of lemon trees surrounded the portico, their swollen yellow fruit ripe in the wet air. Seated underneath the archways, some in chairs, some on the ground, and some standing with folded arms, eyeing the men with barely contained amusement, were women. Dozens of them were waiting, their fingers curling to the men, who were dropping their bags and rushing towards the women, gold glinting in their palms. Wendy's mouth dropped open as they drew closer, and Smith sniggered at her shock.

"Harlot's Grove. Possibly my favorite place in Neverland, aside from the *Night*."

As they drew closer, Wendy could see that some of the women were barely clothed—the one closest to Wendy was wearing tiny triangles of red scales that barely covered her breasts, strewn together with a string of red and pearl beading, a sheer gold scarf wrapped around her waist, covering nothing. Another leered out of a window at Hook as he walked past, her bosom bursting out of a white laced corset, her tiny waist bare atop a low-slung blue skirt. She reached out for Hook as he passed, her fingers gracing his collar.

"How about today, my love? I'll show you something you've never seen before."

Hook brushed her hand aside without looking at her. "Not today, Caprice. Today I'm in the mood for something . . ." His eyes traveled over the group, coming to rest on a copper-headed beauty with dark skin, who was draped across one of the open porticos like a Siamese cat, her taut belly resting on the cool stone. Wendy felt a blush rise up her face at the indecency of these women, their wanton sexuality projected to the pirates like rays of naughty sunshine. The crew swarmed towards the women like bees to honey, their beating hearts like furious wings, hungry and lustful. Hook took his dark beauty with one hand and beckoned to another with his hook, this one a busty blond with a pink mouth. He winked at Smith, who rolled his eyes at the captain, a green-eyed girl with short black hair already hanging off his massive shoulders, her tight lavender dress bursting at the seams. Smith cleared his throat.

"Aye men, you have an hour, and we will meet back here for the quorum of the Scorned. Do not be late or you will be left behind, permanently." He looked around. "Though truthfully, there are worse places to be marooned."

Voodoo was already fiddling with the corset of a women who had draped herself over his shoulders, a happy grin on her face, but her eyes emotionless. A shadow passed over Wendy. Hook was standing over her, the two women flanking either side of him.

"I've gone ahead and gotten one for you, my dear."

He beckoned to an elegant older woman who was watching over the grove from a raised stone platform above.

"Fermina, this is your charge."

The men hooted with laughter as Wendy curdled inside, embarrassed. She turned back to Hook furious, angry at him for his cryptic tales, angry that he would think that she would do this.

"I have no interest in this. No. Absolutely not."

Hook leaned forward, the plume of his ridiculous hat brushing across her cheek.

"Fermina has been in Neverland for a long time. A *very* long time. She may have some interesting things to share with you."

He raised his eyebrows and stared down at her, the implication written across his face. *You need to talk to this woman.*

"Oh."

Wendy took a step back from him, out of the cloud of rose-drenched perfume that was oozing from Hook's whores. The older woman made her way down the staircase towards Wendy.

"Fermina, this is . . . ," he paused for far too long, "Bluebell."

"Bluebell, huh?"

Fermina bent over Wendy with a crooked smile and inspected her face, Wendy studying her in return. Fermina was a handsome woman, curvy and broad shouldered, with black curls that cascaded down to her waist. Her face was lined and weathered with several noticeable scars, her skin brown and taut from the Neverland sun. She was wearing a lacy cream dress with a plunging neckline and a red shawl, her dress downright modest compared to the other women who were happily disappearing into the folds of the grove.

"Fermina runs Harlot's Grove, so show her proper respect."

Wendy heard a shriek and turned around to see Black Caesar marching off with a tiny slip of a woman laughing over his shoulder, passing into the dark shadows of the portico.

Fermina frowned.

"She's an idiot, that one. Sticky fingers. Tell your men to count their gold."

Hook raised his eyebrows before passing Fermina something

inside a black velvet bag. "Speaking of . . . this is for your discretion."

Fermina nodded. "Always, Captain."

Hook strolled into a set of wooden double doors flanked by towering flowers, one woman on each arm and now, incredibly, one trailing behind him. Wendy, who had seen more blatant licentiousness in the last ten minutes than she had in her entire life, burst out laughing at the thought of it, her hysterical giggles rising up and out of her chest, which immediately felt lighter and less burdened. Fermina turned to her, a bemused smile on her face.

"What're you laughing at, lass? You laughing at us?"

Wendy wiped a tear from her eye.

"No, no. I'm sorry, I'm not meaning to be rude. I must look quite insane. It's just . . . what is Hook going to do with those women? Three women? He must be a man of some talent."

Fermina smiled kindly at her, and Wendy felt a sudden rush of want for her own mother, for her soft hands, warm tea, and comforting clucking about her children that Wendy had always taken for granted.

"Don't you worry about Hook, lass. He'll do just fine."

Wendy realized that Fermina probably knew this for a fact.

"Oh, well . . ." She was stammering, flushed and embarrassed. "I suppose."

She was taken with another short laugh, and this time Fermina joined in, her weathered face turned up in joy.

"Come with me, dear—we'll have a drink, and nothing more. I'm sure you could use it after being on that bloody black ship."

She wasn't wrong, and Wendy had desperately missed being around other women, something she hadn't realized until this moment. Talking with another female sounded absolutely divine.

"Yes, I would like that. Thank you."

"Aren't you a polite one? I haven't heard someone speak like that . . . ," Fermina paused, a look of pain crossing her face, "for a long time. Anyway, dearie, let's have that drink and some bread. It's been awhile since I've been paid to sit and chat, and I intend to enjoy it. What shall I call you? I know you're name isn't Bluebell. Hook's terribly bright, but not when it comes to making up names; good Lord, that was terrible."

Wendy grinned before carefully choosing a name that would be familiar to her ears—her middle name.

"You can call me Moira."

Fermina stared at her for a moment.

"Well, that's certainly better than Bluebell."

She smiled, and Wendy found herself following the woman under one of the draping porticos, the overwhelming smell of fruit pressing on all sides of her.

"Come dearie, and let's talk about Peter Pan."

"Peter?" Wendy stopped walking. "What would you know of Peter Pan?"

Fermina paused in the darkness, her eyes now covered in the shadow of the building.

"Oh, I know more than you can imagine about Peter Pan."

The prostitute turned away from Wendy, her broad shoulders giving a shudder in the warm light of the grove. A butterfly fluttered in her hair, its cobalt wings tangled in her thick curls.

"I know about Peter Pan, because I was once one of his Lost Girls."

CHAPTER TWELVE

Wendy tried not to stumble at her words as they made their way under the porticos to a large red stone platform at the edge of the grove where a set table was waiting for them. From there, they could see the edge of the Bay of Treasures and the southernmost tip of the island. Fermina settled comfortably into a plush red chair and began pouring wine into an ornate gold goblet, adorned with swirls of naked lovers embracing. Wendy blushed when it was handed to her, and Fermina burst out laughing.

"Well, aren't you just the most innocent thing I've seen in a while? That's a rarity around these parts."

Wendy shook her head, remembering Peter's touch in the lantern, how he had made her feel like peeling off her clothes every time he glanced in her direction.

"I'm not as innocent as you may think."

She took a deep sip of wine, feeling the cherry and cinnamon notes bounce happily off her tongue. Fermina raised her eyebrows.

"That is good."

She took another sip.

"We haven't toasted yet, my dear."

Wendy put her goblet back down, embarrassed.

"Oh, you're right, I'm so sorry. I just went ahead and drank." She shook her head. "I'm not myself here."

Fermina stared at her, Wendy unnerved by the depth in her wide brown eyes, like roasted hazelnuts swimming in a pool of milk.

"No one is, dearie, no one. I'm actually surprised that you survived Peter's charm with your honor intact."

Fermina sloshed her wine around.

"That is a feat. Perhaps we should drink to Peter Pan."

Wendy made a face. "But he's terrible. Absolutely terrible."

"That he is. But boy is he beautiful."

Wendy couldn't help but smile. "This . . . ," she conceded gently, "this is true."

Fermina raised her glass.

"To the incomparable, dangerous beauty of Peter Pan."

Wendy raised her glass and took a long sip. It went down like warm honey, and she felt her shoulders ease, her body settling into the wide chair. Fermina watched her with a half smile on her face.

"I can see you are biting your tongue. Ask your questions."

Wendy smiled beneath her cup before setting it down beside her and crossing her legs.

"You said you were a Lost Girl?"

"I did, I did."

Fermina took another drink and began tearing at a hunk of brown bread, spreading it with berry jam. Wendy sat up in her chair, the heavy pollen in the air of the grove making her nose itch.

"I would love to hear your story if you feel comfortable telling it."

Fermina laughed. "Oh, I can't get enough of you, dearie! I'm a harlot, and you are asking me if I am comfortable telling a story. I love it!"

She reached out and pinched Wendy's cheek, and the feeling of Fermina's fingers against her face made her heart yearn again for her mother. She unexpectedly found her eyes swelling with tears and looked away, swallowing hard. Fermina shook her head.

"Oh love, you don't have to hide your tears here. Not here, not in front of me." She pulled the scarf from around her shoulders. "Here."

"Sorry." Wendy wiped her eyes. "I miss my mother, that's all. It's silly."

Fermina's smile turned down, slowly, sadly. "I know about that pain, by gods I do."

Her strong profile turned to look out at the bay, out at a sky that was turning more green than gray as storm clouds gathered on the horizon. The air around them buzzed with life; insects and flowers calling back and forth to each other in joyful sexual abandon.

"I was once like you—a carefree girl, with a brave spirit and solid bones. *Fermina* means strength, and I got mine from my mama, and the hot sun that beat down on us. I grew up in Vilanova i la Geltrú, in Spain. My parents were not wealthy, but neither were we poor. We lived in a small but comfortable hacienda, my papa was a merchant, and my mother helped with the cooking at a local hotel. Though Neverland has taken many of my memories, I still smell my mama's *asado de cordero* cooking on the stove, the sound of her humming echoing through the house, the sizzling of her cast iron, the taste of corn in my mouth. It was a good life, a VERY good life, my dear."

Wendy smiled, imagining Fermina as a young girl, shrieking happily in the arms of her parents. "And that is why I will never, ever forgive the bastard Peter Pan for taking me from it. I was NOT his to take! Peter will say that he takes only orphans and children in dire circumstances, but that is a lie. He takes whom he wants, and he doesn't care about families, or lives, or anyone."

Fermina slammed her hand down on a silver tray.

"That was my life! Who was he to take me away to this place?" She gestured angrily out to the island, its beauty always masking terrible truths. "I should have grown up in Villanova, beside my mother. I was her only child, her *milagro*." Fermina shook her head furiously as Wendy watched her with wide eyes.

"Peter brought me here, to Neverland, to Pan Island. At first I was seduced by the freedom of it all, and I fell madly in love with him, though I was too young and he never noticed me in that way. Besides, at that time, he had his fairy with him constantly. They were never away from each other, though I hear he has tired of her now. Peter had brought a large group of girls to the island, twelve of us to be exact. We ran wild with the Lost Boys, playing, fighting, and climbing. For a while, it was a beautiful existence. I'm sure you know."

Wendy nodded, remembering the wild beauty of Pan Island, bursting from the sea like a wet seed.

"It was good, until it suddenly wasn't. Tink hated us and tried to make our lives a living hell. Peter was asking us to do things we didn't want to do. "

Wendy knew exactly what she was talking about.

"At first, he just asked if we would cook him a meal, which we practically fell over ourselves wanting to do since we were all in love with him. Then, he asked if we would cook for the generals, and soon it was all the rest of the Lost Boys every single night without fail. Soon, we were his slaves—cooking, doing laundry, cleaning—can you imagine? Cleaning Pan Island?"

The women both laughed deeply.

"We wanted to be running and playing, fighting the pirates— his war with Hook was a new development back then—and instead I was scrubbing the trousers of every boy and cooking turkey legs over the fire from dawn until dusk. We quietly met as a group and Peter reluctantly agreed to speak with us. After we shyly told him that we wanted to be considered the same as Lost Boys, and that we would no longer be cleaning or cooking for the group, Peter turned us away."

Fermina shook her head, a long black curl flecked with hints of gray falling over her face.

"Peter pulling away from us was like the moon from a tide. He was the sun and without him, we were plunged into darkness. Some of the girls decided that it was worth it to cook and clean just to have his attention and went back to their jobs, an exhausting existence. The rest of us staged a sort of strike—we stopped working and stayed in our hammocks all day. Mind you, I was only eleven at the time, and madly in love with Peter. All the girls were around my age, the oldest one may have been fourteen at the time. We didn't know what we were doing, we didn't know. . . ." She took a sip of her wine, regret playing over her fine-lined features.

"We didn't know that playing with Peter Pan was like playing with fire."

Her wrinkled hands pressed together anxiously. Thunder rumbled quietly in the distance, as Wendy watched Fermina sorting through painful memories behind her thick lashes.

"I'm sorry, I haven't spoken of this in a long time."

Wendy reached out and grabbed her hand, giving it a squeeze. "I'm here."

Fermina smiled at her before bravely continuing.

"One clear morning, Peter asked all the girls on Pan Island if we wanted to go flying with him. We said yes, of course, thinking that all was forgiven." She closed her eyes. "I still remember the thrill of him taking my hand, of the heat that ran off his body and into my own. Tink was there, watching us leave from the Nest, her face twisted with a mix of satisfaction and pain."

"I should have known, I should have known by her eyes."

Fermina wiped a tear with the back of her hand. Wendy's heart thudded dully in her chest and she took another sip of wine.

"He flew us out towards the main island, over the Teeth and down towards the Bay of Treasures. We thought we were going for a fun ride." Fermina wrapped her hand firmly around her glass goblet and took a long drink. Then she wiped her mouth and continued with a dry laugh. "He flew down and dropped us into the Bay of Treasures, about fifty feet from the shore. We were in shock when we hit the water. We surfaced and then we heard the song, felt the scales around our bodies. Five girls . . ." she paused. "Five girls out of twelve were taken by the mermaids before we could all make it to the shore. I heard them screaming as they were dragged under and then there was nothing. I hear that song in my dreams."

Her face grew hard.

"Peter knew that the mermaids would take them. We were his gift to the mermaids, for their silence."

"Silence about what?"

Fermina didn't answer her question, but continued on with the story.

"He left us there on the shore, with nothing to our name. Two of them had just seen their sisters die."

Rain had begun trickling on the outside of the portico, a soft slapping sound that made Wendy feel comforted in the midst of this terrible story, one she understood all too well.

"I ordered my six lost sisters to pick themselves up, and we made our way to the ramshackle buildings that were being propped upon the shore. One of them was owned by Hook—though, truthfully, he owns them all now—and the captain let us stay there—a younger lad he was at the time—in exchange for what we had just escaped from; cooking, cleaning, and earning our keep. I became the leader of the Lost Girls, and it would be many years later that we became known around town as loose women."

She sighed. "Truthfully, I now regret some of the decisions we made to get here. I wish it had been different, I wish that I had my mother to teach me other paths. *But we didn't.* Peter had left us here, with no income, no way to feed ourselves. Is it any wonder that eventually we would find our way *here*? This is no town for children."

Hook said something about that, that Port Duette wasn't safe for children. Wendy was suddenly glad that Michael was back aboard the *Sudden Night*.

Fermina bit into her bread angrily.

"Boy babies are snatched right from their cribs, a few every year. One of my girls, Thea, lost her little boy, Magnus, just last year. Broke my heart. When Hook brings me the man who did it . . . ," Fermina brought the bread knife straight down into the table, "I'll start with his eyes and end at his toes."

Wendy closed her eyes as Fermina continued her story. She didn't want to hear any more.

"Once we were old enough, Hook gave us an opportunity—to run a venue just outside of town that catered to pirates—to him—called Harlot's Grove. He offered me fair terms for rent, and now I run the town's only brothel. I pay my workers fairly and I have strict standards for who is allowed to come in—and who must stay out. We serve Port Duette, and they serve us. My girls have independent means to support themselves, and we are each other's family." She smiled sadly. "We were the last Lost Girls, and from then on, Peter only brought boys to Pan Island. Until now. Until . . . you."

"Does Peter ever come . . . here?"

Wendy wasn't sure why the thought of this was so distressing. Fermina shook her head.

"Oh, no. Peter would never come here. My hatred for him is well-known."

Peter would have to be a fool to come—Wendy could tell by Fermina's face that she was a force to be reckoned with.

"Captain Hook has saved our lives, and though I know him to sometimes be a troubled man, I know in my heart that he is a good one. I would marry him in a fairy's second, if he would have me, though I know his heart is spoken for."

Fermina instantly brought her hand to her mouth.

"Oh, dearie, you must not tell Hook I said anything."

Wendy nodded her head towards the room where Hook had

taken his women and disappeared. Fermina dropped her voice to a whisper, her wine-soaked breath washing over Wendy's face. "Oh those. Those girls are mere trinkets. Meaningless, like all his treasures." Fermina smiled, then reached out her hand and pulled Wendy's face towards hers.

"Now, beautiful Moira, I want to hear your story. And don't leave any parts out. It's been awhile since I have heard a good yarn."

And so Wendy told her the truth—starting with Peter taking them to Neverland and ending with Michael, now waiting on the ship for them to return. She did not tell Fermina about Booth, because right now, Booth lived only in her heart, a soft, warm secret that soothed her soul and mind. Fermina listened intently, and Wendy poured out her feelings. The harlot said nothing as Wendy finished but instead wrapped the girl into her arms unexpectedly, Wendy's head pushed up against her ample bosom. She smelled like summer.

"You poor thing. Peter is a bastard, isn't he? I hope you kill him."

"I don't think I could kill anyone."

"What do you think you are here for, dearie?"

Wendy blinked. "I'm sorry, what?"

"You could if you had to, couldn't you? I thought—SHHHH!"

Fermina's face changed, and she slowly drew a small pistol out of her blouse.

"Someone's here."

Wendy stood quickly, pushing back her chair. Fermina stepped forward, her brown eyes watching the grove. A single planter of flowers, hanging maybe ten feet from them, was rocking wildly. A vine rustled overhead, and a shadow passed over Wendy's face, filtering the golden light beaming through slats of the portico. "Go inside. Now." Fermina leveled her pistol on the crook of her arm and closed one eye. "Move."

Instead, Wendy took a step forward, not willing to leave

Fermina alone to fight whatever lurked in the lush corners. The rustling moved overhead, coming to a rest at a spot right beside Wendy's ear. Orange and pink flowers blew in a soft breeze, and all Wendy heard was the sound of a bee, buzzing happily beside her ear.

A black cat—so dark that it was almost purple—leapt down from the portico, landing with a crash atop their table, sending bites of bread and wine goblets scattering to the floor with a loud crash. Fermina laughed. "Oh for God's sake, Chess, get down." The cat gave an unhappy meow as Fermina put him on the ground and shooed him away with her foot. "Lurks around the grove, listening at every door . . . I swear. . . ."

She waited for the rush of relief, but instead she felt a breath of air rush across her shoulders. By the time Wendy turned her head upwards to see what it was, she realized it was too late. A strong arm reached down and grabbed her wrist, and before she even knew what was happening, she was being whisked upwards, the ground disappearing rapidly beneath her as she looked down onto the shocked, lovely face of Fermina. The pistol trembled in her hands as she disappeared underneath the folds of flora that encompassed the grove.

CHAPTER TWELVE

Wendy struggled as they soared upwards, trying in vain to pull her wrist out of the iron-like grip of a figure clothed in a long, green robe, features hidden by a thin piece of black fabric. Fear pulsed through her veins, her chest constricting, her breaths shallow. Flying itself was terrifying now that Peter had dropped her. The sky was so vast, so high, and it swallowed her whole. The figure spun her around, her face outwards, so that a gloved hand was easily clasped around her mouth. Wendy and her captor flew upwards, up above the grove, up above the shanty roofs of Port Duette, and upwards into the sagging buildings that bordered the jungle. Once on the outskirts of town, they came to rest on a supportive wooden pillar that leaned against one of the larger buildings. The lip of the abandoned building above dangled precariously over the pillar, protecting them from the sky. The figure spoke.

"Don't scream, okay? He'll hear you." The hand came away from her mouth, and Wendy was silent for a moment before lunging to the ground. With one swift movement, she rolled away from the figure, and, after looking around feverishly, grabbed onto the top of a broken wine bottle. She held it out in front of her with a shaking hand.

"Don't come near me!" She snapped. "Stay back or . . ."

The figure pulled at the sheer black mask over his face. Raising her eyes to meet the face, her knees almost buckled at the intoxicating rush of relief that the eyes she met weren't emerald green and seared with hatred. These were chocolate brown, fringed by long lashes and a very amused expression. Still, she kept the bottle raised, one hand out in warning.

"Oy! Wendy! Look at you!" Oxley burst out laughing. "Has being with the pirates changed you that much already? You've only been with them a few weeks! Bravo!"

"Don't come near me!" snapped Wendy. "Stay back!"

Oxley raised both of his hands, the normally happy look upon his face clouding over with concern.

"I will, Wendy. Do you think I would hurt you? Why would I ever do that?"

"Peter did." Wendy's eyes flooded with tears that she quickly blinked back. "Peter hurt me. He hurts everyone."

"Wendy . . . ," Oxley implored as he stepped forward quickly and reached for her. Wendy brought her wine bottle down roughly across his palm before he leapt back with a yowl.

"OWW! WENDY DARLING! You stabbed me! You feisty girl! OY! I was trying to give you a damned hug!" he chortled. "AH! That hurt!" Oxley's hand was bleeding profusely, and Wendy let out a gasp.

"I'm truly so sorry, Oxley, but please stay back. If you could just leave me here, I can find my way back to the Grove. Please don't take me to Peter. We can both still just . . . go."

Oxley shook his head, the bright sun gleaming off the beautiful tribal markings that ran down his face.

"See . . . ," he sighed sadly, "I can't do that."

"You can," she shook her head. "You can."

Oxley reached down and pulled a rolled piece of paper out of a tattered knapsack that was slung across his chest.

"I can't. Because then I couldn't give this to Hook."

He handed Wendy the rolled parchment.

"For the captain only, as soon as you can get it to him." Wendy was speechless, the wine bottle at her side.

"Oh good, I see you've decided not to stab me anymore. Wendy, Wendy, Wendy . . ." He tsked his tongue. "I miss having you on Pan Island, you know? It was so nice to have a lady around. Sort of balanced things out a little, right?"

Wendy looked at the paper and then back at Oxley, the shakiness in her hands subsiding.

"It's you? You're the spy?"

Oxley laughed and rubbed his chin. "Yeah, best be keeping that to yourself for now. Only a few know. Hook, Smith, and Daa."

"Daa?" Wendy thought for a moment.

"VOODOO?" *Of course. Of course. How could she not have seen it?*

"That'd be the one. Though you best know that he hates that name. His real name is actually Nassor. Means victorious. Which we will be, someday."

Wendy's head was swirling as she tried to sort out what she was hearing.

"I thought . . . I thought Abbott was the spy. He helped us escape."

"The only thing you need to know about Abbott is that he's caught on to the fact that Peter is a total arsehole. Most generals do, eventually, but then . . . ," Oxley's voice caught in his throat and he coughed. "Then they die. Like Kitoko, still loyal to Peter even as he led him right into Smith's knife."

"But why? Why you?"

Oxley swallowed awkwardly.

"My dad wasn't always the nicest man. He got caught stealing from a merchant here in town. They caught him, and the penalty for stealing in Port Duette is a slow march off the Teeth—that is, after they almost burned his arm off." Oxley grimaced. "Hook paid his debt to the merchant and then some, in return for a lifetime of service on the *Sudden Night*—half of the debt to be paid . . . by his son."

"Oh, Oxley, that's unfair."

The Lost Boy shrugged happily, never a care on his face.

"It's not so bad. My dad loves the *Sudden Night*, and he will probably continue on with Hook even after the debt is paid, and I'm hoping that someday I can join him on that beautiful, bloated sea beast."

"But until then—"

"Until then, I am Peter's general and Hook's spy, possibly the most-dangerous job in Neverland. It's a good thing I'm clever."

Empathy flooded Wendy's senses.

"Oh, goodness, your hand. Let me see."

Oxley shot his palm out to her.

"It's nothing, it'll heal in a week. Don't beat yourself up about it. Besides . . ." He dropped his eyes. "I didn't *really* know. About Peter, all of what he did to you. I know that Peter is wicked, but he can also be . . ."

Effervescent. Like the sun itself. Like heat thrumming through my veins. Wendy cleared her throat. "Charming."

"Yes, charming. In fact, I rather enjoy his company when he's not being a murderous psychopath." He paused before adding, "Besides, who else is going to protect those boys? Certainly not Peter."

With a hard tug, Wendy tore a piece of cloth from her shirt and tied it around Oxley's hand. When it was knotted, she bent and kissed it.

"Forgive me for hurting you, Oxley, you brave man."

Oxley blushed and glanced away before looking back at her with amusement. "I must say, you look . . . ," he gestured to Wendy, "absolutely terrible in that get-up. I could recognize you from even above."

He rubbed his head. "Hook's good at a lot of things, but apparently dressing a girl like a boy is not one of them. You're lucky I wasn't Peter. He would have snatched you twice as fast."

"Peter is afraid of Hook."

"A bit, but sadly, Peter isn't afraid of much else, and I'm not sure his fear of the *Sudden Night* will last."

There was a moment of silence as they both considered the grim implication of his words. Unexpectedly, Oxley grinned at Wendy.

"Oh go ahead and ask already, I know you aren't that excited to see me . . ."

"John! How is John?"

Oxley's smile faded a bit. "John's good. He's still very loyal to Peter. They have been spending a lot of time together, preparing for something."

"For what?"

"I don't know. Peter has shut Abbott and me out of his inner circle. Lately, he only meets with John, and they spend a lot of time flying around the island, out of our earshot. Peter is getting more dangerous, Wendy. He's restless. More violent than usual— just this week, he whipped four boys for insubordination."

Wendy gasped. She ached at the idea of those young boys, so alone, Peter the only father that they'd ever known. The shattered heart inside of her wept for them, wept for John.

"If you can get to him, get to John, remind him that . . ."

"I can't Wendy. I can't reveal myself to John, or even to Abbott. To anyone. No one can know. It's the only way to keep me safe." Oxley looked around him. "Speaking of which, I should probably go, Fermina is probably losing her mind about what just happened."

He smiled. "What I wouldn't do for an hour with that woman. . . ."

Wendy laughed. "Oxley!"

He gave her a wink. "We better go. Peter's bound to be coming around here sooner or later. He's obsessed with you, you know, and it's driving him mad."

Cold fear crept up Wendy's spine, its claws tickling as it went. She imagined that she could feel him, watching them, watching her. She turned back to Oxley, who was already pulling on his bag.

"That note goes only to Hook, you understand? Not Smith, not Redd, not my daa, HOOK."

Wendy nodded. "Of course."

She reached out her hand to him, and they rose up in the air.

Wendy was silent as he flew her back to the grove, staying low as he weaved through the jungle, out of sight from eyes above and below. He slowed down as they approached the outside of the stone whore house, gently setting Wendy down on a window ledge.

"If you go through that window, you can make your way back to an angry Fermina. The crew is just around the corner in their respective rooms. No dilly-dallying."

Wendy smiled. She had missed Oxley very much without knowing it.

"I won't dilly-dally, you have my word." She tucked the note into her blouse.

"Well, that's one place to keep it." Oxley smiled before saluting her. "I'm off. A traitor's work is never done."

Wendy reached out and took his hand, giving it a firm squeeze. "Oxley. Thank you. I hope that someday we can spend that day on the boat together, speaking as friends without a care in the world."

"I would like that Wendy—especially if wine is involved—but first, we have to save Neverland."

He crouched on the window sill before leaping into the air, leaving a tiny swirl of dust in his wake, quickly disappearing in the eaves and outcroppings of the jangled buildings. Beyond the buildings, through the thick jungle that slithered in between alleys and up the sides of buildings, *Shadow Mountain* loomed over the town. Its manifestation was like a benevolent god, the foothills like its small feet, pattering down to mingle with its congregation. Mist streamed off the top; a trailing pull of white filtered down the mountain and into the jungle. Here, in the quiet stillness, she could hear the peaceful roar of the waterfalls just beyond town, hear the twittering of the animals in the jungle beyond. If Wendy squinted, she thought she could make out a small patch of land, far out on the ocean on the east side. Pan Island. The thought shook her out of her fog, and ducked through the open window, covered with tiny lime geckos. Winding through an ancient building that creaked with her every move, Wendy found her way back to the portico, back to Fermina, and a seething Captain Hook. As soon as she saw him, Wendy turned her head away from Fermina and mouthed the word "Oxley" to him, and watched relief sweep across his face.

Hook cleared his throat.

"It's fine, Fermina. She's alright."

Fermina looked like she wanted to say more, but instead nodded her head, trusting Hook. He stepped forward to speak with her, but was interrupted by the low blast of a horn, its sound unexpectedly causing dread to rise inside of her.

Fermina leapt up from her seat and ran to the end of the sea.

"The *Undertow* has arrived." She raised her pronounced nose to the wind. "I should have known. I can smell it from here, like the stench of a corpse."

Wendy stepped beside her and looked out at the Bay, her eyes finding the ship, like a dark blotch of ink in a gray sky. Though much smaller than the *Sudden Night*, the *Undertow* possessed a certain darkness about it. From the portico high above, Wendy could hear the creaking of the ship, of warped oak buckling under the pressure as the sea became shallower and the ship violently splashed its way to shore. The figurehead on the *Undertow* was a collection of headless skeletons, their bodies mangled together to form a star shape that ran down both the sides of the ship, their legs splaying out where the brown wood met the dark navy of the bulkhead. The boat swung port, and Wendy caught a quick glimpse of oars being yanked inside as it breached the shore. Fermina shook her head with a disgusted sound.

"Animals." She shook her head. "Maison battles the devil inside of him. He deserves nothing more than to drift at the bottom of the sea he calls home."

Hook's eyes rested on the ship. "I couldn't agree more." He practically spat the last sentence, staring out at the *Undertow* as streams of pirates now poured off the deck, making their way swiftly into Port Duette. Wendy pushed back the leather hat she was wearing to wipe at the sweat underneath it. Harlot's Grove was mouth-watering in its ripe abundance, but it was also hot as Hades.

Hook turned to Fermina. "The winds are a'changin'."

She nodded at him, their eyes communicating without words.

The captain curled his hands. "I guess we'll see at the quorum. We best be making our way there now. Go untangle their bedsheets."

Wendy felt a twinge of disappointment that her time with Fermina had been so rudely interrupted.

"I am so glad," she whispered, "so glad to have met you."

Fermina smiled kindly before pulling Wendy against her side.

"I am sure that we will meet many more times, young Moira, though hopefully under much happier circumstances. Keep your wits about you on the *Night*, deary."

Fermina headed back to the closed-off hallway, rapping her knuckles hard against each golden door. A minute or so passed, and then the pirates began pouring back out into the Grove, some half dressed and pulling at their pants, others completely relaxed and composed.

"Maison's here," Hook announced. "Look alive, men! Prepare your pistols and your wits. It's time to make our way to the Privateer."

The crew's eyes shone with a barely contained excitement.

"Aye, aye!"

Fermina gave Wendy's shoulder a firm squeeze before leaning forward.

"I'll see you soon, Moira."

She then pulled a large brass key from her cleavage and, with the crew of the *Sudden Night* waiting behind her, turned a lock on one of the boudoir doors. Hook went in first, followed by Smith, who motioned to Wendy to join him. She ducked her head into the room, which was unassuming—a bed draped with paisley red linens, a dresser with brass knobs and a small mirror.

"Open the door." Hook snarled, and Voodoo, Black Caesar, and Smith reached down the bed, shoving it violently upwards and flipping it towards the side of the room.

"Softer! This is Fermina's property!" barked Hook. "I'll tear off your hands if you break anything."

The pirates grumbled their apologies as they slowly moved a grubby mattress to the side of the room, revealing a trapdoor in the floor. Hook yanked up the ring and the entire floor seemed to lift off the ground, revealing a decrepit winding staircase underneath. Voodoo reached into his bag, lifting out a short torch and lighting it with a match. The torch sputtered and flared, throwing light onto the staircase in short, flickering bursts. Silently, Hook and his men filtered into the hole. Wendy made her way carefully down the slick steps, Barnaby's kind hand leading her down.

"The Privateer staircase. Only crew and captain of the *Sudden Night* get to use it."

"Why not the other crews?"

"Because it's a privilege of the commander of the Scorned."

The staircase ended at another locked door. This time Hook pulled a key from around his neck, its top a skull and crossbones, surrounded by swirling waves of metal.

"Only one key like that in all of Neverland," whispered Barnaby. Hook turned the key and with a hard push, the door to the Privateer swung open.

CHAPTER THIRTEEN

Wendy didn't know what she had been expecting—piles of treasure, perhaps, something like Peter's battle room, but she was surprised to see a very large, perfectly square room, with stone walls in a cool gray. Hanging from the low ceiling in the center of the room, a large bone chandelier—easily larger than a carriage—protruded out in every direction, its crooked arms reaching towards all who dared to enter. Beeswax candles dripped onto a gigantic wooden table, carved into a five-sided polygon, the dimensions of a compass burned into the wood. On the table was a single decanter of red wine, and five clear glasses. The room was filled to the brim with pirates.

"Come with me," whispered Smith, his beard brushing her cheek, "And don't talk." He shoved Barnaby roughly away from her.

Hook walked slowly to the table, pushing out his coat before taking his place at the head of the table, sitting at the largest chair. Wendy thought he looked quite regal, his hat curling over one of his eyes, his medallions gleaming in the candlelight. He looked straight ahead, his gaze unflinching as the other captains made their way to the table. Their crews all gathered in the divided deep eaves of the room, standing and silent as their captains assembled. The air was thick and dangerous. Smith's hands rested roughly on Wendy's shoulders, his hands a little too close to her neck for comfort. He leaned forward and whispered in her ear, his fingers pointing to various men.

"There is Captain Reed Bonney, captain of the *Coral Plunder.* He's loyal to Maison. A soddy git, the glutton that he is." Wendy watched as Reed Bonney took his seat at the table, the chair creaking under his weight. He was a barrel-chested man with set-apart piggish blue eyes and a tuft of blond hair combed over a balding head. His muddled orange waistcoat and brown pants were bursting at the seams, and when he sat, his eyes lingered greedily on the wine. His short, squatty hands, however, didn't move, and he turned his chair away from Hook to avoid eye contact.

Smith's voice continued, "That man in the gold standing next to him is Jaali Oba, Captain of the *Vicious Sea.*" Wendy watched as Jaali pulled out his chair and settled swiftly into it, his fingers tapping violently on the table. He was tall and lean, his skin golden brown, his long dark locks wrapped in green and gold beads. He laid a gigantic golden scabbard on the table in front of him.

"Jaali's Hook's man through and through, and a fine captain. Hook saved his life once, from a Lost Boy with a spear." *Abbott,* thought Wendy. Smith continued. "A good man, though he has a taste for gold and women that is unsustainable. Rumor is that he sails with a harem of seven different women. Why you would want seven women aboard your ship is a mystery to me. If you ask me, one is too many."

He squeezed her shoulders impossibly hard, and she bit her lip to keep from gasping.

Another captain sat down at the table, Smith explaining that this was Xian Li, captain of the *Viper's Strike*—a terrifying man who towered over the other three, one of his bloodshot eyes replaced with a crystallized white jewel. He was completely bald, and an irritated red scar ran from the center of his forehead straight to the back of his neck. Once Xian Li had settled, the four pirates waited in silence, Hook sitting perfectly still, his eyes betraying nothing, Jaali angrily running his hands up and down his scabbard as he stared at the door. The crews of the respective ships stayed silent, but Wendy noticed that every member of the *Sudden Night* rested their hands gently on their weapons. The danger in the air was palpable, and just when it seemed to settle into a simmering calm, the door slammed open and Captain Maison slithered into view. His face was narrow and snakelike, predatory in its very construction. Slicked black hair was pulled back from his slender face by a ponytail, his hollowed cheeks lined with pock-marks and tiny scars. Upon entering, his lips pulled back in a gruesome sneer and Wendy felt revulsion rise up inside of her. His teeth were all sharpened to points, his gums rotted and black. He was missing an ear on the left side, and his hands were covered with black gloves.

"Hallo, gents, did ya miss me?" He tipped an invisible hat. Jaali did not look up from his scabbard as he lobbed sharp words in the captain's direction.

"You're late, Maison. Hook should have been the last one here as Commander of the Scorned. Have you forgotten your manners?" Jaali barked.

Maison pulled his finger along the sword, drawing a small droplet of blood. Then he curled his tongue around his bloody finger.

"I do not appreciate lateness Maison."

Maison sneered. "As if I have ever given a thought to your opinion of me, Jaali."

Maison's men took their positions in the corner of the room. The crew of the *Sudden Night* snarled across the room at them until Maison, with great dramatic flourish, took his seat. Hook stood, and placed his pistol facing outwards on the table. The rest of the captains followed, and Wendy felt a collective breath of relief pass through the various crews. Hook signaled to Smith, and his first mate approached the table to pour the wine. From her place in the corner, Wendy could see Smith's jaw clenched tightly as he made his way forward, the veins in his bull neck rigid and hard.

Hook stood and cleared his throat.

"Our first order of business . . ."

Maison uttered a loud grunt, interrupting Hook. The crews around them gasped.

"Let's not, James. Let's not talk about bounties, taxes, municipalities, or gold. I am sick of these tedious gatherings, these mediocre speeches about Port Duette and her many problems— who owes who, who we've killed, who we will kill, what rum is in shortage, where to put the widows. . . . No. No more of this talk."

Captain Reed Bonney cried his approval with a "Here, here!" as Hook lowered his glass to stare coldly at Maison.

"What would you have us talk about, brave Captain Maison? Would you have us speak of war? Perhaps, of mutiny?"

Hook straightened his spine and took a long sip of his glass.

"No more games. I like to look a man in the eye before I run him through, and you should do the same, though everyone at this table knows you are utterly without honor."

Maison's tongue slithered out around his lips, which were mashing angrily.

"We are all here to talk about one thing, the poison that corrupts the Scorned, the chain—" he gestured madly to his neck, riddled with burns and scars, "the chain that leads us toddling around Neverland, like a bitch following her master."

Smith looked up at Maison.

"Did you just call my captain a dog in heat?" Maison held Smith's stare for a moment before looking away.

"No. But if we let Peter Pan control our fates for a minute longer, we will be his bitch, or more."

Jaali brought his scabbard down hard into the table. "I have heard enough of your grumbling on the matter."

"Aye, and I have had enough chasing this boy around the island, playing games with his Lost Boys! We could be building cities on the outer islands, raiding until our hands were bloody, and our chests bursting with gold, and instead what are we doing? We are playing with Peter and his ilk." He pointed his gloved hand towards Hook.

"We have been slaves to your obsession with the boy, and it has held us back from becoming true rulers of Neverland!"

At his pronouncement, Maison's crew roared with approval, only to be drowned out by the boos of the *Sudden Night*'s larger crew. The three other crews stayed silent. Wendy's hair stood on edge, attune to the dangerous place she found herself in. She ducked her chin, hoping that her hat was low enough to hide her face.

"I've heard rumors, Captain Hook."

Hook wearily raised his voice, though Wendy could hear a traceable anger churning up through his clipped syllables.

"As have I. Still, why don't you enlighten us all with these rumors."

Maison pulled a dagger from his belt and began tossing it back and forth between his gloved hands.

"I'm sure they are just rumors. You know how pirates are. Like a bunch of gossiping whores."

Not a single chuckle resonated through the room.

"Still, they should be addressed. I've heard rumors that you have a girl on board your ship, a girl that Peter wants very much. A girl that could, in fact, be used for a trade deal. Maybe Peter Pan wants her desperately enough to give us something worthy in return."

Wendy's heart sank into the floor, and her knees gave a quiver.

"And what might that be?" inquired Hook, though Wendy knew the answer before Maison even opened his mouth.

"Flight," he whispered, a terrifying delight spreading over his face. "I want to fly, and only Peter Pan can give that to me. For this girl, he might just trade."

Wendy felt a cold shiver pass up her spine, and she bit down on her lip to keep her breathing under control.

"In addition, I also heard a tasty little rumor that you have the last remaining Pilvinuvo Indian on your ship."

There was a collective gasp in the room, and Wendy felt the bodies of the crew of the *Sudden Night* straighten up around her. They were preparing to fight, here in this tiny, closed room where everyone was armed and full of vitriol and hatred. *Apparently, you did not threaten the crew's cook.*

"Now, I know a number of people in Neverland who would be very interested in talking to this man. Not only to satisfy our curiosity, but if we could locate the Pilvi tribe, than we would have a whole new race of people to rule. I must ask—what else are we doing this for? I am tired of ships, of storms and trinkets. I want to rule like kings. And unlike the impoverished idiots that reside in Port Duette, I do not believe that the tribe *just disappeared.* They are here, and your man knows where."

Maison was now standing behind Hook, who was staring straight ahead, his face betraying nothing.

"These rumors make me think that the good leader of the Scorned has something to hide. He's hiding things from us, his men, his Scorned brothers. He keeps the harvest for himself and lets his brothers starve like crows. The worst part is that he keeps pushing this silly war with Peter Pan, and why? For what? Why is Captain Hook so deeply obsessed with defeating this boy? Is it his father? His greed? The fact that Peter took his hand?"

Maison chuckled and leaned on Hook with both hands.

"Being half a man could make anyone lose their mind a bit, couldn't it?"

Hook took a slow sip of wine, and Maison's face twisted angrily at the lack of attention Hook was giving him.

"Who is afraid of the big bad Peter Pan? Hook is. And we deserve to know why. This quorum deserves answers—or it deserves a new commander."

There was a sharp intake of breath from among the crews, along with whispered words that drifted through the crowd like vaporous poison: mutiny, betrayal, war. Hook took another sip of his wine, and stood. Wendy's heart beat furiously in her chest as she waited for him to speak, hoping that his answers would satisfy her own questions.

"Many of you have questions about my relationship with Peter Pan. I can only say this, that he is far more dangerous than any of you could understand. You have elected me as the commander of this fleet, and captain of the *Sudden Night,* her queen."

At that, Hook's eyes narrowed, and the man that he had seen the first day on the *Night* straightened his spine and turned to Maison. His gaze cut through Maison's dripping condescension like British steel.

"I've heard you talk of rumors today. It's funny you should mention rumors, because I have heard some of my own."

"Oh yes?" snapped Maison, twirling his knife in one hand, staring straight at Hook.

"Do tell."

"I heard a rumor of a mutinous captain, who had his ship blown to pieces and who was pulled behind the boat until he drowned, until the fish nibbled at the whites of his eyes."

Maison paled.

"I heard of a traitor aboard the *Sudden Night,* who will soon be joining this captain in a water-soaked grave."

Hook's eyes lay on his crew, accusing and predatory.

"I heard of a man who overstepped his bounds, who knew nothing of Neverland's history and its people. A man who sought power above pirating. A small man who built his ship on the backs of others."

Maison spun at Hook.

"I don't know what you are talking about!"

"I believe you do. And one day, very soon, you will be relieved of your duty."

Unhinged, Maison pushed his dagger up against Hook's cheek. Hook didn't even flinch, his strong jaw steady as he stared down this cowardly captain. A trickle of blood ran down Hook's face. At that trickle, the crews erupted into shouting matches. Wendy, spurned by her anger at the way Maison had treated Hook, found herself shouting terrible insults across the divided crews, gesturing and screaming with the rest of the *Sudden Night* crew, surprised at just how passionate she felt in her captain's defense. She saw now, why Maison had chosen to denounce Hook here, at the quorum. If violence erupted in this tiny room full of pirates, there would be not a one left standing. He had wagered Hook's care for his crew against his own ambition, a brilliant move.

Hook's lips parted, and Wendy watched as he mouthed silently to Maison, "I will kill you." Maison raised his eyebrows and dropped his dagger.

"How about we take a vote then?" Jaali leapt up to his feet, his gold scabbard drawn. "Or better yet, how about we take your tongue for disrespecting the Scorned Fleet with your accusations?" Hook waved his hand towards Jaali.

"No, let the snake get what he wants. We'll take it to a vote. All in favor of pursuing a tribe that no longer exists, ignoring the growing threat of Peter Pan, and becoming grand monarchies of Neverland? Raise your hands, you cowardly bastards."

Maison raised his hand proudly. After a few seconds of tension-filled silence, Reed Bonney, the captain of the *Coral Plunder,* raised his hand as well.

Hook sneered, "Of course."

The room exploded with shouts of "traitor" as the crews now understood that this was something long planned. Wendy felt Black Caesar's hand on her back.

"If things go south . . . ," he hissed, his rotten breath engulfing her face, "lie on the ground, wipe blood all over your face, pretend you're dead, and pray for the best."

Wendy didn't bother to ask whose blood she would be wiping

on her face. Instead she closed her eyes for a moment, remembering the faces of her parents, of John and Michael, and of Booth. She would not die here, in this dark pit of men with swelling egos and loaded pistols. *She could not. She would not.* She shook loose of Black Caesar's grip and stepped forward.

"I'm the girl on Hook's ship!"

The room went silent at the uniquely female cadence of her voice. The fury on Hook's face was enough to turn water to ice as she stepped out of the crowd and pulled the hat from her head.

"My name is Wendy."

Her heart was pounding in her ears, and she struggled to find her voice. Her mouth opened and closed once, but when it opened again, she had found it, and it was loud and strong.

"This traitor Maison wants you to believe that Peter Pan can give you flight. I'm here to tell you that he can't. Peter can give temporary flight, but it ends, either after a few hours, or when he decides to take it."

Her eyes traveled around the room.

"Think about that! You would get flight simply to fall out of the sky at Peter's whim."

She turned to Maison, whose black eyes simmered with rage at her.

"It's positively the silliest idea I've ever heard. Well, besides the idea that Captain Hook is not the best commander to lead you. I'm standing before you today because I want you to know how dangerous Peter Pan is. Peter manipulates the Lost Boys into fighting this war with you. He tried to force me into loving him, and threatened to kill my brothers if I didn't." She could feel the eyes of a hundred pirates taking in every inch of her, some hungry for her blood, others for other, dark, wanton things. "He dropped me from the sky because I wouldn't love him."

Someone from the *Coral Plunder* yelled out, "That doesn't sound so bad, missy! We're pirates!"

Wendy smiled, though her heart churned uncomfortably

inside. She cleared her throat. "It's true that perhaps the bar for morality is much, much lower here."

The pirates chuckled. She turned to face Hook, his face still furious at her for revealing herself, much, much angrier at her than he had been at Maison.

"I believe Captain Hook is the only thing standing between you and an all-out war with Peter Pan." Wendy thought of the fear that lingered in Hook's eyes as he told the story of the overturned *Sunned Shores*. Her voice dropped. "And for reasons you and I don't understand yet—but perhaps Hook does—I believe this is a war you would lose." She paused. "All of you."

With that, she tucked her hair back under her hat and walked back into the safe confines of the *Sudden Night*'s crew. Hook cleared his throat to speak, his face red with anger.

"In lieu of that unwelcome speech, let's continue on with the vote."

Maison stepped out from behind Hook, and made his way back towards his seat, looking like a chastened child. Then he raised his head to Hook, a dead smile on his face.

"No need to vote. It'll be a tie."

His hand was a blur as he pulled a serrated dagger out from his sleeve and without warning or sound, threw it directly into the middle of Xian Li's forehead. The large man looked up at the dagger handle with one confused eye before falling face forward onto the table, driving the dagger in further. Blood splattered the white bone chandelier as Hook leapt out of his seat, his pistol pointed at Maison's head. The room erupted in startled roars as the crews of the *Sudden Night* and the *Vicious Seas* pulled their weapons from their holsters and aimed them at the crews of the *Coral Plunder* and the *Undertow*. Wendy looked around frantically, noting that the crew of *Viper's Strike* seemed quite fine after the brutal murder of their captain. Darting like a cobra, Jaali drew his scabbard and grabbed Captain Bonney, putting the scabbard up to his throat. Hook didn't move, his pistol now pressed firmly against Maison's forehead, Hook's righteous fury blazing in sheer contrast to Maison's amused grin.

"Sorry about that. Things must be done."

"I will shoot you right here," muttered Hook.

Maison clicked his tongue. "See, I don't think so. If you kill me, not only do you leave your crew outnumbered and outgunned, but you also leave Neverland to the whims of my men."

Hook's teeth were gritted.

"You cowardly, spineless, wicked . . ."

"Sonofabitch. I know. And yet, a pirate's gotta do what a pirate's gotta do. So here's what's going to happen. I don't fancy my entire crew dying down here, and neither do you. In fact, now I got three of them to worry about! So, you and your men, and Jaali and his men are going to leave this room. Make your way back to your ships, and go on fighting your war with Peter Pan. In the meantime, as commander of the Scorned, my first order of business is that we get the girl."

The captain brought his hook up to Maison's face.

"And if I defy your order? Because you will pry her out of my dead, cold hook."

"Then you will have denied an order of the commander of the Scorned, and that means war."

Hook smiled, his wide grin curving from one side of his face to another, truly happy in the moment.

"Then I'll see you on the open seas, Commander Maison."

Maison's face fell for a moment, before, with a movement so fast Wendy later wondered if had even seen it, the captain pulled his hook swiftly across Maison's cheek, taking a huge chunk of skin with it. Maison screamed, his hand on his face, dark blood gushing over his cheek, which now hung from his face, a flap of useless skin.

Reed Bonney quickly detached himself from Jaali. "Hook, Oba—take your men and go! This powder keg is lit, and I don't fancy dying in this hole."

Smith raised his voice. "You lit it, Bonney, and you will burn with all the rest."

"Nice to see you, Smith, always a pleasure." Captain Bonney pressed his nauseating comb-over back over his head and smiled at Wendy.

"I hope to be well acquainted with you, lass. Soon."

The crew of the *Sudden Night* made an abrupt surge forward, and Wendy was pushed through a doorway, her feet barely touching the ground, Barnaby shoving her forward into the light.

"Run, run, quickly, my dear."

All the crews were pouring out of the Privateer now, each one taking a different alleyway, all of them sprinting towards their ships. Wendy understood instantly. The ships in Treasure Bay were docked, waiting like sitting ducks. The first crew to get to their boat . . . She let out a cry as her feet pounded the ground. *Michael.* They had to make it. The crew of the *Sudden Night* rounded corner after corner of dark alleyways, following Hook's lead as he zigged and zagged through the streets he owned. Something putrid flowed at Wendy's feet, a creek the color of dried blood, the smell paralyzing, repugnant. Wendy gagged.

"Keep it together, lass!" hissed Voodoo, his breath labored as they ran. "Breathe through your mouth!"

She tried, but the smell seemed to make its way into her mouth, its rotten waste burning her lungs. She gagged again while the men ran, their bodies pressing against her, their shouted curses like a cloud of hatred around her. She flashed back to her children's Bible, still sitting in her nursery in London, filled with draconian images of hell: smoking pits, demons, and darkness. She was here now, depraved men all around her. Their greedy and murderous urges crowded in on her as their bodies pressed tighter around her, and she struggled to breathe.

I am in hell, I am in hell, I am in hell. . . . The streets flew past them as they ran, townspeople of Port Duette scattering out of their way. They crammed into a narrow alleyway, the buildings on either side leaning uncomfortably forward, straining their buttresses and crooked windows as they loomed over the panicked crew. There was a loud bang, and the pirate next to her fell to the ground in a splatter of dark blood. The crew of the *Sudden Night* began firing up the alleyway as they ran, aiming at the glimpses of the *Undertow* crew that she could see running parallel to them. Shots were ringing all around.

"Don't worry about them!" yelled Hook. "Keep running! The *Night* is all that matters!" She saw another spurt of blood in front of her. "Go!"

She screamed, not caring anymore. "Run, dammit!"

They had made it to the edge of town and exploded out from under the leering buildings that had offered them so much protection and into the dense jungle that led to the beach. She breathed in the beautiful, natural light and the sweet air of Neverland as she ran for her life, tree branches exploding overhead, trunks showering her with splinters. In front of her, a younger pirate stumbled, his leg turning over as his ankle exploded. Wendy ran up beside him, hoisting him up against her.

"Come on! I need you to run!" She helped him hobble a few feet forward before Smith scooped him out of her arms and threw him over his shoulder.

"GO!" he screamed. The jungle grew less thick overhead as the blue sky watched their battle from above—two crews, racing for the beach, God knew where the other three were.

"Get to the ship" screamed Smith from somewhere behind them. "Ho, lads! Make ready to weigh anchor! Go handsomely about it!"

"Aye, aye!" the breathless crew replied, sprinting through thick green leaves.

Her feet slapped the wet mud underfoot as she plunged forward, pushing vines and leaves aside, ducking her head every time she heard a shot. Hook's curses rained down from behind her, mingling with the clinking sound of the men's weapons as they bounced against their hips, their legs fervently pumping underneath them. Something besides fear was driving the men frantically towards the *Night*—they were men protecting their home, the love of their lonely lives. She was, indeed, their queen and the crew was almost feral in their desire to be aboard her decks now that the tide had turned so quickly. Smith raised his hand for the crew to run past him, "Go, go! Come on men! I better find sand up your arses tonight 'cause you were moving so fast! Quick as thieves!"

Getting back to the ship was a blur of jungle, of leaves whipping her in the face, of the heavy sound of the pirates' boots splashing through deep trenches of earth and water, of light filtering through the canopy, and of the sweet sound of the sea as they poured out onto the sand. Hook yelled something to Smith, who stayed back near the entrance to the jungle, counting the men. Wendy kept running forward, Hook waiting for her and then running close behind her. She could hear the breaths of the *Undertow* crew right behind them, firing blindly into the jungle as the crew of the *Night* ran up the dock.

"Smith!" Wendy breathed. "Smith!" Hook gave her a grin as he leapt aboard his ship, the crew moving quickly to their positions, hauling off the anchor and hoisting the sails. They ran up and down the deck, flowing like a stream around Hook, who calmly walked up and took his place behind the wheel. Wendy looked back. Smith was still on the beach, lighting a stick of dynamite. Her mouth fell open as he stuck it in the sand at the entrance to the trail . . . and right up against the huge barrel of snakes. Then he sprinted like mad for the ship, a few swift crew members of the *Undertow* emerging from the jungle a couple of seconds later, firing their pistols at Smith as he ran. Then, there was only the sound and the fire, an explosion that made Wendy's teeth rattle. Body parts flew in the air, landing with a bloody stump on the sand, and the snakes were airborne, thrashing their tails as the impact hurtled their bodies up and through the air, their venomous teeth spread wide open.

Wendy would swear later that she heard them scream. Black bloodied snakes rained down on the *Undertow* crew, who were staggering and disjointed. Their screams as the snakes landed on them, bit them, or wrapped around their necks were terrible, but it had worked. The *Undertow* would not beat the *Sudden Night* out of the harbor. Smith ran up the wooden dock, leaping into the air and catching onto the side of the *Night* with both hands. With a groan, he heaved himself onto the ship. Blood was leaking from his shoulder, but he barely noticed the splatters he left behind as he ran up to the poop deck, where Captain Hook was staring at the boats in the harbor through his spyglass. The sun was beginning its slow fall into the sea, and the crew fell easily back into their frenzied work, the deck a place of mass chaos that was intrinsically complex, like a symphony barreling forth from the sails that stretched and billowed. The *Sudden Night* pulled quickly away from the shore, curled back into the protective folds of the waves, speeding away from the pearled sand of Treasure Bay, now flecked with blood and hundreds of wriggling black snakes.

The *Night* sped away from the shore. Smith perched on the railing. "Jaali and his *Vicious Seas* be pulling out, thank the bloody gods, and I don't see *Viper's Strike*, so that leaves the *Coral Plunder* and the *Undertow.*" Wendy could see the ships now, crews running frantically back and forth. Smith dropped his voice.

"Captain, the *Undertow.* You must. Our girl, 'tis trim." Hook stared at the water, his hand gripping the wheel firmly. Smith leaned forward. "C'mon, let's send those traitors' rigs to the bottom of the friggin' seas."

Hook was staring at the two ships, his eyes steady. He cleared his throat. "Mount the swivel guns! Aim everything at the *Coral Plunder!*" There was a moment of silence before the deck exploded with activity, as every single crew member ran to his battle station, their mouths open and panting like racehorses.

Smith was screaming out orders. "Ready about!"

Wendy felt a tug on her pants. She looked down to see Michael, his eyes wide with excitement. She bent down and wrapped him in her arms, crushing his tiny body against hers, taking in the sweet scent of his hair. Instructions to go below deck lingered on her tongue, but instead she took his hand and led him to the side of the deck.

"Wanna see a pirate ship blow up?"

Michael stopped breathing. "More than anything in the world!" he gasped.

"That's what I thought."

The *Sudden Night* swung wide.

"Come avast!" Hook cried. "Ready the cannons."

Smith grabbed ahold of the wheel. "The *Undertow*, Captain?"

Hook lowered his voice. "You know why we won't fire on the *Undertow*." He yanked the wheel away from Smith. "Do you question me, First Mate?"

Smith shook his head. "Never, Captain. Get ready to fire on the *Coral Plunder!*" Barnaby was running back and forth on the deck, the most work Wendy had ever seen him do, yelling out coordinates and nautical terms that she had yet to understand. "Aim Yer Mother's Breasts at their mizzenmast! Eleven degrees north!"

The *Coral Plunder* was pulling away from shore, starboard side reaching for the water when the massive *Sudden Night* breached beside it. There was silence aboard the *Night* for just a moment.

"FIRE!" Hook screamed, and then there was a roar as the cannons began firing, a louder sound than Wendy had ever heard. She clasped her hands over Michael's ears as the smoke drifted across the deck, the ship herself giving a lurch backwards at the force of the guns. The *Coral Plunder's* deck began exploding into sharp slivers that flew outwards, pieces landing on the deck of the

Night. Wendy and Michael ducked down, staring through one of the rope holes in the deck. The *Coral Plunder's* crew was screaming and diving overboard, and Wendy saw more than one body floating face down in the water. Giant holes exploded outwards, one after the other as the *Night* peppered the much smaller ship into slivers. The sound was deafening. Black smoke began to rise from below decks.

"Launch the squealers!" Hook yelled, and suddenly the air was full of tiny black circles, each one the size of an apple. They peppered hard onto the deck of the *Coral Plunder,* their flaming tails streaking through the air like phoenixes. The flame reached the gunpowder inside, and the explosion blew Wendy and Michael off their feet, backwards. Wendy's back hit the mast. The rest of the crew was face down on the deck, anticipating the impact.

"Reload Yer Mother's Breasts!" Smith yelled, and the giant cannon was rolled forward, its nozzle split into two parts. Voodoo was loading a chain into the front of the cannon, linking it with two spiked iron balls.

"NOW!" the captain screamed, and Voodoo lit a flame underneath the cannon before stepping back with a wicked smile. The cannon discharged, and the spiked balls, bound by the chain, whirled towards the mast of *Coral Plunder.* Wendy's heart pounded with excitement, her skin tingling as she watched the chain slice cleanly through the mast of the other ship, the crow's nest falling hard, the man inside of it plunging down into the fiery hell that was once the deck of a grand ship. The ship was torn apart and sinking fast, giving a great groan as it surrendered its weight to the sea.

"Release the chum!" screamed Smith, and two crew members began dumping buckets of bloodied fish into the water. Smith saw Wendy staring at him in horror. "So the sharks finish the job."

When she shook her head, he laughed. "What do you want, dearie? We're pirates!" Hook raised his voice again.

"Back to your stations, men! We mean to make our way to the clear blue!" She and Michael watched as the *Coral Plunder's* mast disappeared into the sea around Treasure Bay. Crowds from Port Duette were pouring out of the jungle now, coming to see what the noise had been, hoping to get a glance at whatever excitement they had missed. The *Undertow* was pulling swiftly away from the dock.

"Quickly, lads! We are going to put as much space between ourselves and the *Undertow* as possible." The crew quickly reassembled themselves, but not before Hook gave one final command. "And hoist the Jolly Rodger!"

Smith turned to him, unabashed glee washing over his face. "Sir?"

"We no longer are a member of the Scorned Fleet, so there is no need to fly that flag. Fetch my father's flag."

Smith appeared a moment later, carrying the white-and-black flag that Wendy had seen that first day in Hook's quarters. They attached the flag to the mainline and pulled it upwards, the black flag unfurling, the white skull grinning as it flapped in the wind. Hook stared at it for a moment, a moment of pride passing over his face, so brief Wendy wondered if she imagined it. Than he looked at Smith's raised eyebrows, answering his question without speaking.

"Maison will be dealt with when the time is right. We are not running, we are planning, and we will ferret him out soon enough. And when we do, he will beg for death, I swear it to you."

Smith gave a delighted smile and ran his hand along the tip of his dagger, turning it then to his tongue. "Indeed, he will."

Barking orders, Smith spun away from the captain. Wendy and Michael began making their way below deck when she felt a hard grip on her arm.

"YOU," the captain hissed, flinging open the trapdoor. He turned on Michael. "Stay here!" Michael scampered off with a fearful look on his face. Without a word, Captain Hook dragged

Wendy roughly down the stairs, her feet stumbling as she fell. He stood her up. "Girl, I don't like to do this."

Then, using his good hand, he back-handed her across the face. The blow cracked hard against her cheek, sending shots of pain up her jawbone and across her brow. Her head exploded in pain, but she didn't fall to her knees. She stood, bent over, gasping and covering her cheek. His breaths were ragged and heavy as he towered over her in the darkened hallway. Fear, like the fine edge of a needle, raised the hair on her arms. Hook looked furious, his gray eyes narrowed, his mouth twisted in fury.

"What were you thinking, exposing yourself to Maison like that? What noble glory did you hope to gain through your righteousness for my cause? And for what? For nothing. You put yourself in great danger, for nothing!"

Wendy steadied herself, her body attempting to right itself from both the blow to her face and the hard rocking of the *Night*.

"I was trying to help you! I didn't know that Maison . . ."

"No, that's right, you didn't know. You don't know anything."

The pain of the slap ricocheted through her head, stoking the quiet fury that had been growing inside of her since the first time she met Hook.

"That's because you haven't told me anything! You keep giving me small particles of information, and it's not enough! I can't help you defeat Peter if I don't even know how or why. For instance, you could have told me that Oxley—"

"Shh, quiet, girl." Hook closed the distance between them, putting his hand over her mouth roughly.

"You never know who is listening inside these walls." His voice dropped, and Wendy could smell his wine-soaked breath as it washed over her cheek. "I didn't know if I could trust you, not yet."

Wendy shook her head. "I have everything to lose if Peter has his way. Whatever it is . . . I will do. But not for you. For my brothers."

Hook crouched down, looking straight into her face, his gray eyes tracing every angle of her hazel ones.

"I believe you. But if you cross me . . ."

Wendy rolled her eyes. "Than you'll throw me out to sea, drown me, drag me, dismember me. Let's get on with it, shall we?"

Hook's thin mouth curled at the end, a sarcastic grin plastering his face. "I do believe you are getting the hang of things around here."

"Will Maison . . . ?"

Hook's smile disappeared. "Maison has the benefit of being mentally unhinged, which makes it much harder for me to anticipate his actions. What he did in the Privateer was a risky gamble. We could have all just as easily died in that dank hellhole."

"Speaking of Maison . . . ," Hook reached into his pocket and pulled out the note from Oxley. He unrolled the scrap, read it for the second time, and then handed it to Wendy with a sigh. "It seems that forces align against us, Miss Darling."

Her heart beat at she unrolled the thin paper, her face still smarting. The ink was blotted and running towards the corner of the papyrus, covered with Oxley's giant, messy scrawl.

"Peter Pan has formed an alliance with Captain Maison."

Wendy closed her eyes. Hook crumpled up the paper and held it up to a burning candle, watching the letters turn into dark ash that sprinkled on the floor of the hallway, the embers sniffing out against the glossy wood.

"Just as I suspected," Hook sighed, rubbing his hook through his black hair, spotted with gray that seemed more prominent than it did a week ago. He turned away from Wendy. "Put something cool on your cheek. Keme will help you, and you'll help him prepare our supper. Tell him I feel like the orange guppy this evening." He looked up through the open trapdoor, at the gray roiling sky above, the clouds bulbous and heavy.

"And you're right. The time has come to trust each other, for transparency and risk. I had hoped to give you more time to come to terms with this life, with what you will have to do. It's time you understood. It's time you asked the question. And when you do, I swear on my dead father that I will tell you everything."

Wendy raised her eyes to meet his, but they were off, somewhere distant, somewhere ancient and terrifying. *The question . . .* Hook had turned back by then, making his way towards the deck. All she could see was the outline of his figure, his frame holding back the growing storm.

CHAPTER FOURTEEN

"Wendy!"

They were back in the cabin now and Michael had wrapped around her legs, and his face pressed up against her stomach.

"Wendy, I missed you!"

"Michael, I missed you, too!"

Michael pulled back, unimpressed with her sentiments.

"Did you bring me something from Port Duette?"

"Ummm . . . ," Wendy paused, the lies coming easily from her mouth.

"I did, it's up on deck. It's a surprise. I'll give it to you tomorrow." She would find something.

"Awww." Her blond little brother kicked angrily at the ground. "But, I don't want it tomorrow."

"And I don't appreciate whining."

"Sorry." Michael grinned. "Okay, you can give it to me tomorrow. But tell me all about Port Duette."

"I will, I'll tell you everything, but first, what did you do on the ship?"

Michael was practically bouncing around the room. "I had such a good time. Keme made us a REALLY good lunch—he made me pancakes! Pancakes, like Mother used to make us, only these ones had a yellow fruit in them, and we put honey on top."

Wendy's mouth watered at the description. "I climbed up to the crow's nest with Hawk. He showed me all the parts of Port Duette that you could see from there: the main street, where the Privateer was, the beach and all the different ships: the *Undertow*, the *Seaward Spit* . . . oh, and he showed me where Harlot's Grove was!"

"Oh he did, did he? What did he say about Harlot's Grove?" Wendy was less than thrilled that the word harlot was now part of her brother's vocabulary.

"That pretty ladies lived there, and that they helped the pirates. But he didn't say what they helped them with. I asked. Clothes, I think."

Wendy blushed, turning her face away to hide her smothered laughter.

"I met someone who lives there, Michael. Her name was Fermina, and she was very kind."

"That's a pretty name."

"She was a very lovely person. I hope to meet her again."

Michael nodded. "After we went up into the crow's nest, I played with some swords for a while and took a nap."

"You played with swords?"

He frowned. "Wendy, everyone does it here."

Wendy felt a sad smile cross her face. He wasn't wrong, and she knew it would be wrong not to let him learn how to use them, here in this world where death came quickly and childhood lasted forever and yet not at all.

The bell in their cabin rung once, a single shrill chime that let them know that Wendy was needed in the kitchen for dinner. She gave Michael a pat on the head as he scampered above deck, and watched the legs that were once round and chubby pound up the stairs, now longer and leaner. His hair was beginning to curl at the ends as it had grown much longer than their mother would have ever allowed, and was turning from honey to white blond in the blazing Neverland sun. His tan skin shone in the filtered light as the sky turned from gray to blue, as night began its slow descent. She blinked, and he was gone, up to a world of pirates and seas, of harlots and weapons. Wendy swallowed the unexpected lump in her throat and gave a shiver, making her way into the depths of the kitchen, to cook for the man who held her prisoner and kept her safe.

Keme welcomed her with a large, soft hug and a genuine smile, and she felt herself falling comfortably into the routine of salting, slapping and seasoning the seared fish that stared up at her with empty eyes.

Night fell heavy and dark on the ship, the azure seas turning to ink, the sea so calm that the light of the stars reflected upon the still waters like a blanket. After dinner, Wendy had been ordered by a grumpy Smith to wash down the deck as the crew member normally in charge of that had been shot in Port Duette and would not be making this—or any additional—journeys. So now she was on her knees, pushing all her strength against planks of wood with a brush that could tear skin from muscle. *This is utterly disgusting,* she thought, spreading the foamy soap over the glossy black planks and then mopping it up, the filth of a hundred boots rising up and over her hands in a brown sludge. Her dress was black from the knees down, a mix of water, waste, and the curdled blood of dead fish. A particularly putrid smell hit her nostrils, and she crawled on her knees to look under one of the cannons. She let out a yelp and leapt backwards at the decaying smile of a black-and-white sea snake that had greeted her there. With a grimace, Wendy pulled the body out, its grinning skeletal face staring at her, its empty eye sockets dangling with rough white scales that turned to dust when she touched them.

"Don't touch the teeth," Owl shouted down from above. "'Tis poisonous! But . . . it might also give you visions of the future, least that's what I heard."

Wendy bit her lip angrily. Pirates and their ridiculous superstitions: the bell held the soul of the ship. Don't step forward with your left foot when boarding a ship. Gold coins must be kept in the keel and silver below the mast. If a wine glass made a sound of its own accord, the ship was about to sink. There were so many of them that she could barely keep track of them, let alone abide by them. Holding her breath, she fished the carcass out from under the cannon and threw it overboard with a splash, ignoring Owl's hooting laughter that tumbled down from the crow's nest, his body perched like a sentinel, his wispy hair blowing in the breeze. She dunked her hands into the disgusting bucket just in case he was right about the poison. *Better filth than death.* She brushed her hands off on her dress, leaving two black handprints at her hips before wiping her face with her forearm.

If her mother could see her now.... Wendy flinched at the thought of her mother, missing her babies. Her hands still disgusting, she clasped them together nonetheless, sending a prayer into the blazing stars above that somehow, some way, her mother would know that they were alive and well. Wendy frowned, looking down at her dress. *Alive, yes. Well...* Her thoughts flitted to John, so firmly in Peter's control. *What would it take to break him of it?* Her mind wandered to a darker place: if Peter had not shown his true colors that night in the lantern, and later by dropping her, would she still be under his spell? A memory of his emerald-green eyes ignited in her mind, followed by his scent, like salty sea air and honey. Her skin flushed underneath her gown, and she turned away from her troubling thoughts.

"You done, girl?" Owl asked.

Wendy nodded. "For tonight."

"Then throw that nasty crap overboard and be on your way." He turned back to his watch.

Wendy slowly made her way below deck, her soaked rags and wooden bucket knocking against her legs as she circled down the Jolly Staircase. She opened a small trapdoor underneath the staircase beneath the bowsprit, storing the bucket and the rags for the next poor, unfortunate soul. The boat pitched starboard and caught her off-guard, slamming her hard into the wall before she tumbled to the ground, a reign of polite curses falling out of her mouth. She brushed herself off before turning the wooden latch on the small cabinet and making her way back down the dark hallway towards the staircase. The boat pitched again, but this time she was ready for it, holding onto the wall as the swell passed. There was a strange thump behind her, but when she looked, it was only a goblet, rolling loose behind her in the hallway. She frowned and made her way quickly to the staircase, her steps lightly rattling the bones, their jaws *clickety-clacking* as she descended down. The long hallway that led to her room was dark, and Wendy thought she heard the softest *whush* of air pass by her, but when she turned her head there was nothing, nobody. Her heart quickened, and she shook her head. Owl would know if Peter was here—her imagination was getting away from her.

She quickly made her way up the narrow passage, lit only by a dim, blue moonlight, to the wall that concealed the secret door. She looked around, making sure no one was nearby, her vision blurred by the pitching of the ship, which caused everything around her to stretch before rolling back again. There was a movement in the dark, but upon a second look, Wendy saw that it was nothing more than a discarded coat, dusty with age, its empty sleeves flapping with the movement on the waves. With a relieved sigh, she reached up in between the bells, gears, and wooden instruments, and her hands found the tiny iron casing. She had barely moved it upwards when she was yanked violently away from the door, a hand over her mouth, a body pressed roughly against hers.

Adrenaline pumped through her veins, and she kicked hard off the wall, shoving the body backwards before bringing her teeth down against the hand. Instead of the yowl she expected, she heard familiar laughter as the cool blade of a knife pressed up against her neck. She felt a warm rush of blood trickling down the collar of her dress and went still.

"See, now it's a good thing I can't feel that bite—it's quite uncouth for a lady, biting! The tar made sure of that. As you might imagine, it wasn't for stealing."

Barnaby's quiet whisper turned her stomach.

"I promise I'll be gentle. If you struggle, you'll just make it worse. This is inevitable, you and me. I knew the moment you came on this ship that this would happen. We're so alike you and I, both from noble families, both stuck here in this tropic hellhole, stuck on this ship with these . . . animals when we would be better off being served by these wretches!"

Wendy whimpered underneath his hand. "Barnaby, please let me go!"

He ignored her and continued. "It's an insult, a disgrace to serve under Hook, under these men, who look at me like I'm a rat among lions. I should be captain of this ship! How dare he command me?"

Wendy's eyes widened as she struggled to breathe, his grip like iron.

"Doesn't he know who I am? Who I was? I am Barnaby Devonshire the Third, an heir to a railroad fortune, and who is he? The son of a dead pirate."

He yanked Wendy's head back roughly. "I've given you plenty of time to come to me, treating you like the lady I can see you are, and yet, you look at me with disgust, shrink back at the touch of my hands. . . ."

Wendy squirmed roughly, her body straining against his surprising strength, her limbs exhausted and weak from her hours of scrubbing.

"Don't scream," he whispered. "You'll wake your brother, and we wouldn't want that. I have no desire to hurt him."

He began pulling her away from the wall, one tiny step at a time, dragging her feet as she used every ounce of strength to pull away from him, even as the tiny prick of his knife dug more painfully into her neck.

"Now will you stop, stop struggling? Can't you see? We were meant to be, I knew it from the moment you stepped aboard, so pure, everything I left behind when I was taken against my will to this place. Now, I can't change my fate here, and, truth be told, I love the *Night* herself, so after we are done, I may have to throw you overboard, but I'll make sure that you won't feel a thing—I promise! And when the captain asks what happened to you, I'll just tell him I have no idea. One more betrayal to Hook, one in a long line of betrayals . . . and soon he'll be undone. God knows his mind is unraveling already."

Wendy squeezed her eyes shut and refused to cry out as the blade pushed farther into her neck. She took a breath and waited a moment, enough to let him think that she was surrendering.

"Good girl . . . ," he murmured, just as she used all her remaining strength to push away from him, her hands shoving his dagger outwards, falling forward. He caught her arm roughly and yanked her back towards him, pulling downwards so she lost her footing, falling to her knees. The blade was at her neck again, this time lengthwise. She could feel it against her jugular.

"You are so feisty! It's so disappointing. I thought perhaps you would just be a lady about this. You should be lucky to be with a man of my standing, whose wealth dates back for generations. . . ."

There was a quick shuffle in the darkness, a muffled thud, and Barnaby fell forward to his knees. Wendy crawled forward and spun around, a sob escaping her throat as she struggled to her feet, her hands trying to stem her bleeding neck. Barnaby lurched to his feet, one blackened hand on the back of his head, his eyes confused. He spun, grabbing Wendy's hand, pulling her back against him. She kicked her leg out, catching the arm that held the dagger, which spun to the floor. She gritted her teeth and brought her closed fist up against Barnaby's nose, her hand exploding with pain at the impact. He reeled backwards, holding his gushing nose.

"You low-class BITCH!"

Two faces emerged from the darkness behind him, one pale and trembling and a full head above where Barnaby stood. The other looked on with glossy eyes, his hands feeling along the wall.

"Keme! Owl!" Wendy gasped, finally finding her voice, her heart thundering so loudly that she was sure the entire ship would be alerted.

"Be careful! He's mad!"

Keme's face was contorted in rage as he grabbed Barnaby, and then threw him backwards, the coward crumpling against the wall like a rag doll. The gentle cook then bent over the wretched man, his large hands wrapping around his throat. A high-pitched sound escaped from Keme's lips as he watched Barnaby contort the harder he squeezed, Barnaby's eyes grew wider as his lips became bluer, his body wriggling as he struggled for air.

"Stop, Keme. Stop!" Wendy's hands were shaking as she reached for Keme's shoulder, one hand on her neck. She wanted him to keep going, and it was that realization that made her raise her voice. "Stop. He's not worth it! Keme, stop! We're better than he is!"

She kept frantically repeating the phrase as Keme's expression softened, and he finally let go of Barnaby, who gasped for breath.

"You filthy monster, you almost killed me!"

In a rage, Wendy picked up the dagger and held it out towards Barnaby. Her hands had stopped shaking, and the fear she had felt had turned to a calm anger.

"Owl, go get Hook. Right now."

"Yes, my lady."

Owl began running down the hallway, his hands feeling his way along the wall. Keme stood beside Wendy, his fists clutching and unclenching, his breathing heavy.

"It's alright, it's alright now," Wendy whispered to him. "I'm okay."

She held the dagger steady, as Barnaby began whimpering, a sound more revolting than his hissing threats.

"Please don't take me to Hook, please, you don't understand, he'll kill me. . . ."

"And I won't cry a single tear," snapped Wendy. "Not for you. We aren't the same, you and I. And even if you had taken me like you desired, I would never be yours. I don't belong to you, or to Peter, or anyone else." She leaned forward.

"Even if you still had your money and your nobility, you still wouldn't be worth one of these pirates' spit. You are nothing, and you will fade into nothing."

The blood pooling down the front of her dress was cooling now, wet and sticky against her skin. Keme motioned to her neck with a concerned glance as footsteps thundered down the staircase. Hook exploded into the hallway, obviously half asleep. Smith followed close behind.

"What on earth is going on here!?" Hook's eyes leveled on Barnaby. "You." He turned to Wendy. "Are you alright?"

Wendy nodded. "I am. But only because Keme saved me."

"So this is it . . . is it?" Barnaby gave a dry laugh through his bruised throat, his eyes on Hook. "You know I betrayed you, don't you? You were just waiting . . ." He coughed. "You're ruined, you know. Everyone is aligned against you, and you can't take your eyes off damned Peter Pan. . . ." Barnaby closed his eyes for a moment.

"And I'll be damned if I won't take something you love too."

Then without warning, Barnaby pulled a pistol from his open shirt. There was a roar of gunfire as Wendy dove sideways, her body crumpling against the wall, her blood soaked hands covering her face. The blast of the guns echoed through the ship, bouncing off the walls and roaring down the hallway. Her ears were ringing, and she raised her head, discombobulated, unsure if she had been shot. She whirled around to see Hook standing still, holding a smoking pistol in his hand.

Half of Barnaby's face was missing, but her horror was saved for Keme, who slumped down against the floor, one hand over his chest, where a bright red blossom was spreading. Wendy gave a cry and knelt over his body, taking one of his large hands in her own, kissing it repeatedly before resting it against her cheek. Hot tears dripped from her eyes and down his palm as she whispered, "I'm sorry! I'm sorry. This is my fault!"

Keme gave her a kind smile and shook his head once before reaching out for Hook, whose face was twisted in sorrow. The captain pushed past Wendy and cradled Keme's large head in his hands, leaning their foreheads together.

"Oh, Keme, Keme, my brother . . . please forgive me. You can't leave me here. Not you."

Keme reached up and wrapped both arms around Hook, squeezing him hard against his chest.

"I couldn't protect you. I tried, I'm sorry, brother . . ."

Keme shook his head back and forth and clasped Hook's hand in his own, laying it on chest, over the wound. Then his mouth moved, slowly, unfamiliarly, his words more breath than sound.

"Lomasi. Lomasi."

A sob escaped Hook's throat. "Oh, brother, yes, I'll take you there. Of course."

Keme gave Hook a wry smile and squeezed his hand. Hook gently crossed Keme's hands over his chest, one hand over the other, as he began humming a strange tune, a tumble of foreign words lilting in the hallway. Keme's face, the pale color of old putty, broke into an ecstatic smile. Hook smiled back at him, the words fading in his throat.

"Please don't go. Please."

There was a moment of silence, and Wendy struggled to keep her sobs quiet, the violence building in her throat. Hook's spine straightened, and he clasped the giant's hand as a croaking rattle escaped from Keme's lips. He opened them once more.

"Love," he whispered to Hook, patting his chest gently. "Love."

Then the gentle cook took a long ragged breath before his body went still, his eyes open and staring at the ceiling, his soul somewhere above the ship, floating out safely among the stars.

Wendy let out a low sob as she curled herself over his body. "It's my fault, it's my fault. Barnaby was waiting here in the hallway, I didn't see him, not once. . . ."

Hook was still as he looked silently on the body, slowly regaining his immoveable composure, his pained face falling back into stone.

"This was not your fault, Wendy Darling. This was only the fault of two men. His . . . and mine."

He nodded to Barnaby's crumbled form, the wall and floor around him a mess of blood and brain matter. Wendy looked away, bile rising in her throat as she looked back with care upon Keme's still form.

How could she not have known? Had she been careless? Barnaby, who at first was such a fine reminder of home, a gentleman.

She leaned her head against Keme's chest, wishing to hear a heartbeat, wishing to feel his great breaths thunder through his lungs, but there was nothing, only stillness in the creaking hallway. It seemed as though the silence would break and stretch them, carrying them also into the great forever, when Smith spoke up.

"He died a noble death, protecting you. That's more than most pirates can hope for."

Owl emerged out of the darkness. "Aye, aye. A finer death was never seen upon the *Sudden Night.*"

Hook was still, his head hanging down, his eyes closed. When they opened, they met Wendy's, and in that moment, Wendy knew him, saw him, not for the terrifying captain that he truly was, but also for the man who was tasked with caring for his crew, for this man who lay dead at his feet. Hook sniffed once and wheeled on Smith, who had reached out his hand to pat the captain's shoulder.

"Don't."

Smith's hand stopped in midair.

"Smith, go cut off Barnaby's hands."

"Gladly," growled the first mate, pulling a long knife out of his boot.

"Then strip him naked and bring the body above deck. Wake the crew, and then cast his body overboard. I want every man on this crew to understand what happens to mutineers. Make no mention of the events that occurred down here with the girl."

He rested his hand on Keme's still chest.

"Owl, get back to your post. We don't want to take any risks. And I trust you'll stay quiet about this—for her honor and yours."

Owl nodded obediently. "Aye, aye Captain, will be my pleasure."

Hook turned back to Smith. "First, help me move Keme's body into the hold."

"Not overboard?"

"No. Not overboard."

His tone implied that this was the end of this conversation.

"Yes, sir."

Hook turned to Wendy. "Make your way back to your room. I'm sure your brother is wondering where you are."

Wendy nodded.

"Wait . . . just . . ." She bent over Keme and lightly kissed his dark lips, his body still warm. "Thank you for saving my life," she whispered, a cry escaping her throat. "I will remember it every day."

Her hand trailed across his forehead. "He was so lovely. So lovely and yet I knew nothing about him."

She shook her head back and forth.

"I'm sorry, I'm sorry."

Smith's strong hands lifted her up and off Keme, and gently nudged her down the hallway until she came back to her door. *The door.* So much had happened—and yet, she had just been here. She felt her face crumpling as she turned the small wheel, the door pulling out from the wall.

"You'll be alright," Smith uttered awkwardly. "Everyone dies sometime."

It was the least-comforting thing she had ever heard, and she let the door shut behind her. She wanted her mother, to feel the wrap of her stout arms around her shoulders, to lean against her mother's chest and feel that everything would be fine. Instead, she was peeling a bloody dress off her body, dried blood sticking to her skin, Keme's blood, her blood on her hands, on her neck. She pulled on a clean nightgown before curling into Michael's bunk, turning her back to his softly breathing body, so that her heaving sobs wouldn't wake him. She cried for an hour before her tears swept her into a fathomless sleep.

Wendy opened her eyes, expecting to see the bottom of her bunk, but instead she saw light filtering through hard wooden slats. She turned her head. More wooden slats, all around her, curving out in an egg shape on either side of her. Her breath became labored as she realized that the air was suffocating and putrid. Her eyes met an iron ring that ran around the top of the slats, sudden horror dawning upon her: she was in a barrel. She began banging her hands against the sides, screaming at the top of her lungs. The rough wood shredded her fingers with splinters as she screamed for help, her gulps of air echoing through the barrel.

"Please, please!"

Something shifted by her feet. Wendy looked down in horror, where a blackness swirled around her ankles. The snakes, she thought. Oh God, the snakes. Something curled up her leg. It moved like a snake, twisting, slithering, but it wasn't solid, rather it was a wisp of something terrible, gas full of malice. It slithered up her leg and her waist, changing form as it went, its grip tightening around her like a python, squeezing the life out of her. Other tendrils uncoiled from the bottom of the barrel, smothering her face, the black smoke covering her head like a bag. Her screams were silenced as she pounded her fists against the sides of the barrel. Suddenly, the smoke around her face lifted, becoming two hands that curled away from her. Through the slats of the barrel, she saw two bright-green eyes watching.

"Peter? Peter, help me!"

He shook his head. "Can't. Can't be stopped. Don't want to."

"Peter, PLEASE!" she screamed with all her strength as the dark smoke began crushing her. She felt her ribs snapping one by one, felt the darkness flowing into her mouth, breaking her legs and arms. The last thing she saw before the smoke clouded her vision was the green eyes, watching with delighted pleasure as the darkness tore her to pieces, muscle from bone.

She woke up with a scream.

Michael rolled over in bed.

"Wendy, what's wrong?"

Wendy's shaking hands traced over her face, feeling her forehead drenched with sweat.

"It was a dream . . . it was a dream . . . ," she was reassuring herself, though Michael thought it was for him.

"Alright. Good night." He rolled back over and was asleep in seconds.

Wendy sat up in bed, struggling to catch her breath. The dream had been as vivid as a memory, almost as if she was meant to have it. With a gasp, she propelled herself out of bed, putting her bare feet on the floor. Moving as quietly as she could, she slipped out of the secret door, locking it securely behind her. She grabbed a lantern hanging in the hallway and ran through the dark corridors of the ship, wanting to rid herself of the fear that the dream had left behind. It lingered inside of her like a dark, beating heart. She raced up the Jolly Staircase, taking the stairs two at a time. All the ship was dark and still, rocking her men to sleep in the folds of her waves. Wendy's bare feet slapped the lush carpet as she ran toward Hook's chambers. There was no knocking. Instead, she flung open the carved doors, the fairy king giving way to her speed and force. The doors slammed inwards, and then Wendy was inside, holding the lantern above her.

"What in the bloody hells?" Hook lurched out of bed, a sword in one hand. "Who's there?"

Wendy approached the bed, the lantern illuminating her sweat-drenched face, her stringy hair, and trembling form. Hook's face changed as she stepped forward. He gripped her arm.

"You're ready. Ask me. Ask me the question."

Wendy gritted her teeth, the memory of the darkness bubbling up, the fear so vivid it could only have come from something real, an awareness hidden inside of her, buried from her view by Peter's glamour and her own need for survival.

"What is the Shadow?"

CHAPTER FIFTEEN

"That is the question, isn't it?"

The captain nodded once before turning back to the bed. He picked up his hook, lying on a plush pillow beside him, and shrugged his sleeve back over his fleshy, red, and irritated stump. Wendy tried not to stare at it, the swinging lantern casting a shifting light over the wound. His face bent into a grimace as he slammed the hook down over the stump. Wendy raised her hand.

"You don't have to put that on. . . ."

"Yes, I do," he snapped. "I hope you understand now that the question could only come from you. If I would have told you myself, you wouldn't have believed it."

He tilted her chin up with the sharp curve of his hook. "We have much work to do and so little time to do it."

Hook walked over to his liquor cabinet and began pouring them both a drink.

Wendy coughed.

"Oh, no thank you . . ."

"Drink it." He handed her a glass of rum. "You need it, after a night like tonight."

Hook downed his glass in a single swig. "And, you'll need it even more after what I'm about to tell you."

Wendy took a small sip; the rum tasted terrible, but it filled her throat with warmth as it settled in her belly. Hook took a breath before settling into his armchair.

"I only know what I know, and what I know is probably very little, gleaned from information gathered over decades. Most of the information that I have comes from a very reliable source, a source that I would trust with my life, but I've also gathered pieces here and there from various folks, folks like Fermina." He sighed. "What do you know about the fairies of Neverland?"

Wendy shook her head. "Not much. I know that Tink is the last, that she heard her family got murdered by the darkness, that's what she called it." Wendy gasped. "The Shadow? The Shadow killed her people?"

Hook gave a nod and continued.

"A hundred years ago, the fairies ruled Neverland. They ruled this world, a world that they had created for themselves, a place called Neverland."

"They created Neverland?"

"Yes. This is going back hundreds of years, but yes. They created this magical place, with unearthly natural delights, and on and on. They communed with nature and nature gave back, in a symbiotic relationship that forever flourished. They had other gifts as well—gifts of speed and strength and flight. They lived in harmony with both Neverland itself and her inhabitants and . . . the Shadow."

Wendy couldn't hold in the intrigue building inside of her. "What?"

"Quiet down. Let me get there. But first—" Hook poured himself another drink, savoring this one with hard sips. "The story stands that Peter snuck into the garden—now the Forsaken Garden—and listened to the fairies sing their mourning song."

"Morning song?" Wendy's heart pounded inside of her chest.

"Hmm, not morning, like the sun; mourning, like death."

Wendy was listening.

"Fairies had immortal life. They didn't age naturally, rather they could choose at what age to be. They could be killed—by violence—but that never happened, for who could kill them? When a fairy was ready to move on, they would call it. The Shadow. In London you would call this death."

An image of the grim reaper came to Wendy's mind, and she grasped her cup with terror.

"Indeed. But this was not your version of death, with its silly scythe and black hood. The Shadow, to the fairies, was a benevolent and loving entity that gently took them into the beyond. They loved it, and I've heard that when it was called, that all the hearts in Neverland would weep as it passed them by. When a fairy decided it was their time to move on, all the fairies would gather together and raise their voices in song, to lift up their weary kin. They would call to the Shadow, and it in turn would take the fairy into its arms, cradling them before taking the body up . . . and beyond."

Hook gestured to the ceiling. Wendy's eyes were wide with disbelief.

"It sounds . . . lovely, like a fairytale."

Hook grimaced. "So I've heard. But humans like us never heard the song, and never knew when the fairies would call the Shadow, and so we didn't concern ourselves with it." Wendy took a long, slow sip of her drink. Speaking of the Shadow made her feel like tiny cold fingers were tracing up her spine.

"So, that brings us to our beloved Peter Pan. The stories say that Peter Pan snuck into the garden, and listened as the fairies sang the song. He memorized it, and then later changed it, and when he was ready . . ."

Hook shook his head.

"He called the Shadow to himself, but not to take him away." He closed his eyes, his voice rising. "He bound the Shadow to himself, and sung it into servitude."

Wendy's voice was trembling now. "But, how would Peter know how to do that? To enslave the Shadow?"

"Some say it was his destiny. Some say he made a deal with the devil. However . . . there is perhaps another answer." Hook gave a sad smile. "I would say it was all three."

"So, he bound the Shadow to himself. Then what?"

Hook finished his second glass.

Wendy waited impatiently. "The Shadow!"

"I'm getting there. Once Peter had bound the Shadow to himself, the Shadow began . . . changing."

Hook stood abruptly, walking over to the massive black fireplace that dominated the room, the crocodile clock ticktocking back and forth.

"What we know from there is a puzzle at best, but here's how I best see it making sense. We don't know how much time passed, but eventually, Peter ordered the Shadow to kill the fairies." Hook sighed sadly. "And they were slaughtered. An entire people, ripped to shreds by the thing they once loved. Even King Qaralius, who was rumored to be of great strength, couldn't defend his people."

"Tink told me that he died protecting her, the last of his race."

"Tink . . . ," Hook growled. "As if what Peter had done wasn't terrible enough, he spared a young Tink and convinced her that he had saved her from the Shadow. She was so grateful, that she gave him all her gifts—flight, speed, and strength—for the duration of her life. They are bound together, in their bones. But the worst gift that she gave him was her own gift of immortality."

"That's why Peter never ages!"

Hook rested his arms on the mantle of the fireplace. "See, death is natural. All humans must die, but when you pervert death, and make yourself immortal . . ."

Wendy finished his sentence, ". . . death becomes twisted. The Shadow is now—"

"Distorted. Mad."

"Does Tink know about the Shadow?"

"No. And I believe that's the only thing that's kept Peter from calling it again. If Tink knows that he controls the Shadow . . ."

"She would never forgive him for killing her people."

"More than that, she may do something dramatic in order to take away his powers."

Wendy shook her head with a sigh, tears gathering in her eyes. "How terrible. Poor Tink, in love with the boy who murdered her family."

Hook stroked his chin.

"I truly think the worst of Peter Pan, and even I wonder if he fully understood what he was doing when he unleashed the Shadow upon the fairies. He was younger then, *truly* sixteen, a child. But now . . ."

"Now he would fully understand. He understood what he was doing when he ordered it to destroy the *Sunned Shore.*"

"I believe that the longer the Shadow and Peter are bound together, the more twisted and deviant Peter becomes. Their darkness feeds off each other, like two rats in a hole."

Wendy's mind was leaping from thought to thought, connections lighting in her mind, so much making sense.

"That's why the Pilvinuvo Indians disappeared! Because they were afraid of the Shadow."

"Yes."

"Are they safe where they are?"

Hook shrugged. "From Peter, yes. From the Shadow, probably not."

Wendy leapt to her feet. "That's why you play this game with Peter! You keep him entertained with this *war* so that he doesn't unleash the Shadow. That's why you fight with scum like Maison about keeping Peter engaged, because . . . because . . ." She turned to him.

"My God. You are protecting everyone in Neverland."

The enormity of his burden made her stumble. She reached out to put a hand on his shoulder but felt only air. This man,

Hook, was tasked with so much more than pirating. The slump of his shoulders, the rings under his eyes, the haunted draw of his cheeks as he stared at the mainland, everything made sense now, and like pulling the veil on her memories, she saw Hook fully now. Wendy had so many questions, but understood now why most of them could wait.

"You're running out of time."

"Peter is getting bored. I can feel it. I was so thankful for your arrival here, a distraction to him, falling in love with you. But I knew the moment that I saw you slumped over in his arms after the Vault that you would soon see him for the monster he is. Peter can't love, can't nurture or care while the Shadow resides inside of him. He consumes all he sees. He only knows how to destroy, and his love for you has made him only more unhinged."

"You're worried he will unleash the Shadow."

"The day will come where he will rashly decide that Tink's gifts are not worth holding back for, and he will risk it. In fact, from what I hear from his relationship with Tink, he has worked long and hard to keep her in love with him while still keeping her afraid of him."

Wendy remembered the bruises on Tink's legs contrasted by the shining love in her eyes.

"I do not believe that she would ever turn on Peter. She loves him desperately. He hurts her and she limps right back." Hook shook his head.

"That is the question—what would Tink do if someone told her the truth? Would she even care? Or would his lies be able to convince her otherwise? He's quite good at telling stories."

Wendy remembered the moonlight filtering down on him as he leapt and filled the Teepee with tales of bravery and adventure, his red hair like a flame.

"Yes, he is quite good with that."

Hook drained his glass. "It's time for another."

Wendy scoffed, "Perhaps you should slow down."

"Do you dare tell a captain what to do on his own ship, Wendy Darling?"

She looked at him clearly. "Aren't we past that yet? I'm trying to wrap my mind around it all and you're lecturing me about manners."

Hook gave her a sad grin. "Yes, well, it's all very scary and all of Neverland hangs in the balance, so I will have another, if it's okay with you."

Wendy looked at his fireplace, watching the flames lick up against an iron poker that leaned inside, its handle a carved lion.

"What . . . what does the Shadow look like?"

"There are only two people who know the answer to that question, and both of them live on Pan Island."

"Ah."

Wendy was quiet for a moment, the impact of this terribly horrifying news echoing around her skull, dulling everything else out while she considered the implications of the truth. A memory crept up from her subconscious: the swirling of navy in Peter's normally emerald eyes, something she had seen a few times. The Shadow, moving inside him, was a part of him. She gasped, remembering something she had seen inside the Vault.

"The room full of instruments in the Vault! You're collecting them!"

Hook gave a slight tilt of his head. "I have to make sure that no one else calls the Shadow. It must be destroyed."

"What does this mean then? It must mean that . . ."

"That to defeat Peter Pan, we have to defeat the Shadow first."

"What if . . . ?" Wendy couldn't believe she was about to speak these words. "What if we killed Peter?"

"Believe me, I've thought about it, every time I see his smug face. But my fear is that killing him would unleash the Shadow, who would then tear Neverland apart, or that Peter, in his dying breath, would no doubt order the Shadow to exact his revenge."

Wendy shook her head. "This is impossible! There must be some way, some way to—"

"And that . . . is the question." Hook coughed. "Do you remember Fermina's story? Do you remember what she said about Peter dropping the girls?"

Wendy thought for a moment. "That Peter sacrificed the girls to the mermaids."

"Have you ever known Peter to give anything freely?"

Wendy shook her head. "Never."

Hook stood, shaking out his long white dressing gown. "Peter did not call the Shadow without help. There is only one race of people that have been here as long as the fairies; one race that knew deep and ancient things about them. I believe that the mermaids know something. Something Peter doesn't want them to speak of."

"How to defeat the Shadow."

Hook slowly put his glass on the side of his chair before leaning forward, looking intensely at Wendy.

"Do you remember, the first night I spoke to you, I told you that I believed you had a purpose here? On the *Night*, here with me?"

"Yes," whispered Wendy, a spindle of terror beginning to churn within her chest.

"I need you to do something for me, something only you can do." Hook's voice was steady, yet Wendy noticed that he was grasping his glass so hard that his fingers were turning white.

"What I'm about to tell you will be somewhat disturbing."

Wendy straightened her spine and lifted her chin, forcing her hammering heart back into place. Sitting like a lady provided some relief.

"With all due respect, sir, since I've arrived in Neverland, I have been dropped, choked, dragged, and stabbed." Her voice faltered. "I held my nearly drowned brother in my arms, praying that God would take me as well. What could be worse than that? Nothing."

Hook gave her a wry smile.

"You may wait to hear what I have to say before you go about pronouncing yourself the bravest girl in Neverland."

Wendy didn't flinch.

"Men are not allowed in Miath, the mermaid city or the land around it, the Gray Shore. The very land itself is poison to us, starting on the low hills above the shore and continuing down onto shoreline of Neverland." Hook swept his hands out, his fingers spread. "That is where they keep Sybella, their rock. Surrounding their lagoon is a vast coral garden, where bright sea flowers grow in the bones of a thousand dead men. The garden extends miles out from the shore. Ships that try to approach it will be ripped to shreds, though a rowboat would be okay to pass overhead—not that it would make it very far. If you enter Miath, the mermaids themselves will attack your ship. They are strong creatures, with skin like stone, much stronger than mortal men."

"I'm aware." Wendy remembered the mermaids' rocklike grip around her waist as she was pulled lower into the depths, the sun slowly becoming nothing more than a wink of light in a fathomless blue. She shivered, as the memory returned, of the black eyes and the open scream, of Peter slicing his way through the water.

"But I can go to the lagoon?"

Hook sat back down, pulling his chair closer to Wendy.

"The coral gardens are fed by one thing, and one thing only—the blood of a virgin. A virgin female."

Wendy took a moment to let his words wash over her before anger erupted from her chest.

"I'm sorry?"

Hook leapt up, his chair flung out behind him.

"We don't have time for pleasantries, Miss Darling! We are running out of time. For the first time in my life, I have something that Queen Eryne needs, something she wants, something she will trade for answers. We must know how to defeat the Shadow, otherwise, what hope is there for us? What hope is there for Neverland? We are held hostage by the Shadow and will lose everything! All it will take is one day when Peter loses control."

Wendy jumped up, her anger as potent as his, all fear of the captain diminished.

"So you want me to go, and die? Just like that?" Hook's eyebrows raised.

"No one said anything about dying, Miss Darling. Now sit back down."

With a scowl, Wendy sat, her arms crossed in front of her.

"I will not sit idly by while you determine my fate."

Hook rubbed his forehead.

"I don't enjoy this conversation any more than you do, but it is necessary." His eyes looked straight ahead. "We must have answers. I need you to go to the Gray Shores, and barter with Queen Eryne. You do not need to give all of your blood, just a few drops."

"And how do I know that they won't just drown me, and take all of it? My blood." She swallowed.

Hook's voice dropped to a whisper. "I have reason to believe that Queen Eryne regrets what happened to the fairies, and I also believe that she fears the Shadow. It is in her best interest to tell you the truth."

Hook shook his head, launching into a diatribe about Peter Pan, but Wendy's mind was far away, floating up and away from the ship. She saw her brothers, playing in the nursery, leaping from bed to bed, sticks in their hands as they pretended to be pirates, or army rangers or fighter pilots. John, picking up Michael and spinning him around by his arms, as Michael shrieked in delight and mock terror. The door of her memory creaked open, and she saw the silhouette of her father, watching his boys, pride etched in the delicate wrinkles of his eyes. She turned back to the captain.

"I'll do it."

Hook nodded solemnly, the words tingling in his mouth.

"So quickly then. I thought you may need some time to think about it." He paused. "Though I'm not surprised. You're a good girl, Wendy."

Wendy turned back to him, the light bouncing off her pale face. "If I do this, you do not have the right to call me girl. Not after all that's happened, and certainly not after what you are asking me to do."

Hook paused, surprised at her boldness. He picked up his glass.

"Cheers, then. To Wendy, a woman."

Wendy turned to head back to her sleeping chambers, suddenly exhausted from the conversation and the liquor that was coursing through her system, dulling her senses to a pleasant hum.

"Good night, Captain."

She heard the faint strains of a lyre being plucked behind her.

"Good night, Wendy Darling. I'll set a course for the farthest northern point. From there, you will walk over the foothills and into Miath. We will be making one stop first."

Wendy turned. "Where?"

Hook reached out with one finger and plucked a string sadly.

"Keme is going home."

At the sound of his name, a sadness took hold of Wendy's heart and carried her out of the captain's chambers, down the Jolly Staircase, and into her bed, snug beside Michael. The pillow was still damp and cold from where her sweat had soaked it earlier, when she had dreamt of the Shadow. She knew sleep would be impossible, and so she lay still as her heart hammered, her body rocking with the pull of the ship as it changed course, heading swiftly into a smothering fog, hiding everything within its swollen breath. She snuggled close to Michael, breathing him in and remembering that there was still some goodness in this dark world.

Chapter Sixteen

The next day passed achingly slowly. Tears blurring her eyes the entire time, Wendy quickly threw together a make-shift breakfast for the men, though without Keme, cooking and the food had literally lost its flavor. The crew stared sadly down at their lumpy, half-seared pile of mush and bleeding berries, a few of them wiping tears from their eyes, others glowering at Wendy as the wind tossed her hair mercifully in front of her eyes. A furious voice barreled down from the helm.

"Eat, you bilge-licking scum of the seas, or I'll be taking your hands as well!"

Wendy raised her eyes. Captain Hook was at the wheel, barely recognizable as the man she had seen the night before. His eyes blazed with renewed passion and his slumping shoulders were gone. Instead, he looked like a rock on the sea—unbreakably solid, majestic, and strong. As she watched him adjust the wheel, his coat flapping wildly behind him in the wind, she realized what she was seeing: hope. For the first time since she had met him, Hook's eyes blazed with renewed optimism, with the joy of forward momentum. There was also a glint of something else she couldn't recognize— joy? *No, it couldn't be joy.* She smiled to herself. Joy on Hook would be like pajamas on a cat, unnatural, unnerving. No, this was something else. Smith's loud bray interrupted her thoughts.

"LADS! Keme's gone, and we best just move on and curse the gods as we go. Now eat your bloody oats before I shove them down your gullet with my fingers."

Black Caesar sputtered over his food. "Damn you, Barnaby. I pray that his soul is resting in Hades fiery seas."

"I always hated that man." Redd angrily spooned Wendy's food into his mouth. "Mutinous scurvy bastard."

"He wasn't even that good of a navigator either. Flanks is better," answered Voodoo.

"Aye, aye!"

As their angry conversation erupted over the table, Wendy felt her hands unclench in relief. Her best was all she could do until another cook was found. And they would never find another Keme. She blinked away tears. *Keme, whose blood was still crusted underneath her fingernails, mingling with her own.* A wave of nausea rushed over Wendy, but she was thankfully distracted by Michael padding up the stairs and up onto the deck, so blissfully unaware of the horrors that had happened outside his door the night before.

"Morning, pirates! Morning, Voodoo! Morning, Redd!"

The pirates grunted in reply, some scowling at their names, but Wendy was sure that she saw a few smiles curve upwards, mostly covered by thick, unruly beards. Her brother brought such sunshine to this dark ship.

Michael stopped at Smith. "Morning, Smee."

Smith growled at him, his mouth full of food. "You better sit down, boy, before I eat all your mush."

"Will do." Michael dramatically saluted Smith, and Wendy saw Smith roll his eyes with something that looked, for a moment, like affection. She covered her mouth to keep from smiling, happy that even when there was blood on her fingers, that tiny cracks of light could trickle through this darkness. She would laugh again. She would smile. Maybe even today. *Maybe even this morning.* The ship rocked hard to starboard, and Wendy felt a hard ripple pass underneath them. Black Caesar leaned over to Voodoo, the two of them always gossiping, reminding her of the girls in her class at St. Mary's.

"Say, where do you think he's taking us? He won't let no one up there but him. Don't recognize this part of the sea, and can't see the mainland, not even through the spyglass."

Voodoo looked up at the captain, squinting his eyes. Wendy still couldn't believe he was Oxley's father.

"We're west, I think. Far west though. He's not even using a compass, from the looks of it." Black Caesar furrowed his scarred brow, his lips cracked and bloody.

"Don't like this."

Voodoo shrugged. "Captain knows what he's doing. Don't ask questions, that's me motto."

"That's 'cause you're stupid, like a sheep being led to slaughter. Look what happened to Barnaby."

"Traitorous letch."

"Yeah, but what a way to go. Wonder we didn't hear him screaming when Hook took his hands."

"Who said he still had a tongue?"

They sailed on for a few hours, Wendy cleaning up after breakfast before spending some time below deck, her thoughts tumbling from London to Neverland and back again. She was considering asking Hook to borrow a novel to help quiet her mind when the *Night* lurched violently to one side, and she heard Hook yelling orders above. Wendy struggled to stay on her feet as she ran up the hallway and the Jolly Staircase as the ship gave a groan, and a ripple ran up the side of the hull. Wendy emerged from below deck, just when Hook was yelling.

"Bring a spring upon her cable, we're running aground!" Without a minute's hesitation, the crew leapt to their tasks like a swarm of worker bees.

Smith yelled out, "Eight fathoms!"

Wendy turned to Redd, who was climbing up to the

mizzenmast. "How is that possible we are at eight fathoms when there is no land?"

He shook his head at Wendy. "Your guess is as good as mine, lass!"

Wendy ran to the side of the deck with Michael to see where they were stopping, but there was nothing, nothing beyond the strange, wet, gray fog that nestled lovingly up against the ship. Land was nowhere on the horizon, and the main island was probably four hundred miles away at this point. *The* Sudden Night *was stopping in the middle of the ocean.* Her heart began to pound at the unknown, the hair on her arms rising as she heard the sound of soft breaths carried on the wind.

"Wendy . . . ," Michael hesitated. "What is it?"

The crew went still on the deck, their voices silenced, their eyes on the captain, who was making his way down from the bridge.

"Smith, bring around a single longboat. And Keme's body please."

Smith snapped his fingers, and three of the crew followed him below deck.

"Wendy, you are coming with me. Michael as well, please."

Wendy tightened her arm around Michael.

"Why? Why do you need Michael and me?"

Hook took her arm roughly, his voice dropping.

"I cannot go into it here. I just need you to get on the boat." He lowered his voice. "It will be alright. Do you trust me?"

Wendy smelled something strange on the air, wafting from Hook's lapel. Sharp and crisp—like soap or freshly laundered clothes? She narrowed her eyes.

"Are we at Miath already?"

"As I said before, we are here to bring our beloved cook home. I'd like you and Michael to be there. Keme liked you both very much."

A trapdoor on the deck flipped open, and the crew members that had followed Smith emerged, struggling with Keme's enormous corpse, his body wrapped up in a white linen shroud blotted with blood. Wendy bit her lip as they laid it carefully on the ground, removing their hats and standing vigil over the still body. Hook raised his chin.

"Say your good-byes, and load him into the boat. Swiftly now, men."

The crew of the *Sudden Night* circled around his still form, their hats in their hands. Not a word was spoken, though the quiet cracking of the sails gave a melodic background to their sorrow. After a few moments, Smith pulled back on his leather hat and coughed.

"All right, men. It's time to get our cook home. Into the boat he goes."

As the crew picked up his wrapped body, Keme's muscled arm flapped out of the side, his large palm dragging along the open deck. Without thinking, Wendy rushed forward, taking his hand in her own and quietly crossing it over his chest as the men held still, their arms straining under the giant's weight.

"I'm sorry," she whispered over his still form. "I'm sorry."

"We all are, lass," muttered Redd. "Now move out of the way."

Wendy stepped back and watched the men gently lower Keme into a creaking black longboat that dangled precariously over the sea on the starboard side. Hawk reached out his hand and helped Wendy step into the boat, her long wrap tangling on the edge of an oar. She reached out her hand and aided Michael into the boat. His excitement about the rowboat quickly disappeared when he saw Keme's body being lowered in beside him.

"Wendy, what is that? What IS THAT?" The terror in his voice tore at her heart.

"Shhh . . . come sit." She patted the seat, and he leaned against her. "Michael, that's Keme." Michael's face crumpled.

"Is he sleeping?" His voice raised several octaves, "Wendy, IS HE SLEEPING?"

Wendy felt the well of strength inside of her weaken, crack by crack, as fat tears filled his eyes. She struggled to pull his chin towards her, his eyes locked on Keme's still form, the bloodstains reflected in his blue eyes.

"Listen to me. Keme died doing something very brave. SO brave, just like you. We cared about Keme, and it's okay to be sad that we won't see him anymore."

She struggled to keep her voice steady. Michael's lip quivered, and Wendy felt her resolve collapsing.

"Did Peter do this?"

"No. He didn't. Barnaby did." Michael crawled into Wendy's lap and wrapped himself tightly around her.

"Don't tell me any more," he whispered between sobs. Slivers of sadness snaked around her heart as she recognized that her brother had seen—and known—more than enough death in Neverland. Hook climbed into the boat, his boots clacking hard on the glossy wood before looking back at his first mate, standing on the deck of the *Night*.

"Smith."

"Yes, sir?"

"If this boat moves, even an inch, I will peel the skin from your body until you beg for death."

Smith couldn't hide his delight at the captain's gruesome threat.

"Aye, aye, Captain. We aren't going nowhere without you."

"Best not, since you also have no idea where we are and you would all die at sea."

"'Tis true, Captain." Smith turned to the crew. "LOWER THE BOAT!"

With a heavy creak, the rowboat launched away from the side of the *Night*, sinking lower towards the quietly lapping water. Wendy kept Michael clutched tight to her chest, his tears for Keme soaking through the top of her thick ornate shawl. Hook sat heavily down, taking an oar in one hand, steering the boat away from the *Night*. She watched Hook's rhythmic strokes, the way that he wound his body down and then back again, propelling the oars forward in a circular motion. Wendy smiled. Hook noticed.

"What's your sneer for girl? Did you forget that we have a body in the boat?"

She shook her head, her eyes flitting to Keme's body.

"No, of course not. I was just thinking that the last time I rowed a boat, it looked very unlike what you are doing now, which is probably why I didn't make it very far."

Hook was silent for a moment before letting amusement cross his grizzled face.

"No, you were about a mile from the shore. You didn't get very far at all."

There was only silence then, cut sharply by the slap of the waves against the boat and the splash of the oars as they drifted away from the *Night,* which faded slowly into the mist. They rowed until only the crow's nest was visible, Hawk's figure like a specter, looking over the rising waves. Wendy twisted in her seat, feeling more uncomfortable the farther away they drew from the *Sudden Night.* Hook's eyes were light and hopeful, though his mouth was twisted in obvious despair, a conflict of emotions playing across his face like a stage. Wendy turned away and rubbed Michael's back, his curls sweaty against her own hair, stiff with salt, wild like the sea. The mist around them became suffocating as they passed through the thick of it. It swallowed Hook and the front of the rowboat, cutting Wendy off for a few terrifying seconds before she was sucked into it as well, the floaty gray so dense she couldn't even see the top of Michael's head. She let out a long breath, the fog in front of her lips swirling in an inky cloud. Then, they were through it, the rowboat passing through an invisible wall, where the fog was left behind them, undulating in their wake. A sudden thump sent Wendy roughly against the grainy sideboard, and the rowboat vaulted up on a sandbank that seemed to come out of nowhere.

"We're here," Hook declared, and then he was gone, the oars left lying in the boat as Wendy untangled Michael from her lap and carefully stepped out of the boat, her dress dragging in the sand. The bank was maybe a half mile wide at most, nothing more than a patch of barren sand with sporadic piles of tall grasses that blew in the wind. The bank was circular, and the fog that had so discombobulated her before now circled harmlessly around the tiny patch of land upon the sea, protecting it from any outside eyes. Wendy took Michael's hand in her own as they made their way up the sloped sand, Hook several paces before them. For once, Michael was silent, awed as she was at this magical little sliver of Neverland. She looked back at the boat, Keme's form unmoving, the white linen darker over the cave of his mouth. She shuddered and turned away, just in time to see Hook drop his sword in the sand and begin running, his boots kicking up sand as he made his way to the center of the sandbank. It was so unexpected from a man that normally moved with such purpose that she stopped short, unnerved by this explosion of movement.

"Why is he running?" Michael asked, surprised. She gave his hand a hard squeeze, but it was unnecessary, for his questions trailed off into the crash of the sea when a figure emerged from the hazy mist.

There was a moment of stunned silence before Michael uttered a single word.

"Oh . . ."

Her legs were impossibly long and muscular, her calves and thighs carved like stone. A loose navy-blue sheaf with gold filigree fluttered around her form, barely covering the body underneath it. Her chest and torso were bound in wraps of brown leaves that ran up between her shoulder blades before circling around the crown of her head. Her thick, black hair, easily long enough to brush the back of her knees, twisted in the wind, circling around Hook as he threw himself at her feet. The captain pressed his face into the sand, his hands clutching at her ankles, before climbing to her calves, his head pressed against her shins. Unnatural light radiated off her copper skin, a hearty golden glow that hovered around her entire being. It rose and fell with each breath she took, and when her hands reached out to run through Hook's hair, his face was lit up in its glorious radiance.

Wendy could see, even from across the sandbank, that Hook was desperately in love with this woman, who could only be Lomasi, the princess of the Pilvinuvo Indians. She sank to her knees next to Hook and pulled his face towards her in a desperate kiss, her glimmering light dulling to a soft glow, flickering between them like the spark of a flame as their mouths met in a passionate, hungry kiss. Her hair fell over her shoulders as she pulled Hook toward her, and with a gust of wind, it covered them both, their faces pressed together, their hands tracing lines of love across each other's cheeks.

Wendy loved Booth, and she had even loved Peter for a short while, but in that moment, Wendy knew that *this love* that she saw between Hook and Lomasi, *this love would swallow them all*, along with Neverland, the stars, and the sea below them. Their passion was palpable, and it barreled across the sand towards Wendy, making her feel in awe and lonely all at once. Lomasi pressed her lips repeatedly against Hook's forehead and then guided his head to her shoulder, where he exhaled mightily, the captain's shoulders unfolding against her bosom. They wrapped themselves around each other, tears of happiness and sorrow dripping off their cheeks. Her glow faded, and then they were just two people, completely lost in each other, the rest of the world blowing away like sand.

Wendy pulled Michael close to her, turning her head away from their fierce display of love, feeling like a voyeur to something so potent. Lomasi's voice finally crossed the sand, a deep tone that spoke of resilience.

"Come, children—I've been eagerly waiting to meet you."

Wendy and Michael shuffled up the sand towards the couple.

Hook rose steadily, pulling Lomasi up with him, their arms entwined as they stood to face the Darlings. Wendy felt very much like a child at that moment, a girl who had not fully understood anything until she saw the look on Hook's face when he collapsed into this woman, his passion and his need so obvious. Looking at Captain Hook had always puzzled her, as if she was seeing a man through the jagged reflection of his soul, but now the mirror was clear, his reflection true. *He loved Lomasi. And defeating Peter meant protecting her.*

Wendy had never felt more self-conscious as she stumbled up the bank towards the princess, who watched their approach with a gentle smile, one hand wrapped firmly around her lover's waist. As they approached her, Lomasi stepped forward, her black hair swirling behind her. Up close, she was even more breathtaking. Her skin was the color of wet sand, etched over strong cheekbones that jutted out from the side of a narrow face. Thick eyebrows arched gracefully over narrow brown eyes, the deep chocolate of the irises blazing against the fathomless black pupils. When Wendy's hazel eyes met Lomasi's, Wendy felt as though she could fall into them, into their wisdom and kindness. Looking at the Pilvinuvo princess felt like coming home to London and climbing back through her nursery window. Safe, as if everything that had been done to the Darling family could be undone with a look. Her pale-pink lips stretched into a genuine smile.

"Ah, the Darlings. Wendy . . ." She bent over and gave Wendy a soft kiss on her cheek, following it with another one for Michael, who blushed from head to toe. She smiled at the boy.

"Are you alright, Michael Darling?" Michael shuffled awkwardly from toe to toe. Wendy heard him whisper something. She turned to her little brother.

"What was that?"

He frowned. "WENDY, STOP!"

Then he looked back up at the princess. "I said . . . you're pretty."

Then her little brother hid shyly behind Wendy's skirt.

Hook laughed. "I'm afraid she's spoken for."

"That was very sweet, Michael, thank you."

Her voice carried out to sea, and Wendy felt it deeply in her chest, like rolling thunder. Being in her presence was shattering. Wendy's eyes met Hook's, and she frowned.

"You should have told me."

Hook shook his head. "I couldn't. No one can know. It puts everything in jeopardy. If anyone knew that I knew how to get to her . . ." He shook his head. "But if I'm to ask you to go to Miath, then you needed to know everything. Even . . . this."

Lomasi was silent, staring at Wendy unnervingly before she spoke. "My brother must have liked you. I can tell you're a kind girl, one who has found herself in what must be the most distressing of circumstances."

Her brother. Keme. A wave of guilt washed over Wendy, and she found herself choking on a sob, as tears pooled at the corner of her eyes.

"It's my fault, what happened to Keme. I should have asked Owl to walk me back, or let him take me. . . ." Despair permeated every natural impulse as Wendy's hands began to shake. "I can't bring him back, but if I could . . ."

The native princess took a step towards Wendy, Wendy's pulse rising as the princess bent over, her eyes level with Wendy's. She reached out a hand and laid it on Wendy's cheek, and Wendy felt her galloping heart quiet. Her full lips parted and a hint of the glowing gold returned to her skin.

"Keme died protecting the innocent. I am very saddened by his loss, but I would not wish it differently. Justice was served, and Keme died aboard the ship he so dearly loved. He did not suffer, nor do I."

The sadness in her eyes betrayed her words. She stared at Wendy for a long moment before brushing a strand of salty curls back from her forehead.

"Do not mistake me for a teller of fortunes, nor a witch or

prophet, or some silly mythic child of the forest. I merely see what I see, and when I look into your eyes, I see . . . sound. Restraint. Mercy." She turned her head sideways and her dark eyes widened. "And I believe that the truest nature of your heart will determine the future of Neverland."

Lomasi pulled back then, and Wendy felt a sudden cold with the distance. Lomasi turned to Hook, reaching her hand up to lay gently across his cheek.

"My love, it is time to see my brother."

Hook nodded solemnly and led Lomasi towards the long-boat. Wendy and Michael stayed still, watching as Lomasi knelt beside the boat with a loud sob, her arms reaching around her brother's still form, her face pressed up against his chest, never rising.

Wendy held Michael tighter as she wished for the sea to rise and carry her far away from this raw grief, so suffocating, the guilt beating in her heart. Unfortunately, the sea stayed where it was, and so Wendy watched as Lomasi wrenched herself away from the body and stood shakily, leaning her forehead against Hook, their tears mingling together, breathing as one. Hook turned her tear-streaked face to his and spoke quiet, secret words to her. Finally, Lomasi nodded before raising her hand in the air and calling into the wind.

"Come!"

Two more figures wearing fabric accented with brown leaves appeared in the darkness, lean males not much older than Wendy who ran past her and Michael without a second look.

"Put him in the boat," Lomasi ordered, and the two men gave her a small bow before heaving Keme's enormous body onto their sculpted shoulders. As Michael and Wendy watched, the two men began making their way across the sandbar, heading the opposite direction that Hook and Wendy had come. Hook wiped Lomasi's eyes with his thumb.

"Someday, he will come and go from you once again, for all

do. On that day, his absence will grieve you no longer. It is not forever, it is just for right now."

She nodded and pressed herself against him, Hook's fingers trailing down her cheeks and down her neck. Wendy watched as a still Keme and the two Pilvi men disappeared into the mist bordering the sandbar.

"Good night," she whispered, to Keme, and she closed her eyes. "Good night, good night."

Hook reached out to her, his hand resting lightly on her arm. Wendy's eyes met his own, steely and firm, gray like the swelling mist around them.

"Bury your guilt, girl. It wasn't your fault."

Wendy stared at him for a moment before surrendering with a nod. *He was right. It wasn't her fault.* And though the grief was real, she knew it to be true. *She was not to blame.* That sin lay with Barnaby at the bottom of the sea. She repeated these words to herself as Hook pulled out his pocket watch and turned to Lomasi.

"Our time is ticking, my love. Soon, the sandbar will be underneath the sea." He sighed. "And my heart with it."

Lomasi raised her eyes to meet his before pressing her lips against his. Hook wrapped her in his arms and pulled her against his chest with a smile.

"I would lose a thousand hours of my life to spend another one with you. I would take a thousand lives to have one of our own."

Lomasi smiled at that. "You wouldn't."

Hook smiled, happy for the first time that Wendy had ever seen him.

"Try me."

Her hair circled around them both. Lomasi stood a bit straighter as she spoke her reassurances.

"Don't despair, dear love. I have great faith that one day you will defeat Peter Pan and the Shadow, and we will be able to live freely, love freely, and our children will splash in the seas of Neverland. It cannot be any other way."

Hook's eyes turned angry. "I cannot live without you much longer. It is an agony worse than any death at sea, this which you have asked of me."

The princess nodded. "I know, and it is the same for me."

She untangled herself from Hook's arms and reached out to Wendy.

"Walk with me for just a moment." Wendy took her arm, feeling the princess's skin, cool and soft, underneath her calloused fingers. "I wish that we had more time together, to truly speak. I want to know you, and I look forward to the day when I can. I believe it will come very soon."

Wendy felt lulled by her voice into a quiet, safe place. Lomasi turned to face her, her wild black hair tumbling over her shoulders.

"When you travel to Miath, take this."

She slipped a tiny bracelet over Wendy's wrist. It was very petite and looked like nothing more than a withered brown bark circle covered with dying leaves. Wendy touched it lightly with her fingers.

"What does it do?"

"It will give you strength when you need it most."

Wendy jerked her head up.

"I'm afraid I still don't understand."

"I can't tell you, because it works differently for each person. When you go into Miath, run your finger lightly over the leaves. It will awaken the magic."

Wendy shook her head. "There is much strange magic here in Neverland."

An overwhelming ache passed through her chest. She wanted to share this magic with Booth, all of it. This regal princess, the bracelet, the ethereal quality of the sandbar—the fact that she wasn't quite real here. Lomasi took Wendy's chin in her hands.

"So young, barely a woman. Would that I could take your place in Miath, I would. But the mermaids would never tell me what they know, nor would they want my blood."

Wendy raised her eyebrows.

The princess pulled her tight. "You are a stranger to our shores, and yet you would risk it all to save the lives of those you don't know. You are very brave, Wendy."

Wendy found her voice, unfurled it from the scared place it had been.

"I don't always feel brave. I feel afraid."

"We are all afraid. But those who decide to act despite their fear change the world for all of us." Lomasi reached out her palm, lying it against Wendy's heart.

"Keep your heart beating, my dear."

Wendy felt cold water licking at her toes and noticed that sea had slowly crept up the bank, narrowing the sandbar to only about eight feet. She stepped out of the water, the hem of her heavy dress dragging in the wet sand. Hook walked towards them, Michael behind him.

"It's time, my love. We must go."

Wendy could hear the desperation in his voice, the agony of leaving her ripping him apart. Hook stepped past the princess, laying his hand on Wendy's shoulders, before he cleared his throat.

"Wendy—I am sending Michael with the princess."

"What?" Wendy wrenched herself free from his grasp and circled her body protectively around Michael.

"No! Absolutely not! He stays with me!"

Michael began crying, clutching his arms desperately around her legs.

"Do not come near us!"

Lomasi stepped forward. "Wendy, we would never, ever take him from you by force. That is not what we want, but I beg you to listen to James."

James. Wendy tightened her grasp around Michael, the waves now cresting over her ankles. Hook's eyes met her own.

"Going with Lomasi is the safest thing for Michael. We are

taking you to Miath, where he cannot go with you—nor would you want him to. Not only that, but it is not safe to be on the *Sudden Night* right now, not with the *Undertow* and Peter Pan lurking around these waters, seeking our destruction. They will not get it, by gods I swear, but they will try, of that I have no doubt. It's just a matter of when." He shook his head sadly.

"The least-safe place in Neverland right now is aboard the *Sudden Night*."

Wendy ran her hands through Michael's blond hair. "But he's with me! I can . . . I will protect him." Even as she said the words, she knew it wasn't true. Lomasi bent over Wendy, who was now kneeling in the sand, clutching her little brother.

"Wendy . . . you cannot protect him from cannons, or even Peter Pan. The time will come when he will come for you—ship or no ship. War is coming to Neverland, and wherever you are, Peter will be there. A pirate ship isn't safe for a child even without all those dangers."

Hook looked pained. "She's right, Wendy. Look at what happened to Keme . . . and to you."

Wendy let out a sob and shook her head. "He's all I have left of my family. I can't leave him alone." Lomasi reached out and stroked Wendy's hair, her subtle glow pouring over them both.

"I will take Michael back with me, to where the Pilvinuvo wait. Captain Maison and Peter Pan don't know where it is. No one does—not even Hook. He will be safe there, I promise. Cared for and loved, under my personal protection. I will not let him leave my sight. We have abundant food and shelter. There are other children he can play with, his age. Wendy—it is the safest place in Neverland, a happy place. Do you trust us?"

Wendy looked at Hook and the princess for a long moment before her heart turned traitorous. *She did trust them.* She clutched desperately to Michael for one last, weak protest.

"But he's my brother."

Hook knelt over her, one arm clutching her shoulders.

"Love protects, even when it breaks your soul apart." He looked up at Lomasi, both of them blurry through Wendy's tears. "I know it to be true."

Wendy picked up Michael and walked a few feet away from the other two, setting him down on the last remaining patch of sand. His blue eyes looked up at her.

"You aren't going to leave me, right, Wendy?" His little chin trembled. "You can't leave me. We're family."

Wendy swallowed her sob, her mouth crumpling in the process.

"Michael. Hook is right. You have to go with Lomasi. She will keep you safe in a way. . . ." Her words were dissolving as she looked at her brother's distressed face, his small features twisted in betrayal.

"You're leaving me!"

His fists began hitting her shoulders. "You're leaving me! Just like John!"

He was howling now. "YOU LIED TO ME! You said you would never leave me."

Wendy brushed his tears away. "I know, I know I said that but . . ."

Her heart twisted painfully as she broke her promise, but also her own last bit of happiness in this world. She knew leaving him would be painful, but it would never compare to watching him die, something she had already done once. For the first time, the safest place for him was away from her. *Her love would have to be enough.*

"Michael. I love you, more than anything in the world, but Hook is right. You aren't safe with me, and the *Sudden Night* isn't safe anymore."

Michael sniffed.

"When it's safe, will I see you again?"

Wendy closed her eyes, and though she knew it was a lie when it came out of her mouth, she said it anyways, a thousand lies wrapped in a bright package of hope.

"I promise I will see you again. And when I do, we will go home."

Michael's eyes brightened through the steady stream of fat tears.

"Home? With mama and papa?"

Wendy nodded and a cry escaped her throat as she pulled her brother into a tight embrace, trying to make her love fall like a protective veil around Michael, her hands trying to remember the feel of his hair, the softness of his cheeks. Water rushed over their feet, and Wendy picked up her baby Michael for the last time.

"I will come back for you, but until I do, I need you to be the bravest boy in all of Neverland. I need you to stay by Lomasi's side and not get into trouble. Can you do that for me?"

Michael nodded.

Wendy cradled his head against her own as she waded through the water towards Lomasi's boat, Hook and his princess a step behind them. One of the Pilvi men reached out for Michael, who pressed hard against Wendy, her heart bleeding out at the clutches of his small arms.

"I love you, Wendy," he whispered, before letting go of her neck. "I'll be a big boy now."

Lomasi opened her hand, and Michael took it with a sad hiccup. She turned to Wendy, her brilliant beauty a comfort in this aching moment. "I will keep him safe until you can. And you, Wendy, you will figure out a way to keep us all safe." She helped Michael into the boat. Wendy reached out and took his hand, but no words passed between them. She squeezed it, one final time, hoping to give her little brother all the love and the hope she had left to give him. Hook reached underneath Lomasi's whirl of hair and gave her a slow, gentle kiss. They then stared at each other for a long moment, without words, their eyes speaking confessions that Wendy could not see. The boat was rocking in the water now, the waves swallowing, inch by inch the last remnant of the sandbar until only a tiny circle was left. Hook nodded his head to the last patch of sand, and Wendy watched in fascination as the sand began to vibrate, giving its final pebbles to the ocean below. A tiny patch of remaining sand filtered into a star pattern, the ground below it dissolved into seawater, and in its place a plant was left standing. The captain bent over, and with a quick pull of his hook, snapped the plant from its rapidly sinking root, before blowing across the top of the bloom. At the touch of his breath, the sand peeled away to reveal a bright-orange flower, splattered with black dots like the work of a frenzied painter. He reached for his love, and she leaned forward as he tucked the bloom gently behind her ear.

"Until next time, my tiger lily?"

She nodded and pressed her lips against his forehead, tears streaming from her eyes. "Until forever."

Wendy turned back and looked at Michael, who was sitting silently in the rowboat, watching her with wide eyes.

"I love you," she mouthed. He said nothing, chipping the last remaining part of her heart into the sea. Lomasi climbed into the boat next to him and raised her hand. Hook and Wendy watched the boat slide away into the mist, only a curling whorl of gray the proof that the two people they loved had ever been there. They didn't speak as they waded through the chilly water back to the rowboat, nor as Hook took the oars and navigated them back to the *Sudden Night*. Wendy stayed silent as the boat was pulled up and onto the side of the *Night*, and ignored the whispered alarms of the crew asking where Michael had gone. Queen Eryne's masthead cleared the way in front of them as the ship lurched forward, Wendy's stomach and her heart going with it.

Hook's booming voice circled out over the deck. "Smith!"

"Aye, Captain?"

"Set a course for the *Gray Shore!*"

A grave silence fell over the *Sudden Night* as her black sails billowed out to meet the wind, and she turned north, on her way to bring Wendy Darling to whatever fate awaited one so bold.

CHAPTER SEVENTEEN

It was three days sailing to Miath, and the *Night* struggled mightily to make its way through the rough waters. The sea was hungry, its choppy waves cutting into the boat again and again, as if it had risen up in defiance of their journey. Making their way up to the mainland was rough, and Wendy saw more men throwing up than she ever cared to see again. She also, had made use of her sick barrel, though to her eternal gratitude, it had been in her own bunk, where she could wretch undisturbed, in a way that was most unladylike. She did her best in the kitchen, helping the new cook, a crass pirate named Cutter Blue, to get the meals to crew, though most paled at the thought of food in their bellies on such rough seas.

On their third day of sailing, the seas relented, and an eerie calm overtook the ship. In her cabin, Wendy pulled her hair up into the messy bun that was now her hair's normal state and rolled up the sleeves of her pleated brown dress. It was time to go above deck. Missing Michael left a terrible ache in her heart, but lingering on it in isolated silence, she decided, made things much worse. The salty air was calling to her, and also a change of scenery was much needed for her dour mood.

The deck bustled with life, most of the crew working, but she spotted a few men enjoying the lulling green sea that lapped so gently at the ship's hull, a lover's caress. The sky and the sea were tinted a pale teal, the water so sparkling and clear that Wendy watched a spotted giant sea turtle, easily the size of a dining room table, swim underneath the boat. She ran to the other side of the ship, delighted to see the turtle emerge underneath the starboard, happily munching a mouthful of dark-green seaweed.

"Look!" She pointed to the nearest pirate, who happened to be Redd.

The old man squinted and raised his eyepatch. "Helps me see with the other," he explained. The wet, black slash where his eye had been moved up and down, revealing the deep hole within in. Wendy had once found it revolting, but now she barely noticed it. Redd peered at the turtle.

"Ah, yes, we call that a Lulu Leatherback! Its shell is oily, and those purple markings make it able to blend in with the coral. Likes seaweed, but it also has been known to hunt crab now and then. Gorgeous creature, ain't she? No doubt she's going to lay her eggs off the Gray Shore." He pointed. "She's headed the same way we are!"

Wendy nodded, breathless at such wild beauty. Redd snapped his eye patch back into place.

"She's outrunning the storm. Lulu Leatherbacks also make a great soup." He licked his lips. "Mmm . . . let Cutter Blue know that we're in turtle-soup waters, and that maybe he ought get to fishin' in his free time."

"I most certainly will not," replied Wendy. "Let her swim and lay her eggs."

Redd patted her hard on the back. "Aye, the weaker sex can be so soft. 'Tis nice to remember sometimes."

"I prefer the words 'vastly intelligent' to soft," smiled Wendy.

"Argh, 'course you do."

Redd stumbled away, pulling his flask from his belt before enjoying a long drink from the sweating beverage. Wendy's mouth watered.

"Enjoy this weather while it lasts—aye, there's a bad storm afoot!" Smith's voice interrupted their conversation, as it always did.

"Redd, ain't no time to be chit-chatting when there's work to be done, you gizzard sea bastard!"

Redd winked at Wendy.

"Let me know if you see any more—lots of sea creatures take shelter near the Gray Shore. It's their little playground. Safe with the mermaids, they are. Lucky beasts. What I wouldn't give to spend a day in their company!"

Voodoo laughed as he walked by, his taut brown shoulders rippling in the sunlight, a thick rope slung across his shoulders.

"If you spent a day in their company, it would be as part of their bone garden, not staring at those pretty black eyes of theirs."

"REDD!" The tip of a whip snapped the side of Redd's arm, leaving a raised welt. "If you've got better things to do at the bottom of the sea, by all means." Smith leered at Wendy just over Redd's shoulder. "Get to work. I'll not tell you again."

Redd limped away, and Wendy turned back to the sea. She could feel Smith's presence lumbering over her, his shadow swallowing her own.

"I don't know what Hook told you about Miath."

"Nothing really at all."

"That's 'cause we don't know much about it. Can't really visit the lagoon just because you feel like it. But, I can tell you something, I've seen them rip men's throats open with their bare hands. They are strong as oxes, and lovely as poison that goes down like wine. You keep your wits about you, girl. Get what you need and get back to the ship."

Wendy was moved by Smith's concern and turned to him with an amused half smile.

"Are you actually worried about me? Could it be that you are coming to like the Darlings on this boat?" She batted her eyelashes playfully at him. "Are you going to miss me, Smee?"

Smith growled in her direction and snapped the whip into his open palm.

"Don't push it girl. I'd still trade you for a fresh mango."

"Why Smith, that is positively the nicest thing you've ever said to me."

"Don't repeat it."

Evening crept in on silent paper feet, and she watched the pale-green seas grow darker. The edge of the horizon where the sun met the sea was a mottled yellow; ominous blue clouds overhead grew heavy with rain. Hook's orders rang down from the bowsprit.

"Batten down the hatches! Deadlight our girl!" and the crew was consumed with strapping down everything they could find. Non-essential crew was dismissed below deck, each carrying their own bucket and a stern warning that if the captain heard a single complaint, they would be pulled behind the ship for the duration of the storm.

Wendy locked herself into her tiny room, missing Michael dearly as she crawled into her cold bed. Unnerved by the growing heaving of the ship, she let her mind drift somewhere she never let it: memories of Peter flooded in, her lust for him and her general revulsion and terror now that she finally understood who he truly was. Part Shadow, part boy. His lies unfolded like the pages of the book before her, and her heart grew heavy with remorse at all that she had almost given him. His grin had passed through her body like a ghost. Her eyes fluttered as she could feel her body grow heavy, sinking into the waves and the straw mattress underneath her. She remembered the night in Tink's lantern, at the heat from Peter's hands that had brushed her skin, his lips trailing fire over her body.

But where her pulse rose at the memory, her brain countered. *He had dropped her. He was responsible for the death of a race, for the death of an endless stream of boys, and he had taken John from her.* Finally, her true heart chimed in, and she fell asleep in the most-comforting memory she had: being wrapped in Booth's arms, the smell of books and coffee grounds upon his skin.

Something was nudging her awake. She sat up with a gasp, flailing her arms wide, clawing out at whatever was grasping her arm. *He was here; he was back. Barnaby had come back for her.* She wrenched away from the arm, shoving herself back in between the bed and the wall.

"GET AWAY FROM ME!" she screamed.

"Good God, Miss Darling," Hook's voice crept into her ear. "We must get you some rum before you go to bed."

Wendy was flustered.

"What . . . why are you . . . ?"

"No time to talk. Get dressed and come up to the deck. I have but a few minutes before I will be needed again. It's a literal lull in the storm."

"I was sleeping, actually."

Hook held his lantern in front of his face, and Wendy was taken aback by the look of boyish excitement in his eyes. He looked positively joyful, an odd grin plastered stupidly on his face. The *Sudden Night* rocked violently to the right, and Wendy grasped onto the mattress to avoid being pitched across the room. Hook barely swayed on his feet.

"Quickly now, landlubber! Throw a cloak over your nightgown and follow me!"

Wendy paused and Hook turned away from her with a sigh. "Oh right. I forgot you are a modest girl. Of course. I'll meet you outside, but hurry!"

His patience was lost as she stumbled upon climbing out of bed, the rocking of the boat throwing her off balance.

"Oh for God's sake, here, take mine. Your sea legs are positively squiblike."

He threw his navy military jacket over her shoulders.

"C'mon, Miss Darling, you're missing all the fun." The captain threw open her hidden door, surging out into the hallway. "Up to the deck!"

The *Night* pitched rough, the bowsprit dipping and rearing its head. Wendy saw foamy water heaving outside the port windows that lined the hallway. She climbed up the Jolly Staircase, her hands pulling her up one step at a time, trying to shake the fog of deep sleep that still clouded her mind. Captain Hook pushed her up and out onto the deck, into a pounding rain violently splattering the deck. Hook motioned to her, and Wendy climbed out, taking her place under an angry sky that crackled with lightning. The *Sudden Night* pitched from side to side as dark clouds obscured the huge moon that hovered overhead, its light hidden from view. The air churned around her, fetid and unsettled, the temperature ranging from warm to freezing within a matter of seconds. The *Sudden Night* heaved and rolled forward, and Wendy was sent tumbling towards the bowsprit. Desperate not to roll into the murderous sea, she clutched desperately to the rigging. Lacerating drops of rain pounded against her face as she watched the *Night* raise itself up on a crested wave and slam back down again. She felt the impact in her bones.

"Why the hell did you bring me out here?" she screamed at Hook, angry at everything, angry for London and Booth, for Peter and John, angry about the Shadow and Michael, so far from her reach. "Are you trying to kill me?"

Captain James Hook did not hear her, no, he would not, because he was standing firm at the wheel of the ship, his face etched with pure elation.

"This is it!" he yelled to Wendy. She tightened her hands around the thick rope, almost slicing her palm open on a hidden scabbard that lay underneath.

"What?"

Hook spun the wheel counter-clockwise and then backwards a few inches, before letting it ripple again through his hands. She felt the response of the *Sudden Night*, moving under his command, the ship skirting along the tip of a wave, each one threatening, each one parting under the great black helm.

"Wendy! Haul yourself up to the crow's nest! Tell Owl that you want to *see the storm*."

"I can see it quite fine from here, thank you!"

Wendy looked back at him, his white shirt soaked and unbuttoned, his gray tipped hair blowing wildly in the wind.

"You're insane!" she screamed. She could barely keep her feet underneath her as it was.

"Go, or I'll throw you overboard!" He glanced at her quickly before his attention turned again to the wheel as a shroud of rain engulfed him. "I want you to understand!"

His voice came out of the downpour, an exclamation of ecstasy, "I love two things in this world, Miss Darling, and you've already met one of them." He turned his head to look out over the violently pitching waves. "It's time you met the other."

Wendy looked up at him, water streaming into her eyes. Hook turned away from her.

"Don't you trust me by now, girl? Climb, and be brave!"

Be brave. Booth's words.

Wendy raised her eyes. The rainwater poured into them, hot like a fever.

"Climb!" He hollered once more as the port side raised up on a swell only to slam back down. A wave of seawater rushed over the side of the boat, soaking Wendy's legs. She pushed her stringy hair out of her eyes.

"Fine! I'll climb." The word was coming out of her throat, and she let it. "Damn you!"

She made her way up to the crow's nest, foot over slippery foot. The *Sudden Night* bobbed like a black cork below her on the incensed sea. Rain poured over her as she made her way up, her hands wrapped tightly around the thick rope that cut into her dainty, dirty hands. Owl leaned over the edge of the crow's nest, his eyes covered with a soaked strip of white linen.

"Aye, girl, c'mon! One slip and you're done for!"

He turned his head to the horizon, to a line of black water, its white caps surging towards the ship.

"This storm's only got about an hour left in it! Hurry up!"

Wendy clenched her muscles and pulled herself up the mainmast, trying not to look down—which was terrifying—or straight up—which was like drowning. She ignored the nagging thought that she was climbing towards her own death.

Why did Hook want her up here? Lightning flashed across the sky, a great snaking root that illuminated the path ahead of them. Wendy reached the crow's nest and was unsure of how to get into the bucket, which gave a terrifying shriek as the boat roiled and rocked in the jaws of the sea. Owl reached down with his meaty arms, feeling around for her hand. Wendy took his hand and then, with a muttered prayer, gave him her other hand. The ship pitched and her legs swung out from under her, and for a moment, she was suspended over the void, with only Owl holding her aloft, the rest of her body dangling over the *Sudden Night*. Then the ship righted itself, and Owl pulled her up and over the sides of the barrel. Wendy instantly wrapped herself around the wooden pole.

"Ah, no you don't. You only have to climb up once more. To see the storm."

Wendy looked over at him, the only man on this ship who actually couldn't see. There was a thick rope in his hands, tethered to an iron clip that had been pounded into the mast. Owl pointed to a single wooden platform—no wider than a large book—that stood right above his head.

"Go on up the platform, girl. I'll heave you up. No, wait." Owl turned his ear to the sky, waiting, listening. "Alright, yes. You're good."

"I don't think so."

She said no, and yet when he reached out his hand, Wendy tenderly stepped onto it. He practically threw her up on the platform, her feet slipping on the wet wood.

"Here ya go!"

The blind pirate quickly looped the rope around her waist, pulling it tight through the iron rung before looping it again around her legs, binding her to the pole. He quickly tied a knot and pulled the rope tight. Wendy's back was pressed up against the thick oak of the mast. She took a deep breath in, not wanting to open her eyes. Her voice quavered.

"This seems . . . like a terrible way to die!"

Owl laughed. "Aye, it would be, though if the ship was going down, we would all die, so better there than trapped below deck, wouldn't you say?"

The pirate opened his arms wide.

"From here, you can see and feel everything." Wendy took a nervous breath as the sea opened its jaws around the *Sudden Night*.

Hook's voice carried up from below, where he was battling with the wheel. A wave crashed over him, but when it settled, he was still standing, from Wendy's perspective like a tall, proud speck of white and fire.

"What do you think, Miss Darling?" he yelled up. Wendy shook the hair and water out of her eyes.

Owl touched her foot, his voice quiet and reassuring.

"Don't look. Close your eyes and feel. *See* the storm."

The lightning flashed above her—terrifyingly close—and she felt the hairs on her arms and head rise. It should have scared her, but instead, she closed her eyes.

The first sound she heard was the waves, beating the *Sudden Night* to death, the harsh collision of wood and water, waves that cut and pounded like stone, each one a threat to the *Night,* each one burst open by her power. She heard the rain splattering the deck, sloshing from side to side, its pattern no longer as random as it seemed before. She could feel it pouring down her face, a holy baptism of salt and sea, dousing her, drowning out any thoughts of home, of Michael, of Peter and Booth.

Thunder rustled quietly once above her, as if it was clearing its throat before releasing a numbing clap of sound and power that vibrated up her spine and into her jaw. It rumbled again, its loud voice drowning out the rain and the creaking wooden heaves of the ship. She heard the labored shrieks of the rudder as it pressed against the great waters of the deep, a song as old as creation; man battling against nature, a man like Hook, who would try and many times fail to bring it to heel. *But not tonight.* The ship dipped violently downwards, enabling Wendy to feel each pitch and incline much more than she had on deck. She heard the cries of the crew below her, and Hook's voice rising above the waves. The sails flapped above her, the hard crack of fabric stretched to its breaking point echoing through her ears. Wendy shook her head, trying to sort her tumbling emotions. The feeling rising up inside of her was foreign, something she hadn't felt for a long time, a feeling that had been buried underneath layers of fear and protectiveness, under longing and the desperate instinct to survive. It tingled through her fingertips and up through her chest, nudging her heart as it went, a reminder that she had once felt it, that it had once lived inside of her.

Wendy opened her eyes in time to see the ship pitching downwards still, down a gigantic wave that roared at them with a white, frothy mouth. The ship plunged forward, down, down into the depths of death and water . . . and then spun starboard, and the wave crashed violently besides them, pushing the ship sideward before she vaulted up and over the wave.

"Yes! Take that you feisty beast!" Wendy let the feeling—that forgotten pleasure: *joy*— overtake her. The weight of sorrow that she had carried since leaving Pan Island was blown off of her shoulders as she stared into the green, penetrating eye of the storm, the maelstrom looking straight at her, seeing right into the insides of her timid heart. Then it called her by name, and she reached out for it. The storm, the danger, the waves, and the water ignited a spark in her chest that reached her face, where it broke into an insane, unfiltered smile. She felt wild and unchained.

Free.

Wendy Darling lifted her arms above her and crowed, her body rocking wildly on the edge of the crow's nest, feeling like she was flying over the chaos below, the line between life and death dangerously close.

Free.

She saw Hook look up at her with a devilish smile. He then lifted his head and crowed as well, facing the waves with a determined stare as water washed over him. The *Sudden Night* heaved her breast forward once again, and Wendy and Captain James Hook continued crowing at the waves, feeling a joy that not even the Shadow could take from them.

CHAPTER EIGHTEEN

The next morning, her eyes bloodshot as a result of the salt water, Wendy watched as two crew members struggled to throw the enormous anchor, covered with barnacles, overboard. The tired *Sudden Night* finally took her rest, rocking softly on the waves that had battered her through the night. The storm had churned the sea, but now it was a perfectly clear turquoise. It sparkled like a gem under a cloudy sky. Hook had docked the ship at the northernmost beach on the west side of the mainland. High overhead, jagged peaks of green blew in the wind. Wendy's eyes rested on the canopied valleys below, at the overgrown path that twisted like a snake through the humid jungle. Her hands shaking a bit, Wendy pulled the burlap knapsack tight over her shoulders.

"Are you sure you don't want to change?" Hook looked skeptically at her blue nightgown. "That doesn't seem practical."

"I will wear what I am comfortable wearing." Her voice dropped. "This is my dress from home. My mother mended it." She pointed to a crooked blue stitch just over her heart. "Here."

Hook nodded once before making his way to the longboat tethered at the port side. Smith climbed in beside the captain, helping Wendy down into the boat. When she looked back at the *Night,* the entire crew had gathered on deck to watch her departure. It was unnerving, and Wendy felt a tear prick her eye as they removed their hats, holding them solemnly against their chests as the longboat began its descent. It was the same gesture they had given Keme.

This was not reassuring, she thought with a grimace, wondering for the hundredth time if she was being led like a lamb to the slaughter.

A pressing sadness folded around her. The *Night* was the only true home she had known here in Neverland, and she was sad to see it pull farther and farther away from her. Hook was speaking, but she didn't hear what he was saying, his voice rolling over her like a fog. The longboat hit the water, and they moved swiftly towards shore.

Wendy turned to Hook.

"I'm sorry. What were you saying?"

His face clouded over with anger.

"Am I bothering you, Miss Darling? Perhaps distracting you from thoughts of iced cakes and warm bedsheets?"

Wendy's narrow eyes met his.

"More like, am I marching towards my death so that you can win a longstanding feud with a sixteen-year-old boy?"

His face flushed with fury.

"I don't need to tell you what you already know. The Shadow is real. Its name was spoken by you, not me. Any decision you make after hearing that truth was your own."

Wendy turned away from him, preferring to watch the *Sudden Night* grow smaller in the distance. The captain sighed before sitting by her, cautiously taking her hand in his own.

"I need to know that you are listening." His voice was soft now, concerned. She remembered all he had at stake, of the weight he carried and what he stood to lose, and she softened her tone as well.

"I am listening."

Hook raised his eyes to the island, so close now that Wendy

could see a group of small striped monkeys scurrying off the beach as their boat grew near.

"Smith will take you as far in as he can, up and over the foothills to where the Gray Shore begins. From there, take the path down the rocky side of the mountain into Miath. It's not far, but you need to move quickly, because you'll be out of my protection for the first time and above the tree line . . . ," Hook raised his eyes, "you'll be vulnerable to the sky."

Wendy swallowed the terror that rose up inside of her. She knew exactly what he meant.

"Peter."

"Yes. Quickly make your way down the rocky shore. Once you pass through Sybella, the great glass rock, you will be in Miath, and under their protection. The mermaids will then deem it appropriate to speak with you. Listen, *only speak with Queen Eryne*—no one else, do you hear me? They are evil creatures, untrustworthy."

Wendy let a small smile trace over her lips.

"I would have once said the same about pirates."

She thought she heard Smith sniffle as he leapt out into the water, pulling the boat onto the rocky sand. Hook's face didn't falter from its intense expression.

"Get to Sybella. You'll know it when you see it. Nothing will touch you once you pass through its arch, but Wendy—get there quickly."

"I understand."

"And once you are in Miath . . ."

"Captain, I know what I need to do," snapped Wendy. She turned to Hook. "I'm sorry, I'm just . . ."

Hook's gray eyes lingered on hers. "I know. Get the answers, and get out. Play to Eryne's pride. Smith will meet you off the shore in the longboat when you are finished. I hope . . . ," he trailed off.

"What?"

"I hope that the Queen's guilt is enough. Anyway, here."

Hook pulled a small present out of his coat. It was wrapped in a rich purple scarf. Wendy unraveled the scarf, gasping when something she had long forgotten fell out of it—a small white dagger, intricately carved and adorned with a tear-shaped blue gemstone.

"I thought that I lost this in the sea, the day you pulled Michael and me out!"

Hook rubbed the stubble on his face.

"I lifted it off your person right after that, as they were taking you below deck."

Wendy cradled the dagger in her palm, remembering its perfect weight. Hook leaned over her. "I have it on good authority from a nameless princess that there is some lingering fairy magic in this gem." His fingers brushed over the sapphire. "Use it if you have to."

"I hope to never use it."

Wendy tucked it into the blue ribbon that cinched her dress before standing.

The captain reached out with his hook, and Wendy took it gently in her hand, feeling the cold steel in between her fingers as he walked her off the longboat. She stepped daintily onto the sand, feeling her stomach turn queasily as her body adjusted itself: land to sea, sea to land. Wendy raised her eyes and looked straight at Hook. He had one leg up on the rowboat, the other planted firmly behind him. His navy military coat flapped in the warm breeze. He looked at the mountainous jungle behind her, his face hardening in concern before turning back to this girl, once his prisoner, now—dare she think it—a friend.

An ally.

His eyes met hers.

"Wendy Darling."

"Captain."

"Come back to my boat. That's an order."

"I sincerely plan on it, sir."

Hook gave a single nod.

"Godspeed, then."

There was nothing more to say then, so Wendy turned away from the longboat and followed Smith down the beach and into the thick swatch of trees. He said nothing to her, and so she quietly walked behind him as he slashed at the trees in front of them with a machete, hacking down fruit trees and green tangles of vines with a ferocity that alarmed her.

"Godforsaken jungle," he muttered, mutilating a bright-emerald-green tree—the color of Peter's eyes, almost exactly—with singular strikes. A dragonfly as big as Wendy's hand landed on his shoulder. Its translucent blue wings reminded Wendy of Tink for a moment before Smith reached out and crushed it in between his fingers. Wendy looked at him with alarm. He shook his head and flung the crumpled insect into the jungle behind him. Wendy heard the pitter-patter of a dozen tiny feet rushing to find their newest meal.

"Pretty buggers. They'll bite you first, and then give you a hell of a rash." He chuckled. "Kind of like the girls at Harlot's Grove."

Wendy rolled her eyes as she pushed back an enormous leaf, its surface veined with mint rivulets. They walked in silence for a few minutes, the only sounds Smith's grunts as he blazed a jagged path through the dense vegetation that surrounded them. Wendy could see the remnants of the sandy path that had once snaked its way through this jungle.

"No one has walked this way in a long time."

"Why would they? Who the hell would be out here? Men can't pass the boundary to Miath without dying, not to mention declaring open war on Queen Eryne, and trust me, if you're a pirate, the last thing you want is the mermaids to be mad at you. They can tear your ship out from under you."

Smith swung the machete upwards, slicing a vine clean at the tip. The vine fell from the tree onto Smith. He barely had time to curse before she saw it shudder before wrapping itself defensively around Smith's arm like a snake. "Godforsaken lancehead vine! Scourge of the damn jungle . . ." He uttered a string of curses as he tore at the vine. Wendy reached out to help him.

"Don't touch me!" he snapped. "It'll move to you!"

The angels and demons that decorated his arms rippled as Smith flexed them hard, one hand ripping at the vine, the other struggling to hack at it without slicing off his arm. Finally, Smith got his hand underneath it and gave a quick, hard, yank. The vine uncurled with an audible hiss, leaving a smear of blood around his forearm. Wendy uncorked her canteen and gently poured water over the wound. Steam rose from his pores as Smith gave a sigh.

"That's nice. Thank you, girl." He raised his eyes to hers, and Wendy was shocked to see that they weren't the black she had previously thought, but rather a deep brown with hints of golden flecks in the irises.

"Your eyes, they're quite pretty!"

Smith stared hard at her for a moment before shoving her backwards. Wendy landed hard on her bottom.

"Ow! Why did you do that? I was just trying to give you a compliment! You're quite rude." She stood up and brushed off her dress. "Your mood has quite diminished."

"Sorry," he grumbled. "It's the Gray Shore. Gives men the creeps." Smith picked up his machete. "We're close. No more talking."

Wendy stayed silent as they made their way towards the top of the hill. By the time they neared the top, Wendy was drenched in sweat, the back of her dress soaked and sticky. Mosquitoes had landed and died on her skin, and she smelled of the jungle: hot, fetid, and alive. The vegetation around them and the canopy of trees above them began to thin out as they climbed upwards. The verdant green gave way to soft silver and gray flowers, until all green had trailed away, leaving just shades of ash. Gray grasses blew at her feet, white flowers darted their rubbery tongues, and crooked white trees reached for the sky, their branches the texture of curdled milk. When Wendy looked backwards, she could see the lush green of the jungle behind her, so stark in contrast to the lack of color all around her. There were no bird calls here, no sounds of buzzing insects or creatures that slithered on their bellies. All was still and ghostly.

As they reached the top of the mountain, the trees gave way to jagged white rocks that started low and eventually rose up around them like whipped peaks of cream. Bleached white skulls, stacked on top of each other, leered at the travelers from the corners of rock formations, or from atop rounded rocks. Broken pieces of sea glass sat where their eyes had been, the skulls now with dead, glittering irises. Smith seemed intent on keeping his eyes on the ground, whereas Wendy looked up, taking in the growing horror that surrounded them, her pulse quickening with each step.

The path opened up as they reached the peak, becoming a wide, sandy swath. A line of skulls ran alongside their feet, marking the entrance like a wedding aisle. Smith stopped hard.

"Those bloody bitches! This line was much farther down last time I checked."

Lying directly across the path was a thick line of human bones and pearly pink seashells. The hazy sun bounced off the beautiful shells nuzzled up close with the remains of what must have been a hundred men. Wendy stopped walking, her breath catching in her throat. Her heart hammered, and she felt weak at the knees.

"Oh no you don't, girl. Don't faint. Take a breath."

Wendy rested her hand on her chest. "I won't faint. I just need . . . a minute."

She closed her eyes and rested her hands on her knees, trying to forget the death that sat all around her. The prying eyes of the skulls had awakened her fear, coaxing it to life, whispering dark unspeakable things. Not wanting to move forward, she called up the image of Michael's face, of what she had to lose if she didn't succeed.

It worked.

Wendy opened her eyes to see Smith towering over her, his shadow engulfing her small frame. "This line is the boundary—I cannot go any farther. From here, there is a path down the rocky side of the mountain. It's not too steep, so you should be able to move quickly."

Wendy turned to him. "So that's it, then."

Smith nodded. He looked at her for a moment before reaching out and awkwardly patting her shoulder.

"I'm ... er ... ," he struggled, for once, with words. "Good luck, lass."

Wendy nodded and turned away from him, facing the downward path to the Gray Shore. Her heart pounded in her ears as she walked slowly towards the line of shells and bone. With a small step, she crossed it, scuffing dirt over it as she went. Smith raised his pistol to the sky, his eyes tracing the clouds. He turned in a circle, taking in every inch of the horizon before turning back to her, a single word dropping from his mouth.

"Run."

Wendy felt her feet move slowly underneath her as she jogged forward, her feet falling faster and faster until she finally was able to pick up speed, sprinting away from the boundary line.

The path down the Gray Shore was a series of escalating switchbacks, followed by a long, flat path. She made her way as quickly as she could down the side of the peak, her feet slipping on the gravel as she went, her hands jagged from grasping rocks to keep her from falling, rounding sharp corner after sharp corner, her feet sending rocks skittering over the perilous edge of the hill. She kept her eyes only in front of her as she ran, names bouncing from her lips with each step, their happiness a reminder why she needed to move swiftly.

Michael. John. Booth. Mama. Papa. Hook.

Wendy.

As she neared the bottom of the foothill, she could see the tip of Sybella peeking out over the boulders. The closer she got, the larger it grew, until she could see it fully, looming above the shore, a great sea-glass rock, a behemoth monolith, flat on the top with rounded sides and a small opening in the middle. Her footsteps pounded underneath her, a rhythm most erratic; her breaths pushed out in gasps.

Why didn't I run more on the Sudden Night*?*

The thought amused her, if only for a second. She pumped her arms as her chest roared its disapproval, her lungs heaving with each step. She reached the bottom, a long stretch to the shore unfolding itself before her, perhaps only a half a mile away.

Almost there.

Her relief was shattered by the sound of a pistol shot far above her, and Smith shouting something, his voice carried away on the wind whipping off the shore. *No. No.*

Wendy didn't have to hear his warning, because she knew it already in her heart.

He was here.

She could feel Peter's presence in the follicles of her hair, lust and hatred rising up in her chest with a murmur of regret and a whisper of terror. If she was blind, she would have known that he had arrived. She sprinted, her feet carrying her as fast as she could go, practically flying now, her legs carrying her closer and closer to Sybella. Her only thought was that she would make it; she would, *she had to.*

Pebbles scattered under her feet as she raced forward, her eyes on the glass, its reflection shifting from green to blue in the filtered morning light. Another pistol shot blasted in her ear, and then another. She ran. A shadow passed over her head, once and again, circling now, like a buzzard. The momentary distraction caused her foot to slide off a small rock in her path and her ankle rolled, sending her sprawling into the dust. Her whole body gave a shudder at the jarring impact as she slammed into the ground. His voice dripped like poison honey.

"Oh, Wendy, you're the opposite of graceful."

The cruel, familiar voice taunted from above.

"Beautiful, yes. Smart, undoubtedly. Graceful, no. Fast . . ."

His voice was close to her now; his lovely mouth brushing her ear.

"Not fast enough."

She slid to a stop, her breaths heaving from her open mouth. A wave of red blood was dripping down her knee. Wendy closed her eyes for just a second, recovering, gathering. Her hand closed around the jagged edge of a seashell.

Get up.

She had barely hit the ground before she was pushing herself to her feet, running again.

His soft voice cut through the air, cut through her mind.

"I can't tell you how nice it is to see you again. I've missed you, Wendy."

Sybella was close now. She could see the distorted skulls, animals and human, that filled the inside of the blue-green glass, their mouths forever open in screams. Instead of the fear that it inspired at a distance, Sybella now pulled her closer, the glass humming with a familiar song, lulling, hypnotic, deadly—that same song that had pulled Wendy out into the ocean. It was that same seduction, only this time she was running for her life, unable to focus and so it drifted past her, curling off her skin like mist off the ocean.

How ironic, she thought, plunging forward, her lungs cutting for breath, that she now ran so desperately towards danger. *It depends,* her mind whispered, *on what is chasing you.*

She heard the air tunneling above her, Peter plunging downwards.

"You can't outrun me, you know," he shouted gleefully. "I'm not sure why we are pretending that you can."

He reached out and tugged playfully on one of her curls. Blood from her knee was splattering the ground with each step now.

She wasn't going to make it.

She saw stars exploding in her vision as her chest ripped apart with pain, her legs trembling with exhaustion. That same body betrayed her now, crying out for her to stop, to surrender to Peter, to his arms and his will. She could take the rest she had so earned; it would be so easy. He was right above her now. She could feel his breath on her face, his scent clean like pine trees and berries, a scent that she had once dearly loved. She felt his fingers brush her cheek.

"You are looking much more . . . rugged than the last time I saw you."

Wendy gasped for air, a cramp piercing her side. She was almost to Sybella, almost there. . . . She reached out her arms. . . .

Peter's voice turned cold.

"I'm not sure I like this new look." He tsked-tsked. "Oh, and you were *so close.*"

Then he swept her feet out from under her. She flew forward, towards the rock, bracing herself to hear the crack of her bones, but Peter caught her midfall. She felt his hands wrap around her waist, felt the ground pull away from her, felt the sudden weightlessness of flight and the heat of his skin.

She plunged the seashell deep into his hand.

Wendy felt Peter's skin give way to the softness underneath, and worried that she would be sick. Instead, she yanked the shell out of his hand and clasped it tightly against her chest. Peter roared and jerked his hands off her waist in surprise. Wendy tumbled roughly to the ground. She landed hard on her side, but scrambled into a crouch before throwing her body desperately forward. Peter lunged for her once more, but she passed through Sybella's open archway, curling her body behind her so that all of her was swallowed beneath its wide curve. As she gasped for breath, the melodious song coming off the rock absorbed her into protective folds. Ancient magic was passing through her skin, inspecting and approving.

The rock wanted her, she could feel it. She pulled herself forward, the archway of Sybella soaring above her. Wendy climbed to her feet, stopping for a moment to stare in wonder at the sea glass that now surrounded her. There was no reflection of her bruised face, only the skull of some forgotten sea monster, its narrow jaws unhinged. Wendy gasped, her fingers trailing inches over the surface. Inside of the glass were *waves*. Tiny waves, moving so slowly that unless you were inches from the glass, you wouldn't be able to see them. Sybella wasn't solidly sea glass—no, she contained the sea. The water was alive, and somehow trapped forever inside of her.

Wendy didn't dare touch the glass, even though every reckless part of her longed for it. Stepping slowly forward, she passed out from under the archway. A short path down to the water continued in front of her, weaving its way in between boulders, the same sky open above her. All was the same and yet, not at all. The air around her changed—it hung with a potent heaviness. There had been a strong wind coming off the sea, and now all was perfectly still. The scent of salt water filled the air, mingled with the fragrance of frangipanis. Wendy looked down, noticing that her knee no longer bled, nor was it scraped. Her wounds had been healed.

"Incredible!" she murmured.

"Isn't it, though?"

Wendy Darling turned around slowly, then leapt backwards with a shout. Peter was right behind her, floating at Sybella's open entrance, perhaps only eight feet from where she stood. The air in the archway between them had a strange quality to it. She could see through it, though it occasionally wavered and leapt, as if she was looking through a fine wall of water. Peter Pan was cradling his bloody hand against his chest.

"You stabbed me." He gave a hysterical laugh. "I'm disturbed, and somewhat aroused."

Wendy said nothing, her eyes watching him as he began to pace back and forth in front of the open archway. His eyebrows lowered, and a look of real concern passed over his face.

"I don't know what you are doing in Miath, or why you would come to this place. This is dangerous, Wendy! Do you really understand what you're doing?"

His voice rose a few octaves.

"Wendy, listen, you're not safe here. Go back to that bastard Hook if you must, but don't go to the lagoon. I'll leave if you promise not to go. You can't begin to understand the deep magic that rests on these shores. Queen Eryne is crazy. They'll kill you!"

He paused, his emerald-green eyes alarmed.

"Wendy—I can't protect you here!"

She narrowed her eyes.

"The only thing I need protecting from is you."

Peter threw his head back dramatically.

"Oh yes, protection from Peter Pan, the boy who only wants to love you."

"You don't want to love me. You want to own me."

Peter's eyes clouded with navy—the Shadow!—before meeting her own. His tone became flirtatious, playful.

"I know the fire that rages under your skin. I know that even though you hate yourself for it, you want me. And if you gave yourself to me, I would consume you and you would let me, happily."

Wendy's skin flushed at his words, knowing they were true. Her eyes traced the fine line of his jaw, the handsome, carefree smile that was plastered across his face, even as blood dripped down his arm.

"But that's not what I want, something that never mattered to you."

Peter sighed, exasperated. "Aren't you tired Wendy? Tired of running? Tired of bleeding? Tired of Hook and his crazed fairytales?"

Peter flew closer to Sybella's archway. She could see the way his red hair curled over his forehead, could see the pale pink of his lips, the gleaming white of his teeth. "Aren't you tired, Wendy, of turning away from your own desires? Don't you see? You and I, we can live together, with both of your brothers, on Pan Island." His navy eyes lit up as he continued. "All that I have could be yours. We could be a family."

An image came to Wendy then, an image from a story she had seemingly heard in another lifetime: Peter, standing over the body of Hook's father, murdered for not choosing Peter over his own son.

"Come and get me then."

Peter snarled, but he didn't move forward. Men could not pass through Sybella, and she could feel the magic humming around her. Peter feared it, this distinctly female power.

"Leave me be, Peter." Wendy turned to go. The air above her was open and clear . . . and somehow safe.

Peter's voice rose, infuriated.

"Soon, you will fall into my arms and beg for my love. I know it. I'll be the only one you want."

Wendy stepped backwards.

"I have to go. Good-bye, Peter."

His beautiful face erupted into a distorted madness as he began screaming at her as she walked away.

"No one turns their back on Peter Pan. No one! Do you hear me! I will kill every living creature in Neverland if I have to. These seas will turn red when I am done. You and your good friend Hook haven't seen anything yet. I swear on the lives of your brothers, YOU WILL LOVE ME!"

His diabolical rant continued, each word a splinter in her heart.

"Do you hear me? I WILL TAKE EVERYTHING YOU LOVE.'"

He kept shouting at her, his voice roaring in her ears, growing ever dimmer as she made her way off of the Gray Shore and into Miath.

CHAPTER NINETEEN

A large cluster of lean, jagged boulders separated Sybella from the shore. Foreboding, they hovered above Wendy's head, their peaks dusted white, not with snow, but with the fine dust of crushed bone. Wendy passed in between the slivers of rock, trying in vain to wipe Peter's blood off her hands and onto her dress. *I will take everything you have.* Though her heart still thundered at the sudden violence of their interaction, seeing Peter was somehow exactly what she needed. *This was why she was here.* It renewed her purpose, her strength. The look in his eyes, the power in his words and touch, this was why she needed to speak with the mermaids, so that one day Neverland—and her family—could be free from his tyranny, from a game built on the corpses of men and boys.

Wendy passed by a series of dwindling rocks, arranged now in a wide circle. Vegetation had started to creep back onto the rocks; white leaves tumbled down the rocks in a cascade of vines, not unlike the green ivy that once crawled around her nursery window.

Wendy . . .

The haunting song that she had heard pulling from the glass of Sybella entered her ears once again: an intimate lullaby that bathed her skin, stripping her bare in the process.

"We've been waiting for you, Wendy. Come to us."

The rocks closed over Wendy's head, and she stopped walking. The path had ended, and ahead of her was a curtain of blue-and-green veined ivy, the leaves thicker than her palm. Crisp notes of the sea filled her nostrils as she peered at the curtain, and the voices of the mermaids rose to a deafening chorus, each singing their own song, each perfectly in harmony with each other. The voices barreled past her, passing her over like a rock in the sea. Wendy looked backwards and saw Sybella twinkling in the sunlight, the waves inside of her pulsing in cadence with the mermaids' song. *They were singing to her, the rock.* She turned back to the curtain of ivy, which blew outwards, opening for her, though she felt no breeze on her skin. She swallowed once, working to quiet the doubts and fear pushed against her chest.

Wendy squared her shoulders and slipped through the curtain, letting the wet leaves brush over her curls. On the other side, a wide lagoon opened up in front of her, perhaps a half mile around. Vibrant colors, almost violent in their lushness, assaulted her from every surface: amaranth pinks and lemony-yellow corals exploded out from under the perfectly blue water; mossy rocks of emerald rose up out of the pool, their round stones covered with purple flowers, their lapping tongues dotted with creamy swirls. Flora covered every inch of the lagoon, and she watched silently as trees dripping with pink blossoms fell leisurely into the pool. There was no beach, no sand, rather just a steep drop off of the moist ground that Wendy stood on straight down into the water. She struggled to regain her focus, her senses assaulted by the beauty around her. A strange high-pitched squeaking emanated from the clear blue water, and she crouched down, peering over the edge.

The water was still momentarily, before something flung a stream of water in her direction. Wendy leapt back with a shriek. A large creature stared back at her, the length of a horse, but shiny and rubbery, with smooth gray skin and a thin, bottled nose. It opened its mouth and squeaked happily at her. There was a small black hole in its head and, when Wendy looked back at it, a thin puff of steam and water ejected from it. Eyes like marbles peered at her, and Wendy felt an overwhelming sense of gentleness from this serene creature.

Cautiously, she lay on her stomach and reached out her hand, slowly reaching towards the creature who watched her with knowing eyes. The animal raised its nose to her fingers, Wendy realizing too late that it was not smelling her, but rather Peter's blood, when it jerked away with an unhappy squeal. It disappeared under the water, and Wendy frowned, missing the peace she had felt in it presence. A dolphin, that's what it was. She had seen them once in one of papa's picture books.

"Come back!" she whispered.

The lagoon was still for a moment before the dolphin vaulted itself upwards, displaying an amazingly sleek form before landing sideways, splashing Wendy with a wave of water. She leapt backwards, water dripping from her nose and hair, and clapped her hands.

"Well done!"

The dolphin gave a playful splash of his fin, soaking her once more and then disappeared under the lagoon.

"Bravo!" Wendy cried, elated.

"I see you've met Maji."

Without looking, she knew it was the queen.

Wendy pushed to her feet, slowly stepping backwards from the edge of the lagoon. The voice echoed across the lagoon, streaming down from the high stone walls, the flowers, the grass, everywhere and nowhere at once. Beautiful and cruel, it cracked Wendy's confidence.

"It's nice to finally meet you face to face, Wendy Darling. We have heard much about you."

The water in the lagoon, previously still, began swaying back and forth in small waves. The waves grew larger, cresting in a

circular pattern that wove around the rocks, one wave crossing through another, creating a small vortex around the rocks.
The entire lagoon vibrated with a low hum, as the reverberating
chorus rang across the water.

Queen Eryne rose out of the center.

Wendy's parents had taught her never to swear, that it was
unladylike and crass.

And yet, her mouth fell open with the familiar words, all of
her proper etiquette falling away.

"Holy Mary, mother of God."

Chapter Twenty

Wendy shrank back from the edge of the water, her eyes blinking rapidly, trying to take in what she was seeing. It was too much, the colors of the lagoon, the blue of the water, and here, a mermaid whose beauty actually burned her eyes. Without her permission, a salty tear rolled down her cheek and splattered the front of her gown. Held aloft by a muscular tail that glistened in the wavering light of the lagoon, Queen Eryne rose over the swirling water, her eyes hungrily resting on Wendy. Buoyed by the push of the water, the queen slid easily onto one of the rocks at the center of the lagoon with a wet slap. She casually curled her fingers in Wendy's direction and three mossy rocks pushed themselves out of the water, sending a handful of chittering blue crabs scurrying back into the lagoon.

"Come closer, Miss Darling. Mermaids are able to see many things, but far away isn't one of them."

Wendy stepped forward, her slipper squishing in the wet ground. The creature that had been so playful now appeared by the queen's side, squirting water over her massive tail, squeaking happily as she stroked its slick maw with a long, pale hand. Moving carefully over the slippery rocks, Wendy started to make her way over to a small adjacent rock that sat close to the queen's mossy throne. The water, once a clear blue was now filled with strange undulations of blue and purple, marked with flashes of black marble. Wendy blinked and looked again as a bubble of horror rose up inside of her. They were mermaids. Under the water, shifting and moving, slithering through one another, hundreds of them followed her steps from underneath as she moved from rock to rock. Wendy stopped walking.

"I think I'll stay here, thank you."

Queen Eryne gave her an amused smile.

"Now that you are here in Miath, do you not think that you're completely at our mercy? Even the pirates fear us, small men looking down from their lofty boats, not knowing that they sail on their death, that the sea whispers their names day and night."

The queen wiggled her fingers as if she were toying with their mortal thread. Wendy settled carefully onto her knees, her blue dress in a circle around her. She tried to keep her face emotionless, but the beauty of the queen was overwhelming, distracting.

The queen sighed.

"Look your fill, child. Most humans will never see what you see, so gaze away. We were designed by the gods, not meant for this world, but our own."

Hook's words whispered in her mind. *Play to her pride.*

"You are indeed beautiful. I couldn't even imagine . . . ," Wendy paused, "not even in my imagination could one create such beauty."

At least there was no need to lie. Cascades of wavy hair fell in lustrous curls around the queen, celestial blue and pale violet mixed with strands of shimmering gold. Atop her head sat a crown of what Wendy at first had thought was coral, but now saw was actually made of human bones. Their crooked arms reached away from her head and pulled towards the jewel of her crown—the skeleton of a seahorse, forever preserved in a glass bubble. Thick lashes of the same blue and violet as her hair set off the queen's ashen-blue and fathomless eyes, which blinked at Wendy. She had a sharp Roman nose and harshly drawn cheeks that pointed downwards to lips covered in miniscule, pearled scales, a multifaceted shade that changed and shifted in the light. When she spoke, her mouth twinkled with stars of jade. Her skin was the palest cream, utterly without blemish, as though she was made of carved marble.

She reminded Wendy of one of Michelangelo's statues—the hard lines, the curved perfection of flesh—that had made her blush when she had seen a picture of it. The queen's large palms, adorned with six fingers on each hand, now smoothed out her hair. She wasn't wearing anything, and Wendy blushed as her eyes moved down her torso to the massive tail that flopped like a gutted fish on the rock. The tail was covered in scales that spread out in a circular pattern, their overlapping colors reminding Wendy of a peacock. Water streamed off the tail and dripped into the lagoon, where dozens of other mermaids were swimming silently underneath, their movements frenzied, agitated. Wendy's hand trembled. Queen Eryne's voice poured over her.

"They won't touch you without my command. Do not be afraid, not yet."

Wendy bowed her head respectfully. It was time to get what she came for.

"Queen Eryne, I have come here seeking answers. Answers that I believe—"

The queen cut her off, leaning forward so that her eyes met Wendy's across the water.

"I know what answers you seek, foolish girl. How dare you come into my lair and presume to tell me what I will tell you? The sea knows all your secrets, every spoken word since the beginning of Neverland. She is ancient and wise, and you are a speck of dirt that she will swallow, and you will pass to nothing." She waved her long arm in disgust. "As they say in your world, dust to dust."

Wendy could not hold back her surprise. "My world?"

"Oh yes, I know all about the world you come from. They are

all connected, though in ways you couldn't begin to imagine. The seas are separate but one, and one wave from Neverland knows every wave in your world's ocean. Waves pass from one world to another all the time, through deep crevasses that comb through the oceans, unknowable, unpassable."

Wendy felt the trace of a smile on her face, somehow comforted knowing that the water that surrounded her here in Neverland was the same water that battered up against Britain's shores. Perhaps her family wasn't as far away as she believed.

Then again, she was staring at a mermaid.

Queen Eryne flapped the end of her tail impatiently against the rock, thin filaments of deep red, soft greens and blues spread out in a feathery texture on the stones.

"Are you, child, aware of the cost?"

Wendy swallowed.

"Yes. My blood, my blood in exchange for answers."

The queen shook her head.

"Not just your blood. Your virgin blood."

She raised an impeccably arched eyebrow, dotted with tiny pearls at both ends. Wendy felt a blush rising up her cheeks.

"Yes."

She beckoned Wendy closer, and Wendy leaned forward, not wanting to get within an arm's length of the queen, who swayed slightly back and forth as she watched Wendy, like a cobra ready to strike.

"We could have had it all already, your blood. It's a pity."

Wendy flinched at the awful memory—being pulled down, the sound of the song as she struggled to breathe. . . .

"Peter saved me that day."

"Peter Pan!" The queen spit the words. "That pompous boy. What right did he have to take what was rightfully ours, what wandered into our home due to their own weak spirit? Bah!"

She waved dismissively at Wendy, and a narrow sluice of water echoed up the side of the lagoon.

"If you only understood the value in your worthless veins."

Her eyes lit up hungrily.

"Your blood feeds our coral garden, one that begins just below your feet and runs out to farthest reaches of the Neverland seas. It provides nourishment for thousands and thousands of living sea creatures, mermaids and anemone." She gestured to the lagoon. "It's what makes these colors so bright. The blood enhances everything it touches, from the crested shark to an oyster shell." She shook her head. "It is most unfortunate that only virgin blood of a girl has the power to make our coral gardens flourish. Daily I wish it was the blood of useless men and boys . . . " she gestured towards the sea.

"Well, between the pirates and the Lost Boys, we would never have to worry again."

Wendy suddenly felt very protective of her pumping heart. She crossed her arms over her chest.

"I have not come to *give* my blood. I have come to *trade* some of it for answers." She cleared her throat. "I must know how to defeat the Shadow."

Queen Eryne snapped her head backwards, rolling her neck from side to side.

"I knew that's what you wanted. I knew that you would invoke its wicked name in front of my sisters."

There was a distressed hiss from under the writhing waters, and a jarring cacophony of notes filled the air.

"The Shadow upsets my people."

Wendy stepped backwards. Fear, its fine fingertips tracing up her spine, crowded her mind.

"We know you must have helped him."

"You know nothing!"

The queen's pitch was high and strangled, and scattered pieces of sea glass that littered the lagoon cracked. The queen raised her head, peering at Wendy from under her massive bone crown, her pale eyes simmering with anger.

"Fine. The deal is struck. Your blood for the answers you desire and then you will know the truth." The queen shivered with anticipation. "I will take what I need and not one drop more."

Wendy struck out her hand, a business move that she had seen her father do many times. The queen laughed.

"You silly girl. The trade is made when the blood hits the water."

She lunged towards Wendy and grabbed her roughly by the arm. Her grip was so strong that Wendy unable to even twist away. Queen Eryne dragged her violently down to the lowest mossy rock in the lagoon before laying her face up on the stone.

"It'll go quickly, passing before you like a dream."

Wendy closed her eyes and mouthed a prayer as she felt the cool water of the rock begin to seep into her hair. Queen Eryne perched above her, Wendy now close enough to smell the nauseating scent on her breath, a potent mix of raw fish and the aroma of fresh flowers. Wendy's arm was stretched out so that her wrist lay above the water, and she gasped in horror as the heads of six mermaids rose out of the lagoon around it. Water streamed from their incandescent hair, and she watched as their eyes changed from marbles of black into the clear, glassy eyes of Queen Eryne. They stretched their hands out of the water, each one holding a conch shell, their singing voices beginning to calm Wendy, even in her distress. The words washed over her, a serene lullaby of the sea and sky, and though her mind protested she felt her heart slowing and her breaths becoming deep and rhythmic.

The queen leaned over her and kissed her cheek softly. "Don't be afraid, sister. You are one of us, though we be of different species, we are both women. Just breathe, and I will tell you what your heart seeks to know: a story of shadows and broken hearts."

Wendy felt something thin and hard slice her wrist. She flinched and turned her head just time to see a bone knife, its sharp tip now tinged with red, drop into the water. A tiny trail of dark red dripped down her wrist and fell into the lagoon below. One of the mermaids, her shimmering blue-green hair pulled up with a comb of jagged coral, looked at the queen. "It is good, your majesty." All the mermaids then looked at Wendy hungrily, and she wished that she had never stumbled into this den of starving wolves.

I will be brave, I will be brave, I will . . .

The queen grabbed her chin, turning Wendy's head from her bloody wrist.

"Don't look at them. Look at me. Hear my words."

And with that Wendy surrendered, letting the queen's words weave her, like silk on a loom. Lulling blue light flickered across the scales on her lips.

"You ask me how to defeat the Shadow, and how to defeat Peter Pan. One I can tell you, but the other I cannot. Peter Pan is simple—the boy is after all, still a mortal, and can be killed as easily as any other man. A knife, poison, drowning. But the Shadow . . ."

The queen leaned back, and Wendy saw two thin gills that ran up the sides of her long neck. They flapped open and closed as she spoke, her words rolling over Wendy's skin like drops of rain.

"You should know that it wasn't my fault, I never meant . . . ," she sighed. "I knew Peter when he first came to Neverland, still very much a regular boy, not able to fly. I met him on a rowboat in the middle of the sea, where he was attempting to fish. He had been singing, and his voice, it called to me. I spared his life in exchange for a song, and he sung me the most-beautiful tale, of an old man called Wick, and an emerald-green shore."

Wendy felt a tendril of nausea curl inside of her. She wondered what version of this story Peter had told Queen Eryne. *A poor child at the mercy of his brothers and sisters? Or had he told her the truth—that he was a rich, spoiled son of the manor, who abused his servants and serfs?*

"I continued to visit him after that, on the shores of his home on Pan Island, and we spoke of many things, many ancient things—intimate things."

Wendy blinked. She was beginning to feel a slight pain creep up from her wrist.

"I invited him to visit Miath under my protection, and he did. We can grant permission to visit our shores to whomever we choose, but we normally extend it to none." She paused. "It had been so long since we had a man in our mist. The decision angered some of my clan."

Underneath the water, Wendy heard the chorus of cries, a lamenting dissent. They were listening to the queen's every word.

"We grew . . . closer. He began to visit here often, and gained the favor of many of us, though there were some that doubted his intentions. I ignored their voices, because this mortal boy confused my mind. He manipulated my emotions through some sort of mortal witchcraft. . . ."

Wendy gasped. "You loved him. You fell in love with him."

The queen gripped Wendy's shoulders, her six fingers digging into Wendy's collarbone.

"Mermaids do not believe in your pitiful human concept of love. In your world, it is used to excuse the most horrible of behaviors. It leads to the downfall of great civilizations, and makes slaves of women. Do not ever again accuse me of love."

The pool had gone silent, and Wendy knew that she had stumbled upon a truth.

Queen Eryne had fallen in love with Peter Pan. Of course.

Wendy was more empathetic that she would have liked to be. She knew how easy it was, how one lingering look from those green eyes could undo any reservation, how one cheeky smile, meant only for you, was the sun shining on the secrets part of your soul, bringing you into the light. Wendy shifted and felt a tiredness seeping into her bones.

How much blood had they taken? How long had it been? The lagoon seemed a bit darker than when she had arrived. Her mouth was dry and crusted.

"The Shadow . . . tell me about the Shadow," she gasped. Queen

Eryne looked sideward, a look of shame passing over her etched features.

"Fairies," she spat. "It all started with the fairies. Prideful, prancing creatures they were. They ruled over Neverland and declared it all under their control—even the trees and the mountains, which belonged to the Pilvinuvo Indians. They declared rule over the rivers and lakes, the seas and all its creatures, though they belong to us. The fairies wanted to rule everything, claiming that their benevolent peace was the best standard for all beings. They knew nothing of our ways. BAH!" Her tail lashed behind her angrily.

"Fairies and their silly songs, that's really who is to blame. Peter Pan was obsessed with them, particularly their ability to fly." The queen scoffed, jealously seeping through her words.

"Flying, like it's such an admirable thing! Soaring through the air like some silly butterfly. Not only do mermaids have the ability to swim, we also breathe in both land and sea! We of the salt water and rock, Peter did not deem us worthy of his admiration, oh no. It was the fairies that he wanted to be like. He had tried to befriend them as he did us, and they would not have him."

She paused, a droplet of water running down her face. A black forked tongue emerged from her lovely mouth and picked it off her lip. Wendy thought she might be sick.

"Though, looking back, I do believe that Qaralius, their king, saw a darkness in Peter that I did not. He was not blinded by the same . . . afflictions." A salmon-pink blush ran up her face. "Peter begged me to intervene on his behalf with the fairies. He was obsessed. I wanted to please him, because he threatened to leave us and never visit again."

An angry moan rose up from below the waters, mournful and dirgelike. Wendy was feeling very, very tired. The queen looked down for a moment at her clan, circling like sharks below Wendy's wrist.

"He was going to leave us. What else was I to do?"

A chorus of angry cries rose up from the water, and the lagoon pitched with angry waves. The queen's voice rose angrily.

"I hear you, my sisters! I know I shouldn't have told him. It was a grave mistake. I have made amends. Quiet your voices!"

The lagoon immediately went still, and the queen sighed.

"I didn't want him to leave. And so I told him about The Song That Calls the Shadow. When the fairies called it, I could feel it moving from wherever I was." Her voice saddened. "Then, its presence was light, and warm. Kind." She shook her head as her eyes narrowed.

"I thought he would mock them for their silliness. Instead, Peter listened to the song, called the Shadow, and bound it to himself. Mad that the fairies had snubbed him, Peter ordered the Shadow to kill them. Perhaps even more importantly, he knew that Qaralius was the greatest threat to his power and he wanted him out of the way."

"But he saved Tink," whispered Wendy.

"Yes. During the massacre he ordered, he ordered the Shadow to spare Tink, and led her to believe that he saved her. In return, she gave him speed, flight, and the ability to never age. I believe that when she did that, Peter's relationship with the Shadow became even darker."

Wendy's eyes fluttered. *Stay awake,* she ordered herself, *stay alert!* The mermaids below her hissed. Something was yanking hard on Wendy's wrist, squeezing the veins of her arm. She flinched.

"And now?" Wendy whispered. The queen straightened her spine.

"I have felt the Shadow stir only once since the fairies were massacred."

Wendy shivered. *The Sunned Shores.* The queen's voice dropped, a quiver unmistakable.

"It is a cold, dead thing, full of malice. It tore through the fairies like paper. They were strong creatures and they were no match for it. I heard their screams from the bottom of the sea, in the deepest trench of our ocean."

The queen looked disturbed at the memory.

"Now we are all held hostage by that same cruel boy, the boy who once played here, in our lagoon. The same boy who once made me believe in fantastic things."

Wendy's voice was barely a whisper. She forced herself to keep her eyes open.

"You fear the Shadow."

"I fear nothing!" The queen tightened her grasp on Wendy's arm. Blood spurted into the lagoon to a chorus of happy mermaid sighs. "But Neverland will never be free, not while the Shadow lies in wait. We are held prisoner in our own paradise."

"Where is the Shadow?"

The queen gave a low hum, its sound echoed off the walls of the lagoon, like the cascade of harp strings.

"It rests now in the Forsaken Garden, that once magnificent fairy city. It sleeps, until Peter calls it once again. And yet, at the same time it resides in the Forsaken Garden it also resides inside of Peter."

Wendy tried to push herself to sitting.

"What is the rush, my dear?" Wendy yanked her arm upwards and was alarmed at how pale it was. Blue veins stood in stark contrast to her white skin. She shivered, suddenly freezing in this warm lagoon. When she looked out across the blue water, she saw hundreds of black eyes watching her, their floating swirls of hair undulating gently underneath the surface. She looked back at the queen and lifted her chin indignantly.

"While I thank you for your story, you still have not answered my question. How does one defeat the Shadow?"

The queen watched her, her clear eyes of glass flitting back and forth over Wendy's face.

"Oh, child. You must know that I can't let you leave here. Your blood is too precious, and my girls are hungry. The seas need the nourishment. A noble sacrifice for Neverland! You should feel lucky to have such an honor."

Wendy pushed herself upwards onto her knees, trying desperately to keep conscious as she her head spun.

"Tell me," she sputtered, "how is it defeated?"

The queen laughed.

"I thought it was obvious from my story. I apologize. It's all inside of the song. First, you must pull the Shadow from Peter. It must be unbound from him in the exact same way it was bound to him."

"And the song?"

"There are only two who know it. The one who bears it, and the one who fears it."

"Don't speak to me in riddles!" snapped Wendy, her patience short. The queen blinked.

"I do not know of riddles. I speak only the answers of the sea."

Her time here was growing short. Wendy could feel the tension rising in the air.

"And once we call it? Once the song is sung exactly as it once was?"

The queen rose up off the rock, slithering her body so that her face was level with Wendy's.

"Then it will be freed from Peter, which might be even more dangerous, for no one will have control over it. The Shadow must be freed and then immediately destroyed."

Wendy shook her head.

"How does one kill a Shadow? How would you kill death?"

The mermaid grimaced.

"With an act of pure light. Only pure light will rend the darkness."

"And what might that be?"

The mermaid queen shook her head.

"I am unfortunately at the end of my knowledge about the

Shadow. I have told you everything you have asked, true to my word."

She cupped one of her hands gently around Wendy's face.

"Now, let me sing you into a soft slumber, and you will pass peacefully from this world to the next, knowing your blood will feed our seas for a hundred years."

Wendy's stomach heaved, and she leaned forward, hands on her knees to avoid a wave of nausea.

"No. No! We had a deal."

Her legs crumpled like ribbons when she tried to climb to her feet. Crawling, Wendy began making her way slowly towards the edge of the mossy rocks, panic rising in her chest.

"I'm sorry, my dear. But this is just how it has to be. A crab that wanders into an octopus den does not leave alive."

Wendy's heart beat slowly. Red continued to drip from her wrist, her own blood mingling with Peter's dried blood. *She had to think of something. Something, anything. Think. Think.* Wendy gasped and lifted her head, forcing her voice to remain strong, not filled with the fear that was swallowing her whole.

"You will let me walk out of here."

"Why would I do that? It's nothing personal, dear. You are a gift I intend to keep."

Why? Why? Wendy closed her eyes for a moment and then opened them with a gasp.

"You will let me go, because the *Sudden Night* sits just off your shore."

"The *Sudden Night* cannot touch us. We have no fear of the pirates." She laughed. "They are just human men."

"They are just men, it's true. Filthy, disgusting, treacherous men. But they are also men with cannons."

"Their cannons cannot touch us here, in this lagoon, nor under the seas."

"No. They cannot." Wendy's eyes widened and a trace of a smile turned up her lip.

"But their cannons can reach Sybella, which is what they are aimed at, as they wait for me."

The queen's eyes flared and the lagoon began to shake with the desperate cries of the mermaids below.

"No. You lie."

Wendy raised her chin.

"Do you honestly think I would come here, without some insurance?"

The queen's face distorted, her eyebrows arching. "You lie!"

Indeed, she would.

"I do not. The *Sudden Night* is my home here in Neverland, and her cannons will take down Sybella in as few as three shots. If I am not on their ship by nightfall, they will turn your precious rock into dust."

The queen snarled at Wendy before bringing her hand down across her face, her neck snapping harshly to the side. Wendy turned back to her, unfazed.

"That's not even the first time I've been slapped this week!" This was Neverland, after all.

"You, you . . . ," the queen was snarling now.

Wendy stared back at her. "My Queen, not even you can stop a cannon once fired." The mermaids howled.

"Quiet! She lies!"

Wendy trembled weakly, her face pressed up against this mermaid whose breath smelled of blood and fish.

"I do not. And what's more than that, don't you wish the Shadow to be defeated? So that you may not live in fear of the day when it wakes?"

The mermaids went silent.

"I know Peter, better than you. I know that he grows more unhinged every day, and that keeping this secret from Tink will one day not be enough for him. He WILL unleash the Shadow again. It is not a matter of if, it is a matter of when. He will lose control, and when he does, it won't be the fairies that pay the cost. It will be the Lost Boys, the pirates, the Pilvinuvo . . . and you. You have everything to lose."

The queen shook her head.

"What you cease to understand is that I will not believe that a polite little girl from another world—one who knows nothing of Neverland—could ever defeat something like the Shadow. Our fate is the same as it was before I gave you any answers."

The queen leaned in. "If the *Night* hurts Sybella, my clan will tear that ship apart, splinter by splinter, and I will personally spread their sorry bones in the coral garden."

"Perhaps. But not before they bring Sybella to the ground, and all the magic within her will spill onto dry rocks. What will the seas say to you then?"

The lagoon was frothing now with activity. To Wendy's horror, the mermaids had begun climbing out of the water, scaling the vertical walls like lizards, their tails holding them aloft as their fingers clawed jagged fissures in the rock walls of the lagoon. Dozens of them were rising up on the walls, rainbow hair and tails streaming water, all of them hissing at Wendy, their beautiful faces marred with rage. Their voices rose up.

"You wouldn't! We can't risk Sybella! Let her go!"

A mermaid with pale-green hair the color of grass ringed with a crown of seaweed pushed herself up on the same rock as Wendy. She had one arm; the other one was a marbled stump, cut clean at the shoulder.

Wendy swallowed. Peter had done that. This was the mermaid that had tried to drown her. She lurched backwards, as the mermaid's eyes met her own.

"I say kill her anyway." The mutilated mermaid licked her lips. "I will tear her apart piece by piece. Think of the blood."

Queen Eryne held out her hand, now protective. Wendy's heart thundered. She tried to focus, but her dizziness made it impossible. The lagoon swam before her eyes, everything a blur.

"Cassandra. Do not interfere in this. Your anger sways your judgement."

"But she . . ."

A loud chorus of mermaid voices drowned her out. "You cannot kill her! Never! Without Sybella we will die. Send her on her way! She cannot fall, lest we fall!"

The queen's voice thundered over the cacophony.

"My clan speaks. We will not risk Sybella."

Harmonic voices gave a sigh, the mermaids on the walls sagging in relief. The queen snapped at Wendy.

"You've made a fool of me, girl. Do you really believe you can change our fate?"

"Perhaps." Wendy raised her hands, trying to ignore the fact that her legs were trembling and weak, her skin stretched like a husk. "You have to let us try."

The queen stared at Wendy for a long moment before raising her hand.

"Fine. Cassandra, back away from her."

"No."

At her defiance, a sudden silence filled the lagoon. All the mermaids jerked their heads towards Cassandra, who hovered close to Wendy. *Too close.*

The queen bared her teeth.

"I will not tell you again, Cassandra. Release the girl or defy your queen's orders."

Wendy took a step backwards, and Cassandra, triggered by her movement, threw her single arm around Wendy's torso. She tightened it, and Wendy gasped—it was like being embraced by stone. Blood pumped in her ears, and she felt finally like she was waking up, like her body was understanding that she, Wendy Darling, was about to die. The mermaids in the lagoon watched silently as this act of defiance played out. They were alert, aroused.

Cassandra hissed at the queen.

"You are weak. You have led us down this path by your fickle heart, turned by a bright-haired boy. You are not fit to be queen."

The mermaids gasped, the scales on their fins rippling with excitement.

"You challenge my reign then? Openly?"

The queen's eyes were flashing now, her marble skin pulsing with radiant energy.

"Do you wish to be queen, Cassandra, of Clan Nautilus?"

The mermaid who held Wendy stared long and hard at Queen Eryne before uttering her answer.

"Yes."

Queen Eryne nodded once, her long fingers smoothing out her hair as she closed her eyes. All the lagoon was still. Cassandra's arm tightened around Wendy's chest as her heart hammered and her legs pumped uselessly.

She was so, so tired, literally drained.

"We fight for the crown then."

Without warning, the queen lunged at Cassandra, forgetting in her fury that Wendy was there as well. Her body hit Cassandra's, and their collision rippled through Wendy, her bones shaking with the impact. All three of them tumbled off the mossy rocks into the lagoon, narrowly missing an outcropping of orange coral that would have torn them into ribbons. Wendy was suddenly in the water, bodies and fins thrashing around her as she struggled to make her limbs work. Cassandra's arm was yanked back from Wendy's waist, and she fell down, in between their tails, frothy water all around. She watched a thin tendril of blood curl out from her wrist, pluming out like a drop of ink. *Ink. Booth.* The water filled with unholy screeching sounds, so different than the songs of the mermaids, this one now full of pain. It burned her ears. Wendy sunk lower. She had tried, she really had, but she was so tired, so very sleepy, and her muscles weren't working the way they should.

The flick of a fin sent her crashing against the underside of the mossy rock before she was pulled towards the swirl of tails and hair, sucked in by the undertow created in their violence. The water cleared for a moment, and she saw Queen Eryne wrap her hands around Cassandra's neck. The smaller mermaid was struggling, her one arm clawing deep scars into the Queen's torso, but it was no use. With a flick of her tail, the queen sailed behind her would-be usurper and held her head out between her arms. Cassandra's body flailed uselessly. She heard the mermaid's cries.

"I'm sorry, forgive me. I was angry! I shouldn't have . . ."

The queen had no use for apologies. She turned Cassandra so that her head lined up parallel to a sharp outcropping of bright-pink coral, its fingers razor sharp, thin, and pointed. Tiny blue fish flitted happily in and out of its caverns. Wendy opened her mouth to scream as the queen suddenly plunged forward, Cassandra's head flying towards the coral, her terrible scream filling up the lagoon as the coral entered through her eyes, face, and mouth before bursting out the back of her head. The water turned blackish red as the cries of mermaids swam in her ears.

She was drowning; water filled her lungs.

Then a hand like stone wrapped around her arm. Instead of sinking lower into the bottomless lagoon, she was yanked upwards and thrown roughly onto the shore. Wendy gasped for air. Someone thumped her chest and flipped her on her stomach. She coughed up water. A mermaid with short plum-black hair was crouched over her. Pale-pink scaled lips, glimmering like pearls opened. Her gold eyes stared straight through Wendy.

"Get out of here. Go! Go and tell the *Sudden Night* to have mercy on Sybella! Run!"

She had no strength to run. She could barely stand, no blood left in her veins. Her wrist was still bleeding. Her wrist . . . Wendy's eyes blinked. The bracelet! Her hand trembled as she lightly ran her fingers over the brown leaves. "I need strength" she whispered. The bracelet began to hum quietly, its brown leaves rustling before pressing themselves hard against her skin. The same golden light that had enveloped Lomasi ran through the bracelet, circling her wrists. The leaves gave a single shake and a surge of energy poured into her muscles, strengthening and hardening them, her body awake and strong. Wendy took a deep breath, feeling her strength return.

The queen emerged from the lagoon, black blood streaming down from cuts on her face and torso. In her hand, she held a tuft of green hair.

"Does anyone else dare challenge the queen?" she roared. The mermaids all bowed their heads reverently before swarming towards her, tending to her wounds.

Wendy scrambled forward, launching herself off the mossy rocks and onto solid ground. She sprinted away from the lagoon, her lungs heaving like a racehorse, her wet feet slipping as she ran, the strength in her muscles propelling her forward without almost any effort on her part. Just before she passed through the ivy curtain, she heard the queen's voice speaking calmly to her from the lagoon.

"If you defeat the Shadow, this grievance will be forgiven, if not, we shall always lie in wait to finish what was started today."

Wendy made her way backwards, easily finding the path that led away from the lagoon. She looked up as she passed the towering boulders the shade of bone, and straight ahead as she ran through a screeching Sybella. She did not linger to feel the slight hint of magic that passed softly over her skin, like the kiss of a silk sheet. As she ran, prayers fell from her lips, prayers of thanks that she had lived. *She shouldn't have lived.* A clever lie was all that had saved her. She shook her head in disbelief.

Who was this girl, running for her life, covered in blood, her ripped dress hanging in shreds around her legs, hair a mangled tumble of salt and spray? She longed for a moment to be the girl she once was, to curl up on her window seat with a book and a cup of tea, proper. Safe. At the same time, her legs pumping violently beneath her, Wendy was also this girl—someone brave, and fearless. A fighter. Free. *She was both*. And she could feel her strength not just coming from the bracelet—which was giving off a flickering light, its power rapidly diminishing, but from deep inside her, from the desire to live at all costs.

She would hold Michael again.

Peter could not win. Above all, he could not win.

Her cracked lips smiled when she saw the rocky beach unfold in quiet glory before her, seaweed strewn across shallow pools, rocky crevasses that bubbled with hot springs. Before them stretched the sea, peacefully concealing the wickedly magic beings that no doubt circled beneath their lapping waves of blue. *Watching*. Smith was waiting for her under an outcropping of rock that hung over the sea. She stumbled out from behind the blindingly bright cluster of boulders, and a happy grin lit up his bitter face. He quickly recovered, his scowl returning, the smile only a memory.

"Hurry up, girl, you've kept us waiting long enough!"

Wendy shakily climbed upwards, her legs faltering many times as she climbed up the steep rock face, her feet slipping on the loose shale. Her arms felt useless, and her wrist ached with a dull pain. She made it to the top of the rock and crawled to the edge, looking down. Smith held his arms out, and Wendy paused. He was a murderer, a thief, the kind of man that she would have walked to the other side of a London street to avoid. He was, indeed, the scum of the earth. And now she gracefully let herself drop off the rock, falling forward, her dress fluttering around her like the petals of a flower, into his thick, tattooed arms.

"I gotcha girl. You'll be alright. The captain will be mighty glad to see you."

Unconsciousness swam behind her eyes, an alluring blackness swirling in her brain. The bells calling her family to Mass were pounding deep inside of her chest. The last thing she remembered was staring at Smith's tattoos, now pressed against her cheek—a demon with a ram's face and a man's body laughing evilly, and above him, a stoic angel wielding a mighty sword, ready to strike. Bright fish swam around them both, the whole scene was tethered to an anchor that wrapped around his wrist. As Smith laid her down in the boat and reached for the oars, and she drifted out to sea in her own mind, surrendering to the lull of the waves, the queen's words etched hard in her memory.

Chapter Twenty-One

When she woke, she saw an ornate canopy of raspberry velvet lined with golden leaves rocking back and forth above her head. She blinked once.

"You're awake."

Wendy turned over and tried to push herself up in the bed, her wrist screaming in pain, along with her knee and ankle.

Hook was sitting beside the bed, his face drawn and pale. Hook reached out and helped her sit up, his hook flush against her back.

"Miss Darling, I must admit, I'm glad to see your face. There was a small part of me that was concerned you would never wake. It really was quite small, relatively. I am the captain of a pirate ship after all, and can't be prone to bouts of womanly emotion. Well, I'm glad to see that my concern was in vain. Here, have a drink."

A glass of rum was handed to her, and Wendy shook her head.

"Water," she rasped. "Water."

Hook shook his head. "Of course." An unfamiliar shape came out of the darkness bearing a jug of water and a steaming bowl of broth.

"Fermina!"

She sat beside Wendy, who greedily gulped the water,

Fermina's long black tresses falling over a yellow robe, smelling of honey and perfume.

"Slow down, slow down. You don't want to get yourself sick." She nicked her teeth. "Those greedy bitches, they almost drained you completely. You've been sleeping for two days." She placed her hand on Wendy's cheeks.

"Though I dare say you're getting your color back now. I see some healthy pink color creeping into those baby cheeks."

Wendy could almost weep at her kindness, at the way she touched her face, just like a mother would, the way she held a spoon to Wendy's lips, prodding and gentle all at once. Wendy sipped the delicious brown broth, crunching the small pieces of green beneath her teeth. Her head stopped swimming, and she took comfort in the familiar rocking of the *Sudden Night*. A temporary home, but a good one nonetheless.

"Why are you here?"

Fermina smiled. "The captain was in need of my medical expertise."

She raised her eyebrows in Smith's direction, who was pacing madly in the corner.

"You may be surprised that a woman trained in pleasure could also be skilled as a healer."

Wendy felt her prejudices fall away.

"No, actually. I'm not surprised at all." She grabbed Fermina's hand. "I am glad to see your face."

"BAH!" Smith exploded from the other side of the room, barreling towards Wendy's bed like an unhinged bear.

"Enough of this drawing room talk! The girl has information for us, and she needs to share it, before she passes out and takes a nice long nap for a few more days!"

Hook held out his hand. "Give her a moment, Smith." He turned to Wendy. "We can wait, if you need more time to rest."

Wendy shook her head.

"No. We've all rested enough." She cleared her throat.

"When Peter first arrived on this island, he befriended Queen Eryne. . . ."

Hours later, when the information had been dissected and documented, after the raised voices of the four had echoed up the corridors of the *Sudden Night,* Wendy and Hook stood together on the bridge, looking out at the sinking sun, its crimson orb sinking into a placid sea. Clouds of white dotted the horizon. Wendy sipped a steaming cup of mulled cider, a luxury beyond belief that Fermina had somehow whipped up in the ship's kitchen. Hook held a wine bottle in one hand, his silver hook looped lazily around the wheel as he tenderly sipped, humming a familiar pirate tune over the waves.

"Do you want to know," he asked, "how I really lost my hand?" Wendy turned to him, the heavy blanket on her shoulders falling loose as she jerked her head up in shock.

"I thought . . ."

"I'm sure you heard Peter's tale. And strangely enough, most of it is true. He did find our hiding place for the *Jolly Rodger* and the *Sudden Night* while it was still being built. He did burn my father's ship, and good men alive with it. As they screamed, he laughed. Or so I've heard."

Wendy tilted her head. "You weren't there?"

Hook took a sip of wine and adjusted the wheel northwest. "I was there, in the caverns, but I wasn't with my men. I was with . . . her."

Wendy knew exactly whom he meant.

"There is a small lagoon, deep in the heart of the Teeth. We've hid treasure there from time to time. There are only a handful of people who've ever been inside of it. We call it the Sanctuary. It's peaceful, quiet, hidden. Swimming in it is something to be experienced, and it is a place to take those whom you . . ."

He cleared his throat, the scars of the memory marring his face.

"You understand."

Wendy swallowed, her voice softening at the pain this memory must have caused him. "Yes."

"I was there with her, a tiny moment of heaven in a lifetime of misery, and Peter found us. He appeared in the cavern and, behind him, I could hear the screams of my men. He floated down, and when he came into the light, I will never forget the hatred on his face. We were already enemies, but I had taken something he wanted desperately—Lomasi. It was the first time he had learned about our love, and the first time, I believe, that his heart was ever broken. With a betrayed scream, he threw himself at her in rage, his golden sword outstretched. I reached out to protect her . . ."

"And Peter cut off your hand."

"Cleanly. It was as if his blade burned hot." He shook his head. "Blood was everywhere. Lomasi was screaming; Peter was laughing. I was in shock, but I picked up my sword with my other hand and readied myself to fight, though I could barely stand. I knew in that moment, that he would kill me, and then her." Hook shook his head. "How does a man, wounded, grounded, fight a boy with fairy powers who can fly?"

He gave a hollow, sad laugh. "It was no contest. He knocked me to the ground. My princess threw herself over me and begged Peter for mercy. I watched his face, watched the delight he felt at his power, at her bowing before him."

Hook narrowed his eyes. "But then his eyebrows raised, and he turned away from us without another word. He flew out of the Teeth, and left me bleeding on the ground, one of my ships burned into ash and twenty-five pirates dead. For so long I wondered why he had turned away. Could it be mercy? Was it love for Lomasi? Regret for killing my father?"

Hook's voice darkened, and malice crept into his tone. "It was none of these things, for these are the feelings that makes one human. When he saw me on the ground, he saw an end to his game, and Peter Pan could not live without that possibility, without this endless circle of chess that we play." He set his bottle down and straightened his jacket, his eyes resting on Wendy.

"When you are ready, we will set our trap, and it will be the beginning of the end, the last move in my game of chess with Peter Pan."

He fluffed out his coat behind him, and before Wendy realized what he was doing, he was down on his knees in front of her. "All these long years, I thought that I could win this game with ships, swords, and pistols. It turns out that I was just waiting to move a girl into the game. You are the missing piece, a girl from another world who I believe has the power to vanquish a devil from our land."

Wendy was unsure of what to do, so she reached out and took his cool hook in her hand.

"I may be the missing piece, but I am no one's pawn. I will do my best, for that is all I can promise. For your family, and for mine."

Hook stood, steely resolve glinting in his dark eyes, his eyebrows narrowed and drawn. "That is all I could ask for. And I promise, that as soon as Peter Pan has been defeated, we will move heaven and earth to find you and both of your brothers a way home."

Wendy closed her eyes. "Please." They were silent for a moment, each swimming in their own memory.

"We should be off the shores of Pan Island in two days' time with this shallow wind. Will you be ready by then?"

Wendy turned to him. "I will." She looked out at the sea, folding itself into the starry night one inch at a time, before turning back to the captain, a man whose name had once made her tremble in fear. She gestured to the wheel.

"May I?"

Hook looked surprised. "This ship wheel was the only thing salvaged from the wreckage of the *Jolly Rodger*. This was the wheel of my father's ship. It has never been touched by a woman."

Wendy smiled and raised her cup, her eyes never leaving his. "And, pray tell, what does that mean?"

"It means—" Captain Hook paused, his upper lip twitching. He looked at Wendy and then back at his ship, the sails fluttering like a black raven.

"It means, oh bloody hell, take the wheel, but don't crash my ship, and for heaven's sake, don't tell Smith. We'll never hear the end of it, and he'll probably shove a sword through your pretty gullet."

Wendy grinned, "Let's hope it doesn't come to that."

Owl's voice carried down from above. "You aren't letting her touch the wheel, are you, Cap'? T'will curse the ship it will!"

"No Owl, she's not, though it's not your position to question me, is it?"

"No, sir!"

"Good, then get back to work."

Hook winked at Wendy and mouthed, "He's blind."

Owl grumbled that he had heard that, and Hook smiled. It was momentary, a whisper of a thing, but it made Wendy's heart swell with hope.

She reached out and wrapped her hands around the wheel, surprised at how cool and wet the wood was, and how her palms fell so naturally around the handles. Her dress brushed the spindle, and Wendy looked at the sky. She heard the cries of seagulls overhead, and her nostrils filled with the smell of the salty sea. The blood in the water was now the same blood that ran through her veins, and it pulled to her. This once foreign danger was now something she returned to, and her hands instinctively turned the wheel as she watched the bowsprit crash through the waves.

The wind caught the sails of the *Sudden Night*, and she leaned forward, headlong into the pitch. Wendy's muscles responded to the needs of wheel without thinking, her body one with the *Sudden Night. She could see.* Hook leaned back against the ship's rail, his face betraying how impressed he truly was. Another wave crashed over the side of the ship, soaking Wendy, but it was unsuccessful at diminishing the smile on her face.

"Keep your hand on the helm. Steady, girl. Steady as you go."

She planned on it.

CHAPTER TWENTY-TWO

Two days later, the *Sudden Night* sat off the shore of Pan Island, a giant tree lumbering a few miles off in the distance. Wendy watched it give a slight shake in the wind from outside the rocking port window. Her fingertips lightly trailed the iron casing around the window, tracing the small metal knots that bound the window to the ship, so strong. So solid. She turned, her ridiculous dress brushing the sides of the narrow hallway.

Fermina had sat with her that morning, preparing Wendy to look as appealing as possible. Her hair had been washed and braided the night before, and this morning, Fermina had set it into lovely waves—light-toffee curls falling over her face, and accented it with a diamond hair comb in the shape of a crescent moon—a gift from Hook. She had a bit of rouge on her cheeks and lips, and though she had politely refused the whale-boned corset that Fermina had offered her, she was tucked neatly and tightly into an opulent blue dress. Silk panels of pale periwinkle draped over her shoulders in a low V-neck, and the tightness of the fabric pushed her bust up and outwards. Frosted silver and gold flowers draped over her left shoulders and crossed over the back of the dress before swirling around the front near her knees and dusting the edge of the dress. It was a heavy creation and utterly useless aboard a pirate ship where it dragged behind her through the endless maze of hallways, often picking up nasty remnants of pirate life in the process—small bones, a clump of hair, a bullet casing.

Now she made her way slowly towards the Jolly Staircase, her heart beating heavily underneath her lungs, dread dragging her feet, making them heavy and slow. She repeated the plan out loud to herself, making sure that she was burying it deep inside her, so that when he—Peter—looked at her that she would not lose herself in his eyes, in his touch that scorched her skin like flame.

"Get the pipes. Get the fairy. Get out."

One of these things could be fairly easy, especially if she was able to get Peter's guard down by convincing him that she was remorseful, and more importantly, totally enamored with him. If she could distract him enough, she could grab the pipes while he was sleeping perhaps, or perhaps during . . .

She shook her head to think of it. The Song had to be called in the same way, and to do that, they would need the pipes.

The other task wouldn't be so easy. She had to convince Tink to tell her the song—the song of her people, the song that called the Shadow—and then to come back to the ship. To do this, she would have to get Tink to trust her, to open herself to the ugly truth that Peter had massacred her people. Wendy was going to have to work through layers of love and self-hatred and an unflinching loyalty to Peter. *Get the pipes. Get the fairy. Get out.* It seemed like a simple plan, and yet, it was endlessly complex.

Impossible, almost.

As she began climbing the staircase of skulls and bones, Wendy wondered how this nightmare would end. No happy ending was assured in this story, not like in one of the princess fairytales that she had so loved Liza to read her as a girl.

Would they be able to quietly call and dismiss the Shadow? Would it be able to be defeated? Would it come to a battle? Captain Maison was still out there, waiting in the shadows for Peter's command. Peter and the Lost Boys—including her brother—had guns, and were preparing for a war. And what did they have?

One incredible ship, one murderous, damaged, love-sick captain, and one blue dress.

Wendy looked down and was mortified to see the apples of her bosom heaving as she walked. One girl in a *very low-cut dress*, a dress that would have made her mother faint. Wendy continued to climb the staircase. *What else was this all for though? If she could never return home, what was the point? To stay here, perpetually in fear for her life from Peter, from the mermaids, from rapist pirate lords?* She paused. No. That was not an option, and so the only way out of this place was to fight. To fight for her family, for her brothers, for her future with the bookseller's son.

Some men had armor. She had a blue dress.

The trapdoor opened before her, and the bright, turquoise Neverland light assaulted her eyes as she climbed out onto the deck of the *Sudden Night*. Wendy smiled at them. *It was time for a bit of theater.*

The crew was lined up on board, their eyes downcast as she walked by, the shuffling sound of her dress cutting through the reverent silence. As she passed Voodoo, he began singing, his rich tenor spilling over the deck.

> *Our anchor we'll weigh,*
> *And our sails we will set.Good-bye, fare-ye-well,*
> *Good-bye, fare-ye-well.*
> *The friends we are leaving,*
> *We leave with regret,*
> *Hurrah, my boys, we're homeward bound.*

The rest of the crew joined in, their male voices rising until they filled the boat and swept out to sea, blowing towards Pan Island. Wendy came to a stop by Smith, who stood at the ready, a scabbard in each hand, his arms crossed over his chest. He looked Wendy up and down.

"'Tis a bit much, don't you think."

She smiled shyly and patted his arm kindly. She saw him blink back watery tears and then he leaned forward.

"You don't have to do this ya'know. We can find another way to kill that boy."

Wendy shook her head sadly.

"No. We can't. Take care of the captain."

She kept moving forward, for she knew that if she lingered for even a second, that her next step would take her back inside the confines of the ship, back to safety, and the endless waiting. *Waiting for a miracle. Waiting for Peter to snap.* Instead she walked forward, towards the captain, dressed in a crisp white shirt, his navy military jacket resting across his broad shoulders. Upon his head sat the captain's hat that she knew he loathed, its bright-red gem winking in the soft light. He reached out his hook, and Wendy took it softly, thinking how the thing that had once terrified her so was comforting, a part of this man and this monster that she had come to trust like a father. She turned to him. He lowered his voice.

"Remember the plan. Don't linger. Don't let Peter into your heart. He can't know why you are there, or we will lose everything."

"I know what I'm doing," Wendy gently reminded him. The plan had been discussed for days—she had no question of what she needed to do, nor what it would cost her. Hook ignored her.

"Get the pipes, get the fairy, and get out. Don't let it go too far. Convince him that you love him and then do what needs to be done when he is at his most vulnerable. And don't . . ."

He paused.

"Don't give up something that you can't get back."

She felt a blush rising up her cheeks. "Please stop talking."

He nodded.

"Best for everyone. Now turn around."

Wendy pulled her hair to the side and turned. She felt Hook slide her dagger beneath the fabric of her dress. He turned her back around.

"If Lomasi and I ever allowed ourselves to have children, in my wildest dreams, I would hope that I would have a daughter as brave as you are." Wendy felt her eyes fill with tears. She missed her father.

"Thank you," she whispered. "And you . . . " she paused, finding the words on her tongue, "you are a good man who has done some very bad things. Perhaps try to do better this time around."

Hook grinned, the smile splitting his face awkwardly. "I'll keep that in mind."

Wendy's eyes narrowed. "Remember what you promised me. No killing Lost Boys."

"I will try my best, but you cannot ask me to not protect my own family if it comes down to it."

Wendy nodded. "That seems fair." They looked at each other for a long moment.

"He's coming," Owl hissed down, from far above the mist. "Get ready."

Hook nodded once at Wendy and turned away from her, his gray eyes full of worry. He cleared his throat. "Let's go, lass."

Wendy held her wrists out before her, and Hook bound them together with a rope, though the knot was quite loose.

She stepped onto the plank.

Hook began to loudly proclaim Wendy's sentence. "Because of her loyalty to the traitor and murderer, Peter Pan, Wendy Darling of London has been sentenced to die by walking the plank. She has shown time and time again that her true heart lies with him, and for this, she is sacrificed to the sea!"

Hook looked up at Owl, who was straining on the crow's nest, his grizzled face turned upwards as he hung precariously, one foot on the nest, one hand grasping a rope. He looked up and then back down at Hook, before gesturing with his hand, up into the clouds above.

Hook turned to Wendy and mouthed silently, "He's here."

Then he screamed, "UP GIRL! ON THE PLANK BEFORE I SPLIT YOU OPEN FROM BELLY TO BREAST!"

Wendy's hands were shaking as she walked forward. The plank was a thick wooden board, leveled against a cannon barrel, and as she walked across it, the bounce of her steps made the board shake and jump. One foot in front of the other, she made her way across it. Hook was right behind her, his sword poking into her back. What should have been threatening was actually a reassurance that he was behind her, only an arm's length away.

The water underneath her churned unhappily, white-capped waves colliding with each other as they barreled against the *Sudden Night*, which took their hits like a weary solider. Wendy looked back at Hook, and he gave her a sad smile, the one that she had grown so familiar with. She stepped forward to the edge. Owl motioned from above, and Hook cleared his throat.

"Wendy Darling, according to the pirate code, you are hereby sentenced to die. Take your step willingly or I shall assist you."

Wendy looked down at the water, and for the first time noticed a dark shape swirling up from below, monstrously huge. It was followed by another. Everything after that happened so quickly. Hook peered over the side of the plank and straightened up, his face white. The first crocodile emerged from the water with an open mouth, bearing its razor-sharp, yellow teeth, set back in black gums that were rotted with age. It snapped its teeth at Wendy as it stared upwards at its intended meal. A smaller crocodile circled around the first, noticeably faster. With a roar, it used its tail to propel itself vertically out of the water a few feet before splashing back down. Hook shook his head violently.

"They usually aren't in these waters. We can't do this. Change the plan!"

Suddenly, Owl was screaming. "It's not Peter! It's not Peter! Stop!"

Hook lunged for Wendy, and that's when they heard Owl's words turn into a terrible, high-pitched scream from above them. The echo of a gunshot bounced off the clouds.

Owl flew down from the crow's nest and landed hard on the deck, his head bouncing to the side with a loud crack. Blood exploded out of his chest wound, and splashed the feet of his crew, which looked on in shock, unable to explain what had just happened. His head was turned the wrong way, and his cloudy eyes were opened to the same blackness he had known all his life. Wendy covered her mouth as a scream escaped from her lips, stepping backwards involuntarily, and feeling the air where the board should have been. Her legs tangled in her dress as she tried to catch her footing, but she pitched backwards, just as Hook threw out his hands to grab her. The last thing she saw was his outstretched hand, reaching for hers, their fingertips inches from each other, but it might as well have been miles. She disappeared off the end of the plank, flailing in the air, her blue dress floating all around her.

She saw the levels of the *Sudden Night* pass before her, remembering briefly that she had once been pulled from the seas onto its black deck, and here, now, she would leave the same way. The dress was everywhere, fluttering around her like a cloud of blue sky, and Wendy barely had time to consider the gruesome death that awaited her. *Would they rip her to shreds? Drown her first? Would she feel their teeth as they descended on her, or would it all be over in a frothy foam of blood?* Her body twisted, and she saw them below her, a mass of green and teeth, and she smelled their breath, rotten and hot.

Oh, mama, she thought.

He hit her hard, moving fast, and the impact was so jarring that she thought she had died. She gasped for breath, unable to see, unable to breathe. She kept her eyes closed, waiting for the pain of the teeth and the ripping to begin. Instead, she felt the wind on her face, and willed herself to open her eyes. She was soaring up, up, up, up and away from the *Sudden Night*, flying, wrapped securely in strong arms. She saw Hook on the plank, watching them rise away from him, his face a mask of surprise and relief. She was moving faster now, soaring upwards. She started to rouse herself from the shock of what had just happened and let her clenched fists lie flat on the back of her savior.

"You saved me!" she sobbed.

There was only silence. She pulled back a moment to look at his face before her lips quivered and she felt hot tears drip from her eyes as she clutched the shirt underneath her hands.

She knew this back, these shoulders, the curls of brown that brushed her face. She wrapped her arms hard around him, enveloping all of him, deliriously happy.

"John! John!"

She began sobbing into his shoulder as he carried her upwards, up through the mist, up through the clouds, until they emerged into a sky of lavender and pale blues, with fingers of pink clouds that stretched far over the horizon.

"John, you saved me!" She hugged him tightly.

"Do you think," he whispered quietly, "that I would actually let you die?"

Her brother then fell silent. She kissed his cheek.

"Oh, John, what is it?"

Finally he cleared his throat. "I'm sorry."

Wendy pulled her head back and looked at him as they turned towards Pan Island. He looked older, much older in fact than the last time she had seen him. His face was drawn and narrow. He had grown a few inches, and his skin glistened with a healthy glow. While his body was strong and lean, his face was heavy. Dark shadows the colors of a ripe plum marked the bottom of his brown eyes, which were hollowed and weary, and his lips were cracked at the corners.

"John?"

"I'm sorry. I've done something terrible."

She took his face in her hands, her brother, and poured out the words that she had wanted to say to him every night since she had left him behind on Pan Island, the words that she should have always known he needed to hear in his insecurities.

"I know that we've had our differences since we have arrived here. All our lives, in fact, but nothing can change the fact that you are my brother. We are a family, even if you don't believe it. I will always be on your side. I believe in your goodness, and I love you."

A sob escaped John's throat as they neared the great tree. "Stop it! Stop talking, Wendy! You don't know anything about me! About my life here! You don't understand anything, and you never will! Just like our mother, so pushy, assuming you know everything."

He remembered. Wendy stayed silent. John had pulled the veil, or more likely something had caused him to remember their life before Neverland. This was a good thing, and she felt hope flood through her body. John's voice dropped to a whisper.

"Is Michael safe? Just tell me that."

Wendy nodded. "He is in a safe place, far from where harm would find him."

"I don't want to know any more."

"John, let's not go back right away. Can't you take me somewhere, somewhere where we can talk?"

John shook his head, his eyes blinking slowly. "Peter is waiting."

Wendy swallowed the arguments that rose up in her throat and let herself just be happy, for a moment, that a part of her family was here, in her arms, his heart beating against her own, the same blood running through their veins, the same memories in their minds. She wrapped her arms tightly around his neck.

"I missed you, you little prat."

She felt him tremble. "I'm sorry, Wendy."

They landed hard on the deck of the teepee. John set her down gently, his eyes meeting hers for a quiet moment. "I'm so sorry," he whispered. "Forgive me."

"John?"

He leapt into the air and flew away from her, disappearing into the thick leaves that hung down over Centermost. Wendy turned around to face the Teepee, her heart thudding in her chest. Every single Lost Boy stood before her, their faces hard, their eyes betrayed. Wendy swallowed nervously.

"Welcome back!"

The Lost Boys parted, making way for their leader. Peter Pan walked forward from the back, dazzling even from a distance, a gold crown upon his head, wearing a new outfit stitched of dark-green leather dotted with maroon leaves. In one hand, he twirled a sword. Wendy let her emotions overwhelm her and let her face fall into distress.

"Oh, Peter!" She threw herself on the ground, bowing before his feet, putting on the show she knew that he would want with this captive audience. *Let the games begin.*

"I was wrong!" she sobbed. "I was . . . afraid and so I tried to escape, but then Hook caught me and . . ." She let out a cry. "The things that I saw, the things that he did! He made me go to the mermaids! He threatened to kill Michael, if I didn't." She saw Owl's head cracking on the deck, and real tears dripped off her nose, and real sobs erupted from her throat.

"I tried so hard to come back to you! I just . . ."

Peter's bare feet stood before her, and Wendy reached out with a trembling hand, laying her palm across his shin. The touch of his skin made the hair on her arms stand up. At least faking her feelings for him wouldn't come without some pleasure. There was that. She dropped her voice to a whisper.

"I just want to be with you. That's all. I will be your queen, if that's what you want. I hope that my foolish behavior hasn't lost all my chances of becoming a girl you could love."

She paused, hoping that she was believable.

"And I just want you to be safe." Peter's eyebrows raised. "I'm glad to see that you have finally come to your senses." He reached down and helped her to her feet, his arm clasped firmly around her waist.

Hook's words rang through her mind as her emotions ran from disgust to desire and back again.

"Make him believe that you want him so desperately that he lets his guard down. Then love him so intensely that he won't notice us spinning a web around him."

Without pausing, she kissed him hard, in front of all the Lost Boys, in front of the world, exactly what she knew he would want. Wendy wanted it to be believable, and so she let herself fall into his mouth, her lips tasting his, like berries, his breath warm as his lips tracing the corners of her mouth. She reached out and threw her arms around his neck, pressing her body against his and feeling him respond in kind, clutching her with both hands, gently at first, and then desperate and hungry. She remembered how it felt to be desired by Peter, how his want for her lit up her soul from the inside, turning her into a pulsing beacon of desire. Heat spread out from his mouth and down her neck, and she felt as though she may burn alive. She pulled her head back with a gasp and looked deep into his eyes. She was taken aback as she remembered just how beautiful they were, a sharp emerald green, bright like sparks of flame. They searched her face, looking for a betrayal, but instead, she saw that he too felt the desire, the satisfaction of getting what he wanted. He ran his fingers through her curls before yanking them roughly.

"Say it. Say you will be mine forever."

Wendy, feeling bold, reached out and bit his lip softly before whispering. "Forever. In every way imaginable."

Peter, unable to control his delight, burst into hysterical laughter before kissing her again.

The boys burst into wild applause. Peter turned her outward

to face them. Tink scowled at Wendy from the corner of the room.

"Our mother and queen has returned to us! Let us treat her with every kindness. Tonight, we will celebrate what we have gained, and what Hook has lost! We will lift our glasses to our Wendy Bird, who flew away only to return to us, just in time to see the beginning of our great war!"

The Lost Boys erupted with feral cheers, and Wendy saw now what she had not noticed before in the waning light: weapons. Weapons everywhere. Guns, knives, axes, swords, and even cannons were scattered haphazardly.

She swallowed. The clock was ticking.

Ticktock.

Peter turned to Wendy. "Before we begin our celebration, I have one more thing for you. A gift to you from your king. Stay true to your words and it will remain…untarnished."

Wendy blushed. "I would be happy to accept whatever gift you have for me, and many more."

Peter looked Wendy straight in the eye. "Say that you love me."

Wendy stepped forward, hoping that her shy voice would convince him of the truth.

"My feelings for you have only grown in our absence. Being with Hook made me realize that I can't imagine my life without you in it." And then, a truth.

"You are the fire that burns me alive."

Peter's eyebrows raised, and a devilish grin crossed his face.

"I'm glad to hear it. Boys, bring Wendy her gift."

They shoved him forward with a bag over his head, and he fell to his knees at her feet.

"Take it off!" Peter ordered, his eyes narrowed with malice.

With a shaking hand, Wendy reached out and pulled the black burlap off his head.

A cry escaped her lips. His face was bruised, and a thick line of dried blood had crusted on his forehead. Still, the bright-blue eyes that she knew so well peered up at her, and Wendy feared that her actual heart might burst from her chest and splatter at his feet.

Booth raised his head.

"Wendy?"

Checkmate.

Please look for the finale in the series,
Wendy Darling, Volume Three:

 SHADOW

ACKNOWLEDGMENTS

This book was a beast.

A water-logged, free-sailing, nautical beast that pushed me maniacally through a world of ships, pirates, and ancient mermaid lore. Luckily, I have a great ensemble of people to help me untangle these sailor knots, all to whom I owe my thanks: My agent Jen Unter who listens and works and builds bridges for me to cross. PR visionary Crystal Patriarche and her incredible team at Sparkpress: Megan and Taylor, Kristin and Wayne. To my writing partner Mason Torall—The Sudden Night is better because of you. To beta readers Patty Jones, Amanda Sanders, Erin Burt, and Jenn Lehman, who were brilliant in their critiques and kind with their praise. To my story editor Erin Armknecht, who never fails to find the unintentionally hilarious lines in the manuscript and has seemingly vast reserves of support. For my own mermaid clan of fierce women: Elizabeth Wagner, Cassandra Splittgerber, Katie Hall, Kim Stein, Sarah Glover, Emily Kiebel, Karen Groves, Nicole London, and Erin Chan. Finally, to my family, who believe endlessly in my work and still act excited at book signings: Cynthia McCulley, Tricia McCulley, Ron and Denise McCulley, Butch and Lynette Oakes.

And to Ryan Oakes, who is the rock my waves crash around, and to Maine, who is every horizon.

About the Author

© Erin Burt

Colleen Oakes is the author of books for both teens and adults, including *The Elly in Bloom* Series, *The Queen of Hearts* Saga (Harper Collins 2016), and *The Wendy Darling* Saga. She lives in North Denver with her husband and son and surrounds herself with the most lovely family and friends imaginable. When not writing or plotting new books, Oakes can be found swimming, traveling or totally immersing herself in nerdy pop culture. She is currently at work on another fantasy series and a stand-alone YA novel.

Wendy Darling, by Colleen Oakes $17, 978-1-94071-6-96-4
From the cobblestone streets of London to the fantastical world of Neverland,
readers will love watching Wendy's journey as she grows from a girl into a
woman, struggling with her love for two men, and realizes that Neverland, like
her heart, is a wild place, teaming with dark secrets and dangerous obsessions.

Running for Water and Sky, by Sandra Kring $17, 978-1-940716-93-0
Seventeen-year-old Bless Adler has only known betrayal—but then she falls
in love with Liam. After a visit to a local psychic and a glimpse of Liam lying
in a pool of blood, Bless now has 14 blocks to reach Liam and either beg him
to fight for his life, or say good-bye to the first person who made her want to
fight for her own.

Blonde Eskimo, by Kristen Hunt $17, 978-1-940716-62-6
In Spirit, Alaska on the night of her seventeenth birthday, the Eskimos rite of
passage, Neiva is thrown into another world full of mystical creatures, old traditions, and a masked stranger. When Eskimo traditions and legends become
real as two worlds merge together, she must fight a force so ancient and evil it
could destroy not only Spirit, but the rest of humanity.

Within Reach, by Jessica Stevens $17, 978-1-940716-69-5
Seventeen-year-old Xander Hemlock has found himself trapped in a realm of
darkness with thirty days to convince his soul mate, Lila, he's not actually
dead. With her anorexic tendencies stronger than ever, Lila must decide which
is the lesser of two evils: letting go, or holding on to the unreasonable, yet
overpowering, feeling that Xan is trying to tell her something.

The *Alienation of Courtney Hoffman*, by Brady Stefani $17, 978-1-940716-34-3
Fifteen-year-old Courtney Hoffman is determined not to go insane like her
grandfather did—right before he tried to drown her when she was seven. But
now she's being visited by aliens who claim to have shared an alliance with
her now-dead grandfather. Now Courtney must put her fears aside, embrace
her true identity, and risk everything in order to save herself—and the world.

ABOUT SPARKPRESS

SparkPress is an independent, hybrid imprint focused on merging the best of the traditional publishing model with new and innovative strategies. We deliver high-quality, entertaining, and engaging content that enhances readers' lives. We are proud to bring to market a list of New York Times best-selling, award-winning, and debut authors who represent a wide array of genres, as well as our established, industry-wide reputation for creative, results-driven success in working with authors. SparkPress, a BookSparks imprint, is a division of SparkPoint Studio LLC.

Learn more at GoSparkPress.com